Ascension of the Chronicle

Chronicle of Ceres, Book 5

CL LaVigne

This novel is 100% human created.

For permissions, contact:

CL LaVigne

cindy@cllavigne.com

Cover Designed by MiblArt

Ascension of the Chronicle

(Chronicle of Ceres, Book Five) - 1st Edition

www.cllavigne.com

www.facebook.com/CLLaVigneAuthor

ISBN (paperback): 979-8-9884845-8-5

ISBN (eBook): 979-8-9884845-7-8

"Ascension of the Chronicle" signals the final installment of the pentalogy "Chronicle of Ceres," a storyline that dropped into my mind in 2018.

I would never have published the first book "Beginning of Tomorrows" if it hadn't been for the encouragement of Jimmy "Super" Flanagan.

A writer himself, Jim understood my angst and nervousness regarding my project.

He provided the nudge I needed to soar on my own wings. He told me, "Just publish it and send it out into the universe. You'll learn so much after you do that."

He was right. With each book I've completed, not only did I learn more about the writing industry, but I learned more about myself.

I celebrate Jim in each book by including a Flanagan's Pub. Jim loved everything Irish and this was the perfect way to ensure he'd always be a part of my writing journey.

Jim is with me in spirit – my muse if you will – as I write each day.

Contents

Meet the Characters

The characters in the Chronicle of Ceres pentalogy revealed themselves as I wrote the various novels.

I don't do outlines. Instead, I choose to let the individuals tell me the story as I write. Hence, many characters emerged when they needed to carry the storyline forward.

Here is the wonderful cast and the books in which they introduced themselves:

Beginning of Tomorrows, Book 1

- Darrius Dagda (benevolent Cererian)
- Prasad (benevolent Cererian)
- Chance Kemp (Keeper of the Records)
- Kai Kemp (Keeper of the Keys)
- Fenna "Fen" Kemp (Guardian of Peace)
- Hilliard "Hilly" Kemp (Guardian of Battle)
- Stygian Chernobog (Yfel Brethren leader)
- Curtis Dawson (Hilly's husband)
- Jeff (Kai's husband)

Denali Rising, Book 2

- Jake Pierson (Keeper of the Word, Shaman)
- Lolo (Jake's bush plane that is a spiritual entity)
- Samuel "Sammy" Taylor (A nahwiht, meaning "nothing")
- Aaron Aningan (evil Cererian)
- The Sentinel Boulder (earth spirit that binds the Word to Jake at the age of 8)
- Great Mother Denali (earth spirit)
- Raven (Hilly's spirit animal)
- Everild, Thane, and Benedict (Yfel Brethren who kidnap Curtis)

Shasta Beckons, Book 3

- Benedict (becomes a benevolent Cererian)
- Axel (coyote earth spirit, Kai's spirit animal)
- Troy (bigfoot earth spirit)
- The Leohts (orbs, Kai's ancestral family)
- Mount Shasta (earth spirit)

Bluestone Shadows, Book 4

- Janet Kemp (Chance's wife)

- Wyatt, Maeve, Myla (3 of Chance's children)
- Alden Stark (benevolent Crerian)
- Gabriel Telfer (Chance's cousin)
- Hildred (white stag, Chance's spirit animal)
- Balor & Cary Atwood (twins, Yfel soldiers)
- Ryan Pierson (Jake's father who became an Yfel)
- Yr Wyddfa (Welsh earth spirit)
- Bran, Dylan, and Ellis (the giants of Mount Snowdon)

Ascension of the Chronicle, Book 5

- Miriam (Ryan Pierson posing as an earth entity)
- Galena (a sacred sister who resides in the Circle of Calm)
- Bodhi (white bison, Fen's spirit animal)
- Robert "Bob" Downs (benevolent Cererian)
- The Senator (Cererian)
- Orion, Mason, and Luther (Cererians, High Order of Truth)

Chapter 1

The Medicine Wheel

Guardian of peace, a warrior stands.
The Big Wheel turns again.
Healing, atonement, and visions, the quest begins.
The time is nigh. The battle approaches.
Gather the troops and reclaim the forgotten throne.

Fen floated on a cushion of air.

Where am I? she thought.

Moments earlier, as she sat in the English cottage surrounded by her friends and family, someone rushed at her. She threw her hands up in surprise but relaxed when she recognized her old friend, Prasad.

Come with me, Prasad had instructed telepathically then he gripped Fen's hand.

That was her last memory.

Now she was alone and drifted on her back with her eyes closed while being soothed by the warmth surrounding her. Sandalwood wafted by.

Prasad's favorite incense, she thought.

Contentment filled her heart. Prasad would never harm her.

Fen glided through the void, buoyant as if floating in a pool of water, yet lighter as though her body skimmed along gentle air currents.

There was no urgency.

She was at peace.

The sweet scent of sandalwood drifted by again.

She smiled, thinking of Prasad, the Cererian she had dared to fall in love with. A man who willingly journeyed to the Land of the Dead and traded his life so her sister could live and fulfill the prophecy.

The granon! Her heart hammered as she remembered the Cererian plant that contained Prasad's life essence. *I left it on the dresser in the cottage. I need it.*

Fen, an androgynous voice echoed in her head.

Fen tried to open her eyes, but she couldn't.

Fen, an ensemble of voices, male and female, telepathically called out a little louder.

Floral notes floated - chrysanthemums and tulips.

Mother? Fen thought. *Mother loved pink tulips. Did I die in the cottage? Is this the afterlife? Mom, are you reaching out to me from beyond the veil?*

Be at peace. You are safe within the embrace of your ancestors, the voices replied.

Am I dead? She thrashed with fear, trying to wake up.

Chanting began.

Starting low, the rhythmic cries grew louder while a distant drum beat a measured tune. The familiar melody thumped in time to Fen's heartbeat and she hummed the tune. The cadence of the chanting and drumbeats lulled her into a peaceful reverie.

Then silence.

"Awaken, Fen," a female voice requested gently.

Fen slowly opened her eyes and squinted in the dazzling sunshine. She held her hand up to shield her eyes. Gently swaying red and yellow blossoms of Indian paintbrush and coneflowers towered above her.

She propped onto her elbows and gazed around.

She was still alone.

A warm breeze licked at the beads of sweat on her face. Above her, popcorn clouds moved lazily through an azure sky.

"Hello?" she called out. "Is anyone there?"

The wind rushed through the wildflowers, and they rustled a reply.

Fen rose and stretched. A patchwork of red, yellow, and orange blooms bled into the horizon in all directions.

"Where am I?" she said aloud.

"You are home," a female voice answered.

Fen whirled. A woman appeared ten feet away. A friendly smile and dark eyes with gold centers softened the stranger's tan face. Long, dark hair cascaded over her shoulders and spilled down the front of a sleeveless beige shift that kissed the tops of her knees. Red dust coated her bare feet.

"Welcome home, Fen," the women said. "I am Miriam. I…we have been waiting for you."

"We?" Fen asked. A hesitant smile flickered across her face. She sensed no malevolence from the being in front of her, yet she couldn't detect benevolence either. *It's as though this person doesn't exist,* she thought.

"I, we, it's all the same," the woman responded.

Is this a dream? Fen mused.

The young woman laughed. "This is very real."

"You read my mind," Fen admonished. "That was wrong. You should have asked permission." Fen shuffled backward and glanced around nervously. The flower meadow had disappeared. Instead, a dry red desert stretched toward the distant mountains.

Fen narrowed her eyes. "If this is real, then how did I get here? I was in England minutes ago."

"Your ancestors brought you," the being responded.

"How?"

"We were guided by the beacon you wear around your neck." The young woman pointed to Fen's necklace.

Fen touched the tiny dreamcatcher pendant. "This? This is how you found me?"

The woman nodded. "Yes, the Guardian boulder protected you with his amulet. The moment you put it around your neck; it sent ripples into the universe so we could locate you."

"But why? I was with my family."

"Because you are in danger. The darkness would have found you had we not intervened."

"What darkness? Stygian?"

"Walk with me, Fen." The woman extended her hand.

Fen hesitated. "Where's Prasad? He came to me in the cottage. Where is he?"

"Once he delivered you to your ancestors, the Cererian returned to the Land of the Dead."

"And where are we?"

"You are suspended in the magic of the sacred medicine wheel."

Fen frowned. "This *is* a dream. A place I've concocted while napping at the cottage."

The young woman gripped Fen's hand and squeezed. "Do I not feel real?" She brushed her fingertips across Fen's forehead. "Do you not feel my gentle touch?"

The woman spread her arms wide. "This place is a sacred sanctuary that has been in existence since the beginning of time. Our ancestral home hovers between the dimensions of the physical world and the great ether." She gazed upward.

"A dimension," Fen repeated. "My friend, Jake, can shift into the dimensions."

"Jake Pierson cannot enter this space," the young woman snapped. "The shaman is not a member of our ancestral tribe. Come with me and let me introduce you to the great healers who lived before you."

Reluctantly, Fen allowed the woman to pull her forward. After several steps, Fen stopped.

"Is something wrong?" the young woman asked.

"The darkness you spoke of. Can it enter this place?"

The woman gathered Fen's hands and gazed deeply into her eyes. "No evil will find you here, Fen. You are home. You are safe."

Chapter 2

Fen's Disappearance

"Fen can't disappear without a trace!" Chance roared as he dashed upstairs.

"Chance!" Jake shouted. "Stop and listen to me for a minute."

"She's not upstairs!" Chance bellowed. "Did anyone look outside?"

Chance hurdled the railing and landed hard in the foyer. "I'll search outside."

"Stop!" Alden held up his hand and blocked the front door. Chance grimaced and rushed the Cererian.

Snap!

Alden snapped his fingers.

Chance stopped mid stride. His lips curled back in a snarl, and his eyes narrowed on Alden. One arm was pulled back, ready to drive a meaty fist forward.

"Cool," Kai said as he joined the group in the foyer. "Is he aware we're here?"

"He's perfectly aware," Alden said as he moved away from the door. "I've just stopped him in his tracks, so to speak." He whispered into Chance's ear. "Now, if I release you from this suspended animation will you sit down and let us talk to you?"

"Uh." The strangled reply was the only sound Chance could manage from his frozen mouth.

"Was that a *yes*?" Kai asked.

Alden waved his hand and released Chance's head from the magic.

Chance twisted his head at Alden. "Let me go you son of a bitch!"

Alden snapped his fingers, and Chance froze again. This time his mouth was wide open, his teeth bared like a wild animal ready to bite. Alden shook his head. "He's not quite ready to listen to reason. Why don't we go back into the lounge and discuss our next move."

"Uh!" Chance grunted.

Alden stopped. "Do you want something, Chance?"

"Uh-huh."

Alden ambled into Chance's line of sight. "You'll calm down and do as I say?"

"Uh-huh." Chance's eyes vibrated with emotion.

"Alright, I'll release you. But be forewarned, I'll suspend you instantly if you don't behave." Alden snapped his fingers.

When Alden unfroze him, Chance lurched forward and crashed into the door. He crumbled to the floor and pouted.

Alden squatted next to him. "Chance, we all want to know where Fen went, but let's discuss it in an orderly manner and not run off half-cocked." Alden gripped Chance under his arm and hefted him to his feet.

"Come on. Let's go talk with the others." Alden pulled Chance down the hallway and into the lounge. "Sit over there." Alden guided the magician to the sofa and gently pushed him back into the cushions.

"Everything is sorted, Darrius," Alden reported.

Chance sat on the couch rigidly, his arms crossed in front of his chest, his jaw muscles bunching.

"Very well," Darrius began. "Jake, please explain what happened to Fen."

Jake gazed out the window into the garden. A slight drizzle fell against the glass. He turned and faced the others. "Fen has been claimed by her ancestral tribe."

"How the hell do you know that?" Chance barked as he sprung from the sofa and sprinted at Jake in a blur. The two men stood chest to chest. "How the fuckin' hell do you know where my sister has gone?"

Chance glared, but Jake averted his gaze and moved past his friend. "Fen is no longer in England. She is with her ancestors. And no one will be able to find her."

Defeated, Chance returned to the couch. His hands fidgeted in his lap.

"How do you know?" Darrius asked.

Jake turned back to the garden window. "I saw them coming," he whispered. "They arrived on the currents of the storm." He turned back to Darrius. "They left the same way within a second."

"How could they take Fen without us seeing them?" Alden asked.

Jake smiled a cock-eyed grin. "Magic. The pendant she wore was a beacon that allowed her people to locate her."

"Did they teleport?" Benedict asked.

Jake shook his head. "Nah. Her people are not of this physical dimension. They passed by all of us and took Fen in plain sight."

Darrius nodded. "They exist at a higher vibration."

"Yes," Jake replied.

"But Fen is of this physical world," Alden argued.

"She *was*. But she has transformed. She exists on a different plane. One I can't enter. One no Cererian can enter." Jake faced Chance. "Your sister is safe in the arms of the Healers."

Chance glanced up at Jake with sorrowful eyes. "Will she come back?" he whispered.

Jake sighed and looked out the window. "My gut tells me no."

Kai joined Chance on the sofa and wrapped an arm around his brother. "It's you and me, Big Brother." He nudged Chance.

Chance elbowed him back hard.

"Ow!" Kai yelled. He shoved his brother with both hands. Chance retaliated, grabbing Kai and rubbing his knuckles into his scalp.

"Take that, you little pest," Chance growled.

Jake sighed and walked away. "Things are back to normal," he uttered as he passed Darrius.

Jake strolled into the kitchen and took the Woodford Reserve from the shelf. He grabbed three tumblers and placed them on the kitchen table. He sat down and poured bourbon into all three glasses.

He held one but didn't drink. Instead, he swirled the golden fluid and silently counted to himself. When he reached ten, he glanced up as Chance and Kai slid into the kitchen, pushing and shoving each other.

"Care for a drink?" he asked.

"Why not," Chance answered. He snatched the glass and slumped into a chair.

"Sure." Kai slid into a chair next to his brother.

"To Fen," Jake said, raising his glass.

"To Fen," the brothers chorused.

The men sipped in silence.

Chance gazed at his drink. "That's it then?" he said.

"What is?" Kai responded.

"The world won't know peace," he answered. "Without Fen, I can't restore my crystal to its seat of power. Without my crystal and Fen's crystal, peace will never be restored to Earth."

Jake refilled the tumblers. "You believe that?" he asked then he tossed his drink back.

"Yeah, of course I do," Chance replied. "We can't do shit without Fen."

"Appears that way, doesn't it?" Jake acknowledged.

"Isn't there something we can do?" Kai asked. "I assisted Fen at the Guardian boulder in Denali and in Wales. Maybe there's something we can do with just me?"

Jake shook his head. "Nah, it's gotta be Fen. She's the reader of the symbols."

Kai swirled his drink. "Is there a way for Fen to help us from where she's been taken?"

"Don't be an idiot!" Chance shouted punching Kai's arm.

"Your brother's not wrong," Jake noted.

"What?" Chance responded.

"Fen may be on a different plane, but we can still work together."

"How?" Chance asked skeptically.

"Hold your hand up," Jake instructed.

"Why?"

"Just hold your hand up."

Chance thumped his elbow on the table and held his palm up facing Jake. "Now what?" he demanded.

Jake placed his palm against Chance's and then closed his eyes. Soon a white light glowed around their hands.

"Hey! What's going on?" Chance yelled, whipping his hand away.

"Oh, I get it," Kai said as he placed his hand against Jake's. Soon, a soft light glowed around their hands. Kai snatched his hand away. "You see, big brother, we have our own conduit between the dimensions." He pointed at Jake. "Fen may not be able to join us in the physical plane, but Jake can bring our worlds together."

"I still don't get it." Chance pouted.

"Remember how you and Fen used your combined magic to penetrate the Land of the Shadows when Hilly and I were held hostage?" Jake asked.

"Yeah."

"Same principle. Your power penetrated a space no one else could go. That's what we'll do with Fen. We'll combine our power, so she can join us at your Guardian boulder."

"Ah," Chance said, nodding. "I get it. Will that work?"

"Definitely," Jake answered confidently. "But it will involve water." Jake grinned and downed his drink. Then he stood and left the kitchen.

Chance turned to Kai. "It will involve water? What the hell does that mean?"

Kai shrugged. "You know Jake. He's always messing with you."

Jake strode into the lounge and found Darrius, Alden, and Benedict facing each other. "Sorry, I didn't mean to disturb you," he said as he ambled to the garden window. "I need a change of scenery."

The Cererians followed Jake as he passed by and then reconvened their telepathic discussion.

The trial begins in two days, Darrius noted. *I think we should all be there to ensure justice is served.*

What about Jake and the Kemps? Alden asked. *We need to ensure they are escorted on their journey.*

We could insist they stay here until our return, Benedict added. *Besides, with Fen removed from this plane, how will they be able to accomplish uniting Chance's stone with its Guardian boulder?*

Jake whirled and faced the Cererians. *Because I've figured out how to unite Fen with her brothers.*

"How were you able to jump into our private conversation?" Darrius demanded. "I cloaked it."

Jake winked at the Cererian. "Interesting, eh? Ever since Fen and Chance bombarded me with their combined power, I've found that I can easily listen to your conversations, cloaked or not. Don't worry, your secrets are safe with me. Besides, I wager The Cererian Prophecy reveals more to me than all of you put together." Jake smiled and pivoted.

He opened the door leading into the garden. A damp, chilled gust rushed through the opening. He paused before walking out into the rain and shutting the door behind him.

The Cererians stared after him.

"What do you make of that?" Alden asked.

"Like everyone else, Jake is transforming," Darrius replied.

Chance and Kai remained in the kitchen.

They had stopped drinking in favor of scrounging for leftovers in the fridge. They settled on cold fried potatoes and mushy peas when Jake re-entered.

Sopping wet from head to toe, Jake lingered in the doorway.

"Raining?" Chance asked.

"A bit," Jake responded. He grabbed a dish towel and slumped into a chair. He briskly rubbed his hair.

"Any reason you chose to go out in the rain?" Kai asked.

"To clear my head," Jake responded as he patted the towel on his shirt and pants. A small puddle pooled at his feet. "Walking in nature frees my mind. Besides, I didn't want to be around them anymore."

"Them?" Chance asked.

"The Cererians," Jake replied. "I'm tired of their interference."

Kai raised an eyebrow. "Interference? Have they done something?"

Jake draped the towel around his neck and hung on to the ends. He narrowed his eyes at Kai.

"Well...um...what I meant..." Kai stammered shifting his gaze from Jake.

"What's got your jockeys in a jumble?" Chance demanded.

Jake stared at the table. "Things are happening fast. I would rather not be joined at the hip with a Cererian every time I make a move."

"What's happening fast?" Kai asked.

Jake slammed his hands on the table. "You're just full of questions today, aren't you, Kai?" He pushed away from the table, and the chair slammed up against the range. He leaned forward and glared first at Kai and then at Chance before storming out of the kitchen.

The brothers watched their friend leave and shared a puzzled look.

"Jake's upset about something," Chance noted as he stood up.

"I wouldn't go after him," Kai added. "He might slug you."

Chance marched out of the kitchen and found Jake standing in the lounge staring out the window. He held his hands behind his back. The Cererians were nowhere to be seen.

"At the risk of being throttled, what the hell is going on with you?" Chance asked from the safety of the doorway.

Jake sighed and dropped his head. "I need to find Hilly."

"Oh. Can you sense her at all?"

Jake shook his head. "Lord Yr Wyddfa is holding her prisoner behind the magical veil at Mount Snowdon."

"How do you know she's a prisoner?" Kai asked as he strolled in.

"She'd be here if she wasn't being held against her wishes," Jake reasoned.

"The giants were healing Hilly and refastening the blue opal," Kai added as he joined his brother. "Perhaps they're taking longer than originally thought."

"If she was free, she'd find a way to reach out," Jake insisted. He turned and faced his friends. "She'd reach out to one of us and let us know she's okay.

"Why don't we travel to Snowdon and find out for ourselves," Chance suggested.

"We can't," Jake replied.

"Why not?" Kai asked.

"Because I said so." Darrius said as he walked up to the trio.

"I thought you left for Ceres," Jake said.

"Soon," Darrius responded as he gazed at the three men. "So, you're planning to leave the cottage, I see."

"Yes," Jake replied. "There's too much to do, and we won't get it done hanging out in England."

"I would prefer you remain here until we return from the trial."

"It's in our favor to leave now. We need to prepare for uniting Chance's crystal with its Guardian boulder," Jake replied. "The Yfel will hunt for us regardless of Stygian and the twins being tried on Ceres. There are hundreds more Brethren waiting for us to make a mistake."

Darrius and Jake studied each other for several moments.

"Very well," Darrius said. "Leave the cottage, but don't go to Yr Wyddfa's kingdom. Hilly will contact you when she's well enough to travel."

Jake turned away.

"Do we have an understanding, Jake?" Darrius asked. "Jake?"

Jake whirled, his tanned face was flushed red. "Yes," he seethed through clenched teeth.

Alden and Benedict strode into the lounge. "We're ready when you are, Darrius."

"I'm ready," he replied. "Jake, I'll contact you as the trial progresses."

Jake jutted his chin at Darrius and turned away.

"Thanks, Darrius," Chance mentioned. "We appreciate that. I hope all goes well."

Darrius smiled weakly. "I hope so too."

Without another word, the Cererians disappeared one by one.

"Now I understand your 'Cererians are shitty' monologue in the kitchen," Chance said to Jake. "I thought there was going to be a nuclear meltdown between you two."

"What's our plan, Jake?" Kai asked.

Jake stared into the garden.

"Since you don't need Hilly to find the Guardian boulder—" Kai began.

"Don't tell me my job, Kai!" he snarled.

Kai held his hands up. "Okay, okay. Be grumpy. Get it out of your system because we have work to do."

The room grew quiet.

Chance shifted his gaze between Jake and his brother.

Jake returned to staring out the window. The drizzle ended, and sunshine filtered through the gray clouds. "We leave tomorrow morning," he stated softly.

"Okay," Kai responded. "Where are we going to?"

"He can't tell us," Chance added.

"I can tell you where we're going to meet up," Jake said. "Kai and I can fly, but then there's you, a flightless bird, unless you can flick to a known location."

"So where are we going?" Chance asked.

"To The Nine Muses," Jake responded.

Chapter 3

Leaving England

THE NEXT MORNING, THE men met in the kitchen for breakfast.

Jake arrived an hour earlier and brewed a strong pot of coffee. He eased back in his chair and sipped his second cup while watching Kai spar with the eggs and bacon sizzling in the skillet.

"Take that, you dastardly dragon," Kai joked as he flipped the food onto his plate with the spatula. The food spat grease at him.

"Morning," Chance grumbled as he ambled into the kitchen. He snatched a strip of bacon from Kai's plate.

"Get your own," Kai complained as he sat down. "You're such a moocher."

"Whatcha make for me?" Chance asked as he gazed around the kitchen. "I'm hungry too. Didn't you make enough for all of us?"

"Do I look like your personal chef?" Kai pushed food into his mouth. "Get your lazy ass over to the stove and cook something."

Chance attempted to steal another slice of bacon, but Kai rapped the back of his hand with his fork.

"Ow!" Chance wailed. He sauntered to the coffee pot grumbling under his breath. After shoving two slices of bread in the toaster oven, he returned to the table with a large mug of coffee. He slurped and glared at Kai.

Kai chewed, swallowed, and smiled at his brother. "Not a morning person, are you?"

Chance growled and hunched over the coffee, allowing the steam to warm his face.

Jake tilted back in his chair. Chance and Kai continued to bicker, but he wasn't listening. He focused on Hilly. Time and again, he mentally reached out to her only to receive silence.

The last time he saw her was on Mount Snowdon when she was pinned against the boulder with a gaping hole in her neck. He was helpless then and felt useless now.

"Yo, Jake!" Chance bellowed snapping his fingers in front of the shaman's face.

Jake jerked. "What?"

"I've been trying to get your attention."

"Why?" Jake sipped his coffee.

"I thought we should talk about our plan?"

Jake looked past Chance, into the garden, and watched a wren flit among the tall flower stalks.

Chance shrugged and gave Kai a puzzled look.

"A plan, Jake..." Chance continued. "Remember how you held me captive in the lounge and forced me to hammer out a plan to find my crystal? Having a plan was goddamned important then. What about now?"

"Yep," Jake responded and leaned forward. The front legs of the chair thudded to the floor. He jumped to his feet and poured another cup of coffee. Then watched the autumn breeze blow the remaining leaves off the trees.

Chance and Kai exchanged a glance.

Kai filled his cup and sauntered beside Jake. The two men sipped in silence. Although Jake peered outside, his eyes were glazed over and unfocused.

"Jake, is everything okay?" Kai asked.

Jake sighed, and his shoulders rolled forward. "Kai—"

"Yes?" Kai interrupted.

Jake looked at his friend with tired eyes. "I'm okay."

"Alrighty then," Kai said as he returned to the table.

"Guys," Jake began as he turned around and leaned against the sink. "I'm doing fine, but these last few days have been shitty. My father lured me into a battle through so many dimensions that I lost count. Then I woke up in the arms of Kai, Fen, and Darrius with no recollection of how I got there. Then I was forced to watch Aaron torture Hilly, and I couldn't do a goddamned thing to stop him—" Jake gripped the edge of the sink so hard his knuckles blanched.

"I don't know if my dad is dead. I hope he is, but he's a tough son of a bitch. And I don't know if Hilly is okay."

"She's also tough," Kai added. "She's the toughest person I know."

"She is." Jake agreed, staring at the floor. He smacked the edge of the counter. "Enough reminiscing," he blurted. "Time to get our shit together and head home."

"Now, you're talking," Chance said. "What's the plan?"

"We'll meet in the living room of The Nine Muses," Jake explained. "Kai and I will fly over. You can flick over."

"Perfect," Chance replied. "I haven't practiced my flicking much, so I'm anxious to try it on The Nine Muses. I know exactly where I'll materialize...right in front of that massive old fireplace."

"Oh yeah," Kai said. "The one that was never lit, even when the weather was freezing."

"Sounds wonderful," Jake lied.

"Oh, you'll love the old homestead," Kai said. "Huge mansion and luscious grounds on a cliff above the Atlantic Ocean."

"I wonder what condition it'll be in," Chance pondered. "Has anyone kept an eye on it since we left?"

"Good question," Kai replied. "I assumed the Cererians would have posted someone there since it is a major hub for portals."

"Oh?" Jake asked.

"Yeah. The short story is the Yfel targeted our parents after Dad got a little sloppy with his travels," Chance explained. "Stygian destroyed a central portal in the front yard and then sickened our mother with some Cererian disease."

"I had no idea," Jake said.

"Yeah, there's a lot of history in that old house..." Chance trailed off.

"You can tell me more when we get there," Jake said. "Now, about our plan, once we arrive, we need to ensure the house is protected. Then we lay low until Darrius, and the others return."

"What?" Chance bellowed. "We're going over there to sit on our butts and wait for the Cererians? Then what was all that crap about leaving England? Why not stay here and then go together?"

Jake held up his hands. "Easy, Chance. There's a reason. Once we arrive at The Nine Muses, I need to go gather information to bring you and Fen together at the Guardian boulder. I need to explore my options. Plus, I need to get familiar with the area. So, while I'm off doing that, you and Kai will be manning the mansion."

"How long will you be gone?" Chance asked.

"As long as it takes," Jake replied. "Hopefully, no longer than a few days."

"Okay," Chance said. "While you guys are flapping your arms across the ocean, I'll arrive first and canvas the house."

"I wonder if Darrius and Prasad's magic is still cloaking it from the Yfel," Kai mused.

"Stygian still found it despite their magic," Chance scoffed.

"Because of Hilly," Kai added. "Their blood connection changed everything."

"True. Still, I'll check out the old place and reinforce it with my own special magic."

"Should we inform Darrius?" Kai asked.

"No!" Jake barked. He noticed his friends' startled faces and added, "What I mean is I don't want to bother Darrius. He'll be busy with Stygian's trial and providing testimony."

"Sure," Chance replied. "But when are you going to let Darrius know where we went?"

"When I decide he needs to know," Jake answered.

Chapter 4

The Nine Muses

CHANCE MATERIALIZED INSIDE THE foyer.

Dust swirled in the dim light. He turned slowly and reminisced. Childhood laughter echoed in his head as he recalled the epic hide-and-seek games he played with his siblings late at night.

He froze when he faced the gaping black maw of the stone fireplace. Fear squeezed his heart like the cold fingers of a malicious spirit pulling him from the past. A shiver raced up his spine when he saw the family oil painting above the mantel. Layers of dust muted the once-vivid colors, and the picture appeared bleak and forsaken. It depicted an ancestor clad in full armor, standing on a beach and raising a sword into the stormy sky. When he was a kid, he had concocted fairy-tales around the lone figure never expecting that the scene would, one day, become his reality.

The battle with Stygian on the beach steps from The Nine Muses replayed in his mind. Chance, Kai, and Fen had thrust their blades, they barely knew how to use, through their sister, Hilly, as she lured Stygian inside her body.

Though the battle had occurred seven months earlier, adrenaline surged through Chance's veins as though he was still fighting.

His mouth went dry, and he gagged.

I need a drink, he thought then he rushed to the nearby study.

The room was exactly as he had left it seven months ago and, thankfully, the decanters were still full of bourbon. He poured some into a glass and held it to his mouth. His hands shook violently, and the tumbler clicked against his teeth as he sipped. He set the glass down.

Beads of sweat peppered his forehead, and he gasped for air. His heart galloped.

Fuck, a panic attack! He plopped into a chair and put his head between his knees.

Slow breaths. Slow breaths.

Moments later, he raised his head. A distant memory of Darrius, Prasad, and his siblings gathering in the room and discussing war strategies tugged at him. He sighed. He checked his pulse. His heart had slowed, and his hands no longer trembled.

"Come on, Chance. You've got this," he said aloud. He stood and snatched the drink from the counter and gulped it. He winced as the bourbon burned the back of his throat.

He poured another one.

"A little early for binge drinking, isn't it?" Kai asked as he entered the room.

Chance jerked.

"Jumpy, big brother?" Kai teased.

"Kai!" Chance grabbed his brother in a bear hug.

Kai pushed him back. "You okay? I just saw you ten minutes ago in England."

Chance stared at the floor. He could feel the heat of embarrassment creeping into his face. He turned away and grabbed his drink. "I'm fine." He tossed the bourbon back.

"Pour me one," Kai said. He pulled the curtains open and daylight flooded the room.

Chance handed Kai a drink and they stood in silence gazing at the calm Atlantic Ocean.

"Where's Jake?" Chance asked.

"On his adventure."

"The asshole couldn't stop and say hello to me?"

"He's got a lot on his mind. He's not fun to be around. He abandoned me halfway across the Atlantic and rocketed out of sight."

"Yeah," Chance agreed. "Something's pestering him, and I don't think it's only Hilly."

"He almost died, Chance. Even Darrius nearly gave up hope on healing him."

"I didn't know that. Thank goodness for you, Fen, and Darrius."

"His obsession with Hilly *is* interesting though," Kai added. "In Alaska those two tormented each other, but in England, something changed..."

"I think Jake knows a lot more than he allows us to believe. I think he's more in tune with the Prophecy than Darrius."

Kai raised an eyebrow. "Yep." He turned and set his glass on the counter. "Come on, Chance. Let's check out the house."

Chance gazed at the decanter.

"We can drink later," Kai added. "Let's go, I'll race you upstairs like the old days." A mischievous grin spread across his face.

Chance loved a good challenge, and Kai's smugness added fuel to the fire that burned in his belly. Chance slammed his glass on the counter, the sharp sound scattering the dark memories. Then he dashed out the doorway. His legs pumped furiously as he climbed the stairs easily, four steps at a time.

Kai soared after him. Flying in front of his brother, he curled a finger and taunted. "Looks like you're losing."

"Get out of my way, you annoying insect!" Chance bellowed as he swatted at Kai. The men reached the second-floor landing at the same time. Neither of them was out of breath.

"Tie!" Kai shouted.

"You're nuts. I got here first," Chance claimed.

A strong gust of cold wind rushed by them.

"What the hell?" Chance said as he looked down the hallway. "Did you feel that?"

"Yeah. I think a window's open."

"For seven months?"

"Let's check it out," Kai suggested. He pushed Chance ahead of him. "You go first."

The two men crept down the hall toward the bedrooms. When they reached the end of the corridor, they glanced left and right.

"See anything?" Chance asked.

"Nope."

"You go right, and I'll go left," Chance said. "Check the bedrooms." They split up. As they checked each room they shouted, "All clear!" Until finally, they reconvened in the main hallway.

"That was weird," Chance said. "It was a gust of cold air, but the windows are secure."

"Except that window in Fen's old bedroom," Kai added. "It's always been a little wonky and never closed all the way. There's a bit of a breeze blowing in, but not like what we felt."

"Interesting," Chance mused as he rubbed his chin. "Let's check the kitchen. Maybe there's food still there."

"After seven months, I wouldn't want to eat it," Kai added.

The men used the back staircase that led directly into the kitchen. Chance flicked the light switch, and the overhead lights flickered on.

"You check the fridge, and I'll look in the cabinets," Chance suggested.

Kai pulled the fridge door open. "Yikes! There's only a shriveled cantaloupe in here. How about you?"

"Cans of vegetables and baked beans. Oh, and a package of pasta."

"I wish Prasad was here," Kai said. "He was a marvel in the kitchen."

Meow.

"Did you hear a cat?" Kai asked.

"Yeah. It sounded like it came from that direction." Chance ambled into the dining room with Kai close behind. They searched under the table and behind the buffet but found nothing.

A blur of red dashed out the door.

"What the hell was that?" Chance said, dashing into the living room. "I don't see anything."

Kai yanked the brocade curtains aside. Brilliant sunshine streamed in and illuminated dust vortices swirling throughout the room. He sneezed several times.

"Remember when we first arrived here?" Chance asked. "There was that odd cat that checked us out. I think its name was Pyewacket."

"You know Pyewacket was Darrius...right?"

"Of course I do. But maybe he came back to spy on us."

"He wouldn't leave the trial. And Darrius would let us know if he was going to join us."

Meow.

"Shit!" Chance yelled as he whirled. "Where is that fucking cat?"

"Sounded like it came from the foyer." Kai hurried toward the fireplace.

"I don't see anything," Chance said. "I'm getting tired of this game."

A blur of red dashed into the study.

"I saw a fluffy tail!" Kai shouted as he chased after it. "Shit. Nothing's in here."

Meow.

"Damned cat's outside!" Chance shouted as he ran for the front door and yanked it open.

"Stop!" Kai yelled. "Don't go outside. The house is protected, but the grounds aren't. Remember what happened to Hilly when Mr. Spatz lured her outside."

Chance filled the doorway, leaning across the threshold enough to peer right and left. "There's no cat." He stepped back inside and slammed the door. "I'll reinforce the magic just in case I broke the Cererian protection spell." He signed sigils in each corner of the doorway.

"Good morning," a male voice whispered.

Chance and Kai whirled, their hands raised and ready to fight.

A short man with flaming red hair and rosy cheeks stood between them and the study. A friendly smile filled his face, and he looked at them with bright, cheerful eyes. His hands relaxed across his large belly while his fingers tapped his paunch rhythmically.

"Relax," he said. "I won't harm you. Let's see. You're Chance Kemp and you're his brother, Kai. Is that correct?"

"Who the hell are you?" Chance growled.

"I'm Robert Downs, but you may call me Bob."

Kai gently touched Chance's arm and lowered it. "It's okay, Chance." Turning to the stranger, he asked, "Are you the benevolent Cererian assigned to this house?"

"Yes, Mr. Kemp."

"Call me Kai."

"And call me Chance. We heard a cat. Was that you?"

Bob nodded. "It's the Cererian way of investigating. Darrius sent me to keep an eye on you." He scanned the room. "I believe there were supposed to be three of you. I don't see the shaman, Jake Pierson."

"I haven't seen him either," Chance snarled.

"That's most disturbing that the shaman isn't here. I'll need to advise Darrius that there's been a change in his plan."

"No!" Kai shouted. "Um...what I mean, is that Jake will soon be here. He had business to take care of. We wouldn't want to bother Darrius over something trivial, would we?"

"Yeah," Chance agreed. "When we left England, Jake told us he was taking care of a few details and would arrive a little late."

Bob's gaze shifted between Chance and Kai before he pursed his lips and said, "Fine. I'll give the shaman an hour. If he doesn't show by that time, I'll need to report his absence to Darrius."

Kai exhaled audibly.

"I imagine both of you are hungry," Bob said.

"Yes!" they chorused.

"I can take care of that."

"We've checked the kitchen," Kai noted. "There's nothing but cans of old vegetables."

"Please go into the dining room," Bob instructed. "You'll find a nice selection of food waiting for you."

"We were just in there," Chance argued. "There's no food."

"Follow me," the Cererian said. He opened the door, and the savory aromas of roasted meats wafted.

The brothers were transfixed by the spread of food on the table.

"I wasn't sure if you preferred ham or turkey, so I made both," Bob said.

"My god," Chance uttered as he walked around the table, snatching bits from each dish and popping them into his mouth. "Look Kai. There are two bowls of mashed potatoes."

"Check out these fresh rolls," Kai said, He tossed one to Chance who shoved the entire bun into his mouth.

"I assume you're pleased?" Bob smiled.

"Yes!" they said in unison.

"Excellent. I'll leave you here while I inspect the house and ensure all the protection spells are in place." He narrowed his gaze at Chance. "And I'll make sure the front door is secure. It's fortunate that Kai stopped you before you negated our protection spell."

"I reapplied magic," Chance mumbled as crumbs fell from his mouth.

"That was thoughtful of you. But I'll recheck all the entry points." Bob closed the door as he left.

Chance snatched a turkey leg and stood by the window gnawing on it. Juices dripped down his chin and onto his shirt.

"Interesting man, eh?" Kai asked as he joined his brother. His plate was piled high with mashed potatoes with gravy puddled in the middle. Various vegetables spilled all around the mound.

"Um," Chance grunted.

"How long do you think he followed us around the house?"

Chance smacked his lips and swallowed hard. "The more important question is why didn't we sense his presence in the first place?"

Kai nodded. "True."

"We need to keep an eye on this one," Chance warned.

"Aren't you being a little too suspicious?"

"You say that as though it's a bad thing."

"Perhaps you're right. We need to be cautious until Jake gets back."

"*If* he comes back."

"What do you mean?"

"Jake's pretty pissed right now. If he returns, I'll be surprised."

"He has an obligation to you and Fen."

"I know, but not being able to contact Hilly is gnawing at his insides. I wouldn't put it past him to fly to Yr Wyddfa's kingdom, despite what Darrius said." Chance piled more food on his plate and sat down.

The brothers ate in silence, except for an occasional muffled belch from Chance.

"I was thinking of calling Jeff," Kai blurted.

"You can't call—" Chance began. "Oh, yeah, Dad's landline. I've been without devices for so long, I forgot about the phone here. I'd love to hear Janet's voice."

They looked at each other for several seconds before they bolted from the table, wrestling each other to open the door and then raced to the phone on the table in front of the fireplace.

"Me first!" Kai yelled grabbing the phone off the table and running as far as the cord would allow. Chance batted at Kai as he dialed.

"Hello?" Jeff answered.

Kai's eyes watered as he put the receiver to his ear and turned away. "Hi, honey. It's me," he whispered.

Chance sighed. Reluctantly, he returned to the dining room. Kai would be a while. When he reached the door, he looked back at his brother. Kai had curled into the chair with his knees pulled up against his chest while cradling the phone with his shoulder. He absently twisted a lock of hair with his finger.

Chance entered the dining room and closed the door behind him. Tempting piles of meats, potatoes, and desserts lay before him. He sat in front of his abandoned plate and tapped his fingers, deciding on what to eat next.

"It's not easy," a male voice whispered.

"Shit!" Chance exclaimed as he pushed the chair away and stood ready to fight again.

Bob sat at the other end of the table, his hands resting on his ample belly.

"Fuck, Bob," Chance yelled. "Don't creep up on me!"

"Sorry," Bob replied. "I thought you were aware of my presence."

Chance narrowed his eyes at the Cererian. For a fleeting moment, he wondered if Bob was mocking him about his earlier comment to Kai about not having sensed the Cererian's presence.

They stared at each other.

Bob broke the silence. "The house is secure."

"That was fast," Chance replied. "You were able to check every entry point by yourself?"

"Of course. I'm efficient. I see Kai is catching up with his husband."

Chance glanced at the dining room door and then back to the Cererian. "I suppose you can see him through the door."

Bob grinned. "As a matter of fact—"

Chance pounded the table with his fist. "Stop!"

The Cererian's smile grew wider. "You seem perturbed."

"Who are you?" Chance demanded as he clenched his fists.

The door opened and Kai entered. "What's all the shouting about?" He glanced at Chance's menacing posture. "Chance...are you okay?"

"I don't trust this...this...Bob!" Chance seethed.

"Why?" Kai asked.

"Because I'm not like your friend, Darrius," Bob answered. The Cererian ambled around the table. Chance glared at his every move. "I possess different traits than the other Cererians you know, and your brother is suspicious."

Chance grimaced. "How do we know you're not an imposter? An Yfel or perhaps even Ryan."

A rich chuckle filled the room as Bob held his sides and laughed. "Oh, Chance. You are a tough one for sure. Did you question Benedict's validity? His unusual appearance is unlike any other Cererian. Did you question Alden's credentials when he showed up unannounced at the English cottage?"

Bob vanished.

"Shit," Chance said. "Where'd he go?"

"Behind you," the Cererian answered.

Chance whirled with his hands ready to deliver a bolt of magic. Bob grabbed Chance's hands and squeezed them together like a vise. "Careful, magician. Your emotions will be your undoing."

"What the fuck?" Chance growled as he thrashed against Bob's grip.

"I can hold you like this all day, if needed," the Cererian noted. He released his hold at the same time Chance pulled back. "But I choose not to." Momentum sent Chance crashing backward into his brother, and the two men crumpled to the floor.

Chance leapt to his feet, but Bob had disappeared.

"You pissed him off, big brother," Kai said. "What's your problem with him?"

"I don't trust him. He plays games. First as a cat and then popping in and out like a ghost. Something's odd about him."

"Bob's got a point," Kai replied. "Every Cererian we've ever encountered has been different in appearance and abilities. Call Janet. Talking to her will make you feel better." Kai sighed. "Talking to Jeff was exactly what I needed. He always knows what to say to make me feel better."

"I *do* need to call Janet," Chance agreed. He snatched a couple of rolls and burst out of the dining room.

From the doorway, Kai watched Chance dial and then he smiled when his brother whispered into the receiver and slumped into the chair.

Kai closed the door and went to the window, quietly gazing at the cloudless sky. A thin grin appeared on his face. "I know you're here, Bob," he said and turned.

The Cererian sat in a chair at the head of the table.

"Unlike your brother, your intuition appears heightened and far superior," Bob observed.

"Careful, Bob. *Like* my brother, I also have my doubts about your intentions." Kai leaned toward the Cererian. "I'm keeping an eye on you."

"Your caution has been received," Bob said plainly. "I will resume my duties in protecting this house and its occupants." Bob rose, bowed toward Kai, and vanished.

"Little prick," Kai said under his breath.

Chapter 5

A Prisoner Behind the Veil

"Do you have to watch me *all* the time?" Hilly complained.

The young giant, Ellis, stood in the chamber doorway with his head lowered. Pink tinged his cheeks. "I'm sorry. The laird wants to make sure you have everything you need."

"If that was true, Lord Yr Wyddfa would release me," Hilly argued.

She glared at Ellis from her perch on a square-cut boulder in the middle of the room. A wool blue and green blanket covered Hilly's shoulders and draped over the rock she sat upon. The chamber's ceiling soared high above her and was transparent, a natural window to the night sky's sparkling stars.

"I've been a prisoner in this cell for several days," Hilly said. "Why can't I talk with Lord Yr Wyddfa?"

"I'm sorry," Ellis apologized. "The laird was very clear on my duties."

"It's inhuman," she muttered as she turned her back and crossed her arms.

Ellis scratched his head and sighed. "But ye are not human. Ye are a Firewalker witch."

Hilly whirled. "What do you mean I'm not human?"

"Ellis, step aside!" Bran barked as he shoved his brother against the wall. He strode up to Hilly and glared at her. "Lord Yr Wyddfa wants to talk wid ya."

Hilly squared her shoulders. "About what?"

Bran reached for her arm but she violently shrugged him off. She leapt from the boulder and backed against the wall.

"You're nuttin but trouble, ye are!" Bran growled as he stomped toward her. He curled both hands into thick fists and lunged.

Hilly dodged the behemoth tucking under his arm and running to Ellis who guided her behind his large body.

"Ya little bitch!" Bran snarled.

"Bran, watch ya temper," Ellis cautioned. "The laird wouldn't want his guest harmed or upset by yer antics, would he?"

Bran stopped and huffed. His fingers straightened and curled at his side. With each breath, a wave of foul stench wafted. Hilly held her nose. "Then ye take the witch to the laird. I'm dun wid er." Bran snorted and exited the chamber. He stormed off, his footsteps sounding like rolling thunder.

Once Ellis was sure his brother had left, he led Hilly back to her seat. "I apologize for Bran's behavior. He's been gruff ever since we were wee lads."

Hilly smoothed her clothes and smiled. "Thank you, Ellis. You're very kind."

Ellis's cheeks flamed crimson.

"May I ask you a question?" Hilly asked gently.

"I suppose...if I know the answer," the giant replied.

"Why did you say I wasn't human?"

"Ow!" Ellis grabbed the side of his head and winced.

"Is everything okay?" Hilly asked as she touched his arm tenderly.

"Aye. I'm fine. The laird just yelled into me brain. He's impatient and wants to meet with ye now. Follow me, please." Ellis entered the corridor and walked several feet before turning back. Hilly hesitated in the doorway. He extended his hand and curled his fingers. "Please come wid me. The laird will be cross if I don't bring you to him."

Hilly glanced to the left, the direction Bran had departed. There was no sign of the angry giant. She slipped her hand inside Ellis's massive palm.

"Thank you for healing me," she said as she lightly touched the blue opal at her throat.

"'Twas me and me brothers working together," Ellis replied. "And it was the laird who led you back from the Land of the Undead."

"I am very grateful." Hilly squeezed the giant's hand and gazed at him. The tips of his ears glowed red.

After navigating the main rocky corridor, Ellis guided Hilly down a narrow passage. The temperature increased noticeably.

"Why is it so warm here?" Hilly asked.

"'Tis usually chillier, but the laird didn't want you to catch a cold," Ellis replied.

Hilly swiped her brow. "Feels like we're in the tropics."

"I wouldn't know about that place," Ellis replied. "I've never been outside Wales."

The double doors to the laird's room loomed twenty feet high and wide. Constructed of thin layers of rhyolite, the fine-grained surface appeared tan with streaks of dark gray quartz snaking through the massive slabs. Carved symbols covered each side of the entranceway.

"These markings are as old as time itself," Ellis said as he pointed toward the gateway.

Hilly studied the doorway. "Some of these seem familiar."

"As they should," a male voice responded.

Ellis dipped his head, and Hilly straightened as an entity floated toward them. Hues of purples and blues fluttered throughout the transparent veil surrounding his rocky body.

"I know you," Hilly said as he drew near. "You were with me in the Land of the Undead."

"I'm Yr Wyddfa. You decided to trust me and return to this realm."

Hilly glanced at the massive doors. "You said these symbols should be familiar to me. Why is that?"

The spirit gestured toward the carved wall. "These are the markings on the hearths of all earth spirits. Denali surely had these etched in her chamber."

"Yes...yes, they were there. Only they were chiseled in ice." Hilly stepped forward to touch a nearby symbol.

Ellis grabbed her hand. "Please don't. These are sacred."

Hilly studied Ellis and then the entity.

"Ellis is correct," Yr Wyddfa noted. "Ancient magic was employed to carve them. Each marking is connected to the ones on either side. To touch one would disrupt the energetic flow of the spell."

Yr Wyddfa waved a hand and the massive doors opened. Dust and gravel fell to the ground as they rumbled apart.

Hilly peered inside. An immense cavern, the far walls not even visible, loomed in front of her, and a hint of sulfur wafted.

"Welcome to my lair," Yr Wyddfa said as he drifted through the doorway.

Hilly followed but stopped when she realized Ellis wasn't behind her. She turned around. Ellis smiled and raised a hand as the doors rumbled shut.

Hilly stared at the closed doors.

"Please, Firewalker...join me," Yr Wyddfa said as he floated up a massive structure of rocks and boulders that flowed upward like a spiral staircase. A throne of bluestone slabs and pillars dominated the top. He gazed down at Hilly twenty feet below. "Please join me," he invited. "You may take the stairs, if you wish."

Hilly studied the slabs that formed the steps. Each one was perfectly cut to the same length, depth, and height. Then she looked upward at Yr Wyddfa who smiled gently at her. He extended a hand and curled his fingers, beckoning her.

Hilly lifted her arms out to her sides and lifted from the ground, spinning slowly until she reached the platform and landed softly.

The laird had taken a seat on the throne. "You may sit over there," he said gesturing toward a rough-hewn bench. "I'm sure you have many questions."

The top of the seat had been scooped and sanded to a smooth depression. Hilly sat cross-legged and gazed at Yr Wyddfa.

"Are you comfortable?" he asked.

"Yes, thank you," she replied.

"Your earth mother, Denali, is anxious to have you back on her slopes."

"You've spoken with her?"

"Yes, she campaigned for me to intervene during your capture and torture at the hands of Aaron. But, as you know, The Cererian Prophecy forbids interference."

"I'm aware." Hilly brushed her lips with her finger absently as she remembered Aaron removing her mouth. "It touches my heart that Denali reached out to you on my behalf."

The ethereal cloud surrounding the entity pulsed in bursts of blues and purples. "Earth spirits are quite attached to their children," he responded. A broad smile softened his angular, carved face.

"Do you feel that way about Chance?" she asked. Hilly looked around the space. Besides the staircase and throne platform, the cavern was void of any furnishings or structures. Luminescent balls peppered the walls at various levels and pulsed a steady yellow glow. Above her loomed a transparent ceiling like the one in her chamber. It was night. Stars and planets blinked in the inky void.

The laird nodded. "Yes, the relationship we have with our magicians is unique and unbroken."

She returned her gaze to Yr Wyddfa and found him staring at her, his eyes like dark slits. "You have a question you want to ask but dare not," he remarked.

Hilly tensed. The question had been on the tip of her tongue since Ellis led her there.

She took a deep breath. “Why did Ellis say I wasn’t human?”

“Ah,” Yr Wyddfa replied. “My young giant misspoke.”

“Oh?”

“It’s hard to explain.”

“I have time.”

The entity smirked. “So, you do.”

Yr Wyddfa drifted from the throne and hovered in front of Hilly. Flashes of blues fluttered throughout his transparent shell. He studied Hilly as she stared back at him. “Do you feel human?”

Hilly’s forehead furrowed. “That’s an odd question.”

He sat on a nearby rock. “Is it? You should have no issue answering it.”

Hilly gazed at the floor, considering everything that had happened to her—Stygian, the vision quest, her magical powers. She lightly touched the blue opal nestled in her neck. Flashes of Denali and her magical raven fluttered through her mind. “I *am* human,” she whispered.

“So, you *feel* human?” Yr Wyddfa asked.

“I feel the way I’ve always felt. I feel like me.”

“Is Shasta’s earth child, Kai, human?”

“No. He's a leoht, but he was raised human with Fen, Chance, and I.”

“Is Chance human? Is Fen?”

“What are you getting at?” Hilly’s angry reply surprised her. “I’m sorry. I didn’t mean to raise my voice.”

A low chuckle echoed around the great hall as Yr Wyddfa’s aura sparkled in greens and purples. “I toy with you. I apologize for that.”

“I’m not human, am I?” Hilly whispered.

“You are a Firewalker witch, a shaman, and a magician. You possess powers beyond the limit of the world’s populations. You have watched your abilities grow exponentially over these last six months. When Darrius performed your Revelation, he pulled the plug out of the dam holding your memories at bay. With the Cererian’s fogging magic removed, you realized who you really were.”

Hilly listened to Yr Wyddfa. She soaked up every word. "I'm not human," she admitted. "I'm something different."

"Are you disappointed?"

"No. I've always loved who I am. To me, I'm no different."

"But you are very different, Firewalker. You and your siblings are unique. Another way the Prophecy works behind the scenes. How many humans do you know who interact with earth spirits?"

Yr Wyddfa chuckled again. The tone was rich and endearing, not mocking.

Hilly relaxed.

"Come with me, Firewalker. I'll show you around my kingdom. And then, you will return home to Denali." He leaned forward and took her hand. His fingers felt like icy stone.

"I'm going home to Denali?"

"Yes, she insists that you meet with her. She made me promise. And as you know, I don't break my promises."

"What about Jake and my brothers? We need to take care of the remaining family crystals."

"The shaman is quite perturbed that you've remained behind the veil here on Mount Snowdon. He is preparing to leave England with your brothers."

Furrows creased Hilly's forehead. "But I want to join them. It's my responsibility to be with them."

Yr Wyddfa held up a finger. "Protocol, Firewalker. Your earth mother is your priority at this moment. Once she has seen you are safe, then you can join your friends."

"You're holding me hostage like Aaron."

"Oh? Am I torturing you? Have I removed your mouth and the blue opal that keeps the voices quiet? Patience, Firewalker. I have much to show you. Walk with me, and I shall reveal the secrets of my kingdom."

Chapter 6

Clash of Wills

ONCE THEY WERE OVER the mid-Atlantic, Jake rocketed out of Kai's sight and doubled backed toward England. Five minutes later, he arrived at Mount Snowdon and landed on a snowy slope near the cave that led into the bowels of the mountain. There Jake paced outside the entrance.

Darrius's warning not to return to the laird's kingdom ran through his mind. Challenging the earth spirit on his home turf was a bad idea. Any match between a supernatural entity and a magician, even a powerful shaman, would end in a big bag of hurt...if not death.

But he had to try...he needed to find Hilly.

He reached out mentally to her.

Hilly, can you hear me? I'm coming to get you.

A cold gale blasted from the cave. Jake staggered back and fell to his knees. Bending into the stiff wind, he found his footing and trudged toward the entrance, his hands shielding his face from the bite of sleet.

Was that your warm welcome, Lord Yr Wyddfa?

The wind abruptly subsided as a light dusting of snow drifted upon the landscape. The temperature plunged below freezing.

There had been no reply from Hilly and Jake couldn't sense any living thing inside the cave. But he knew Hilly was in there. Was the earth spirit interfering with his ability to find his friend?

You test my patience, Yr Wyddfa.

Jake touched the hilts of Cathal and Cadmar, his battle daggers that lay secure in their sheaths upon his back. He sucked in a deep breath and marched into the cave.

Suffocating darkness engulfed him. Even the faint light filtering from the outside vanished in the inky void. Jake inched forward relying on his hands and instincts to find any obstacles in his way. Slowly sweeping his arms back and forth, he crept further down the dark corridor.

He stopped.

Light flickered on the wall ahead.

Creeping cautiously toward the pale light, he held Cathal and Cadmar in front of him. After a few steps, he entered a small antechamber illuminated by a single torch. Shadows from the flames danced across the rocky walls.

Something's not right, he thought. The hairs on Jake's neck bristled and goose bumps raced down his arms. He tensed.

You should not be here, a male voice warned telepathically.

Jake looked over his shoulder from where the voice appeared to have come from. There was nothing but a wall.

"If somebody is here, show yourself!" he demanded as he stepped into the middle of the small space, swinging his daggers back and forth menacingly.

"I have always been here," the voice proclaimed. "For millions of years, I have stood my ground and not yielded. You, shaman, are not welcome here."

"Who are you?"

The flame on the torch flared and illuminated the nearest wall. A two-dimensional shadowy figure loomed large like a dark entity creeping along the rock's face.

"Who are you?" Jake yelled as the form flickered along the wall within the shadows of the flame.

"I am Lord Yr Wyddfa," the voice called from behind Jake.

Jake whirled around.

Nobody was there.

"You hide in the shadows Yr Wyddfa. Are you afraid?"

The torch flared again and illuminated the entire room. An ethereal figure hovered in a far corner. It floated toward Jake.

Jake gritted his teeth and clenched his daggers.

The spirit stopped in front of the shaman. Flashes of purples and blues filled the aura around its body. "Knowledge of your arrogance precedes you, Shaman. You should know your place in this world."

Jake gripped Cathal and Cadmar harder. He assessed his adversary. The supernatural being appeared carved from rock, and he wondered if his weapons would have any impact at all. As an earth spirit, this being also possessed the supreme magic of the world. Jake knew that no one, not even another earth spirit could subdue Yr Wyddfa.

Jake sheathed his weapons.

"Wise decision, Shaman," Yr Wyddfa commented.

"Where's Hilly?" Jake demanded.

"Straight to the point. So, I shall give you a direct answer. Go home."

Jake took a step forward. "I need to know she's okay."

"My giants healed her. She rests and will soon be reunited with her earth mother, Denali."

"Hilly needs to tell me she's okay. I want to make sure she's not being held hostage."

A low chuckle echoed off the walls.

"You accuse me of holding the Firewalker against her will?" Flashes of crimson burst throughout the entity's aura.

Jake clenched his jaw, biting the words that yearned to fly out of his mouth. Offending an earth spirit was not a good idea. "I need to see and hear she is well."

Yr Wyddfa cocked his head. "Ah, there's that look again. I first saw it when you gazed upon the Firewalker as she was being tortured by Aaron Aningan. It's the look of deep concern...of love."

Jake dropped his gaze as the heat of embarrassment filled his body. He attempted to cloak his true feelings, but it seemed the entity was able to probe deep into his soul. Jake collected his senses and stared directly into Yr Wyddfa's eyes. "She and I are warriors. I only wish to ensure my comrade is well. I need to see it for myself."

Yr Wyddfa rubbed his chin. After several moments, he raised an arm and the torch flared again. He pointed toward a wall. "Behold, she has been observing you the entire time."

Jake's eyes widened as he saw Hilly standing on the other side of a transparent stone barrier. He ran to her and collided with solid rock. Blood trickled down the side of his face.

"She stands on the other side of the veil, Shaman," Yr Wyddfa explained. "It is the barrier between the magical realm and the world of man. You cannot enter."

Jake placed his hand flat on the wall and spread his fingers. Speaking slowly, he mouthed, *"Are you okay?"*

Hilly placed her hand against the transparent wall opposite Jake's palm. She nodded.

Jake faced the entity. "I want to talk to her. *Please*, let me talk to her."

Yr Wyddfa smiled. "All you had to do was ask nicely, Shaman. I will enable speech between the two of you, but no contact. The entity waved his hand and nodded at Jake. "Say something to her."

"Are they treating you well?"

Hilly smiled deeply. "Yes. They've been kind. They healed my wounds and my emotional scars." She pulled the scarf covering her throat down and revealed the blue opal.

"Is it your decision to stay here?"

Hilly glanced at Yr Wyddfa before responding. "Yes. Denali was instrumental in Lord Yr Wyddfa and his giants intervening on my behalf. I will be leaving soon to join her in Alaska."

"When will I see you again?"

Hilly's eyes misted. "I'm not sure. But you'll be the first to know when I can rejoin you and the others."

"It's time to go, Shaman," Yr Wyddfa curtly remarked.

"Just a little more time..."

"No." The entity waved his hand, and the transparent wall disappeared.

Jake pounded the rocky barrier. "Hilly!"

"She can no longer hear you."

Jake faced the entity. "I better not hear that you've done something to her."

"Or what? There is nothing you can do to me, Shaman. But there is so much *I* can do to *you*. Be careful with your next words."

Jake stared at the ground as his thoughts raced. Hilly appeared healthy and not stressed. She would have given him a visual cue if something was amiss. He glanced at the entity. Battling an earth spirit was not a good idea. "Okay, Yr Wyddfa, I'll do as you ask."

Jake turned to leave and stopped. "Would you give something to Hilly for me?"

"What is it?" the entity asked.

Jake opened his shirt pocket and withdrew an item. He held it up. A faint sweet scent wafted.

The entity cocked his head. "A lupine bloom? What is the significance?"

"Hilly will know."

"I will grant your request." The entity reached forward and plucked the dried flower from Jake's fingers.

"Thank you, Yr Wyddfa," Jake replied. Jake dipped his head in respect and departed.

Yr Wyddfa stared after Jake. *There is hope for you, yet, Shaman.*

Jake hurried down the corridor and exited the cave into a blinding snowstorm.

Fucking Yr Wyddfa probably conjured this up as a passing shot, he thought. He glanced into the tunnel. For a moment he considered marching back in and giving the earth spirit a piece of his mind. *Not worth the trouble,* he reasoned.

He shielded his eyes from the stinging snow and launched into the sky. Minutes later, he soared over the Atlantic heading toward Massachusetts. As he passed over The Nine Muses, he telepathically messaged Kai. *I'll be about an hour. Tell Chance.*

Moments later, Jake alighted on top of a butte in central Wyoming. Crouching low, he gazed into the distance. It was autumn, but the remnants of a recent heat wave lingered. He wiped his brow with his sleeve and scanned the landscape looking for something...or someone.

His head snapped in the direction of the Big Horn Medicine Wheel half a mile away. A small figure stood near the center cairn of the sacred circle. The person hadn't been there a moment earlier.

I seek Fen Kemp, the Guardian of Peace, Jake reached out telepathically.

Who are you? the figure replied.

I am Jake Pierson, the Keeper of the Word.

The figure disappeared. *Where did you go so fast?* Jake thought.

"I am here," a female answered.

Jake whirled to find a petite woman with long black hair wearing a beige cotton sheath. Dark eyes with gold centers stood out on her tanned face. She was barefoot and took a step toward Jake. The top of the butte was covered with sharp stones, but her face gave no indication that she suffered as she stepped forward.

"I am Miriam."

"I need to talk with Fen."

"She sleeps within the medicine wheel." Miriam pointed to the sacred circle in the distance.

Jake followed her gesture. "I can clearly see she is not in the circle."

Miriam smiled gently. "No, she is not," she acknowledged. "But you already knew that, didn't you?"

"It's important that I speak with her. She's needed at the Guardian boulder for the Crystal of Earth."

"Fen is with her people, the Healers. She cannot be disturbed."

"Without Fen, we can't restore the crystal to its seat of power. The world will never know peace."

Mirian lowered to the ground and patted the dirt beside her. "Please sit, Jake." She drew her legs up and adjusted her shift so it covered most of her skin.

Jake plopped to the ground and sat cross-legged with his hands draped across his knees.

"What a beautiful view from this perch," she said as she gazed back at the sacred circle.

Jake studied Miriam's face. It was serene and peaceful. With her smooth skin and youthful appearance, Jake figured Miriam was in her twenties.

She cocked her head at Jake. "I'm older than time itself, Jake Pierson. As I sit before you in this realm, I exist in ten other planes and yet I do not exist at all." She tucked a loose lock of hair around one ear. "I'm aware of your mission for the chosen four. I...we have been waiting patiently for a millennium. But Fen is no longer of this dimension. She sleeps in the arms of the Healers."

"The Word is clear about what must be done," Jake stated.

Miriam peered into his eyes. "You are conflicted. You are a man of purpose, of commitment and you yearn to see the earth crystal reunited with its Guardian boulder, but feel that the world has turned on you and stopped you from gaining that which you seek. You are impatient. But now is the time for patience and reflection."

Jake exhaled loudly through pursed lips.

Miriam giggled. "This is hard for you. Sitting...talking...reflecting." She gazed skyward. "I don't spend much time in this world. It's serene and beautiful."

"Where do you come from?" Jake asked.

"I come from the land. I am born of all living things."

Jake touched her hand. His finger slid through her palm as if she didn't exist at all. "You're a spirit," he remarked.

"I am energy." She swept her arms wide. "I am filled with the same energy that creates the life around you—the trees, the rocks, the animals."

"You came from the sacred circle. Is Fen within that medicine wheel on a different plane?"

Miriam gazed at the ancient circle of stones and nodded.

"Will she ever be allowed to come to this plane?"

Miriam shook her head. "No. She has evolved to a much higher level of being."

"If she cannot come to me, may I go to her?"

"No. You have not evolved enough to be included in that world."

Jake dropped his head and sighed. After several moments he set his jaw and looked intensely at Miriam. "Please help me, Miriam. Tell me how I can complete my mission."

Miriam tapped the side of her head and grinned. "You are a clever shaman. You already know how *you* can accomplish it. But to include Fen, you will need me as an intermediary. All you had to do was ask for assistance and not demand answers."

Miriam stood and brushed the dirt from her dress. Jake joined her. "Are you taking me to see Fen?"

Miriam shook her head. "You haven't been listening. Fen sleeps with her ancestors. This is a not a short nap. While she slumbers, she is being fed the knowledge of the Healers, her tribe. The process takes as long as it takes for her to retain the information." Miriam walked to the edge of the butte and gazed out at the vista. "Answers to our questions arrive at the precise time we need them. No sooner."

"But we need to restore the remaining crystals and bring peace to the world. We need Fen."

"My dear shaman, you should understand by now that we have no control over what has occurred, nor can we plan for the unknowns. The only thing we can control is the present. And today you will *not* see Fen." Miriam raised her hands to heart center and bowed toward Jake. Then she vanished.

Jake balled his fists and screamed, "Dammit!"

A bald eagle shrieked. The raptor circled overhead before soaring eastward.

Jake sighed. *I suppose that's a sign I'm supposed to go to The Nine Muses.*

A girl's giggle floated on the wind, and he glanced toward the sacred circle. Miriam stood at the central cairn and raised a hand toward him.

Jake waved back.

Miriam vanished.

Chapter 7

Returning Home to Denali

Lord Yr Wyddfa and Hilly strolled through a brightly lit corridor.

"It's been a week since you arrived in my kingdom, Firewalker. It's time for you to return to your earth mother, Denali. My giants report that you have made a full recovery." The entity glanced at Hilly. "Is their assessment correct?"

"Your giants have been most kind and have treated me with deep respect," she replied.

The laird halted. "Including Bran? He can be quite grumpy."

Hilly looked up. "Bran has had his moments, but I think he really does care about me." A gracious smile lit up her face.

"That pleases me," the laird responded as a flurry of purple and blues flashed throughout his aura.

"I'm looking forward to seeing Denali. It's been a long time since I've been on her slopes or gazed into her eyes."

"She's anxious to see you too. She's a peculiar earth spirit. Not very trusting, is she?"

"She's accustomed to getting her way. You've been a gracious host, but I'm sure Denali will be critical of everything that you've done for me."

"I agree. If the situation was reversed, I'm sure I would be distrustful of any information she provided me about any of my earth children."

For an hour they chatted while walking through a network of rocky tunnels carved from solid bluestone. Eventually, they emerged into a cavernous space. Bran, Dylan, and Ellis awaited them. The three giants bowed as Yr Wyddfa passed.

"Firewalker, we have reached the end as well as the beginning." He pointed toward a glistening black wall. "In front of you lies the separation between my realm and the land of humans. On the other side of this barrier is where you may open your portal to Denali." The entity touched the rock, and it shimmered into translucence.

Hilly's eyes widened. On the other side of the veil, she observed three deer foraging for food in a pine forest. A hare jumped into view mere feet from the barrier, stood on its hind legs, and stared at her, its nose twitching furiously. "Can it see me?" she asked.

"Nature's creatures are all magical and this furry one can see you, though you stand on this side of the veil."

"There was a forbidden boundary on Shasta," Hilly mused. "My brother, Kai, could penetrate it, but I was not allowed."

"Why not?"

"Axel, the coyote, told me I couldn't enter. He told me only Kai would be able to penetrate the veil."

The laird chuckled. "Axel is a trickster to his core. I know of his antics. He's been warned to stay off my slopes, but my giants have seen him frequently regardless."

"You mean I could have followed Kai through the veil?"

"Yes. You are a Firewalker witch and have the means to come and go to the realms of all earth spirits." He chuckled again. "Axel is a scoundrel."

Hilly thought back to her journey with Kai and Jake on the slopes of Mount Shasta. She recalled anxiously waiting for her brother's return from beyond the veil. When she had stared at the rockface she was convinced she could see and hear Kai, but Axel's warning had kept her from trying to penetrate the magical world of Shasta.

"Well, I'll be..." she whispered.

"We've all been outwitted by Axel at some point," Yr Wyddfa admitted.

"Even you? An earth spirit?"

Dylan laughed out loud and then clamped his hand over his mouth. Yr Wyddfa gave him a cross look and then chuckled again. "Yes, even me. There is no malice in that coyote but some of his antics can be quite embarrassing."

The hare suddenly bounded away.

"It's time, Firewalker," Yr Wyddfa announced. "Denali grows impatient to see you."

Hilly turned and faced the giants. "Thank you again for healing my wounds and for resetting the blue opal into my neck. If it wasn't for your healing, I would be dead or might have gone insane." One by one, she gestured for them to lean down so she could kiss their cheek.

"Welcome," Bran grumbled.

"Our pleasure," Dylan remarked.

"Honored to be of service," Ellis said, his cheeks flaming crimson.

Hilly turned to Lord Yr Wyddfa. "I appreciate you intervening on my behalf." She dipped her head and flashed him a smile. "One day, I would like to return to your kingdom and listen to the stories about the history of this land and how it came to be."

"It would be my pleasure to entertain you," the laird responded.

She looked at everyone one more time, then whirled and walked through the translucent wall without hesitation. Once on the other side, she turned around. The veil was no longer visible, but she could sense eyes were watching her. She thrust her hands into the air and invoked the powers of the north, the east, the south, and the west. A huge portal opened in front of her, and she trotted in.

When the portal re-opened, Hilly exited onto a snowy slope. A cloudless azure sky loomed above her. Fresh snow covered everything. She drew in a long breath. The air was crisp and clean, and a pang of familiarity caught her in her throat.

She was home.

CAW!

Hilly glanced up. Perched on a rocky overhang was a large raven. It was the spiritual animal Denali had gifted her to help identify disingenuous people.

CAW!

The corvid ruffled its feathers and cawed joyously at her arrival.

"I'm happy to see you as well," she called out.

The raven launched into the sky and soared above Denali's peak until it became a mere pinprick in the beautiful blue sky.

It's been too long, she thought as she surveyed the land around her.

Hilly. Denali's voice drifted through Hilly's mind like a gentle breeze

Mother, Hilly replied. *I've returned home.*

Come to me, my child.

A thunderous rumbling shook the slope. Snow and boulders tumbled from their high perches. Familiar with Denali's unusual manner of welcoming her, Hilly deftly avoided them by jumping sideways and flying out of the way. She sought refuge under a rocky overhang just as a large crack appeared in a rockface opposite her sanctuary. After tortuous groaning and grinding, the fissure split the rock in two and revealed a narrow passageway.

Join me, my child, Denali urged.

Without hesitation, Hilly shimmied through the crack and entered a damp cave that smelled dank and musty. Snowmelt trickled down the walls and ran into a small pool of milky water. The moment she passed through the entrance, the rock fused together with a grinding groan, and the room was plunged into darkness.

Follow the path, Denali instructed. *I'm anxious to see you again.*

Though she couldn't see anything, Hilly trotted easily down the passageway, relying on her intuition to guide her. She brushed her hands along the tunnel walls, and images of her first visit fluttered through her mind like the frames of an old movie.

The corridor ended abruptly but Hilly's instincts prevented her from colliding with the rock in front of her. She slid her hands along the walls until she found a small opening two feet from the ground. It seemed to be just high enough for her to wriggle through on her back.

She bent down and peered through. A faint light flickered from the other side. *It's never easy to see Denali,* she thought as she recalled her first visit, which involved shimmying through a narrow crevice of jagged quartz that slashed her body.

She placed her broadsword, Raven, onto the ground near the opening. Then she maneuvered onto her back, clutched Raven to her chest, and wriggled through the hole headfirst. The space was tight, but she managed to reach the other side with only a few scrapes.

A breath caught in her throat when she stood and found she was in Denali's throne room. The massive chamber soared twenty stories above her. Thousands of quartz crystals jutted from the ceiling and walls, illuminating the room with brilliant sunshine that filtered through their faceted sides.

A waft of sulfur burned her nostrils. A fissure filled with fast-moving lava snaked through the floor and stretched into the distance. In the middle of the immense cavern, a gentle waterfall, born from the snowmelt, cascaded from the ceiling to the floor where it disappeared underground. Gnarled black tree roots protruded from the ceiling and walls like twisted fingers.

Beside the cerulean water stood the Great Mother. *Come to me,* she beckoned.

Mother! Hilly launched into the air and soared high above the hot lava zigzagging across the floor.

"Welcome, my daughter," Denali called out as Hilly touched down beside her.

Formed from white granite, Denali wore an ice-crystal gown, the interlaced frost appearing like delicate lacework. Her long, dark hair was twisted into a bun held in place by selenite sticks, and ringlets cascaded down her angular cheeks. In one hand, she held a slender, selenite wand, and a crystalline crown sat atop her head.

One blue opal eye peered out from a delicately sculpted face. She gazed at Hilly with intense love.

"Come to me," Denali said as she spread her snow-white arms wide.

Hilly folded into Denali and the icy entity hugged her tightly. When they parted, frost had formed on Hilly's eyelashes and hair.

Hilly gazed into Denali's face, taking note of the vibrant blue opal eye staring back at her. Hilly touched the gemstone in her throat, then stroked Denali's face where the other eye had once been located.

"Through your sacrifice of the blue opal, the voices have remained quiet," Hilly said. "Without your generosity, I may be dead or completely mad."

"When Aaron snatched the opal from your throat, I could feel your pain and anguish," Denali said. "Then when your siblings cast your soul to the Land of the Undead so they could dispatch the Yfel, I feared you would not be able to find your way home. Fortunately, Lord Yr Wyddfa guided you back."

"Yr Wyddfa told me about his promise to you."

"Yes, Yr Wyddfa was kind for looking after you. I doubted him, but he delivered on his promise and returned you to me. Come. Let's talk about more pleasant things." Denali sat upon a bench carved from solid ice. She patted the slab. "Please, sit and tell me about your adventures."

Despite the chilly seat, Hilly felt warm, fueled by the love between herself and Denali. After some consideration, she spoke. "Aaron forced me to release Stygian."

Denali nodded. “Yes, I know. Yet Stygian punished Aaron for his cruel treatment of you.”

“What *has* happened to Stygian?” Hilly asked. “I can’t recall what occurred.”

“Chance and Fen successfully propelled him back to Ceres where he is standing trial for his crimes.”

“Chance and Fen? Together? I wasn’t aware their powers were that strong.” Hilly sighed. “I should be on Ceres. I’m a witness to Stygian’s crimes.”

“Darrius, Benedict, and Alden are the only witnesses needed for his trial, which is underway as we speak.”

“What will be the outcome?” Hilly asked, a note of uneasiness in her voice.

“You know I can’t share that information with you.”

Hilly dropped her head and looked at the floor.

“You seem troubled,” Denali noticed. “Are you worried about Stygian?”

“No!” Hilly answered quickly. She shook her head and added, “Perhaps.”

“Ah. Stygian’s blood runs through your veins. You have a natural affinity for the Cererian.”

“But that’s wrong. He’s murdered so many.”

“And yet, you fear he will be killed for his actions.”

“Yes,” Hilly whispered.

“If he’s found innocent, would you want to see him? Would you want to join him in the brotherhood...become a Brethren?”

“No! The Yfel are despicable. I don’t condone anything they do.”

“Stygian is their leader. He has killed more magicians than any other Brethren soldier. Do you not find *him* despicable?”

Hilly dropped her head. “He is blood of my blood. Since I released him from his interdimensional cell, he has attempted to enter my mind. Six months ago, when I first encountered him at The Nine Muses, he could easily enter my body. But my powers have strengthened, and he can no longer come and go as he pleases."

Denali chuckled.

"You're laughing at me?" Hilly pouted.

"I find it amusing that you protest his intrusion, yet there is a strong desire to know him better."

Hilly blushed and turned away.

"I've struck a chord," Denali teased.

"It's complicated," Hilly answered. "I detest what he is, but he's my family. Kai and Chance found their original families, but I never will. I am the last Firewalker, the last of my kind. But I carry Stygian's DNA. He's the closest thing to a natural family I will ever know."

Denali nodded. "Yes, I understand." She leaned closer to Hilly. "Do you recall what I've always told you about making decisions? Trust your intuition because it will never betray you. If you are compelled to seek out Stygian, then you must explore that avenue. But do so only if that's truly what lies in your heart."

"Your advice has served me well in the past," Hilly replied.

A stillness settled between the earth spirit and her daughter.

After several peaceful moments, Hilly spoke. "I've made a decision. If the situation presents itself, I'll speak with Stygian."

"Do you feel safe in his presence?" Denali asked.

"I do. He's had opportunities to kill me and didn't. When he first appeared as Mr. Spatz, the bedraggled cat caught in the rain, he lived in our house for months and never harmed me."

"But he attempted to seize your body at The Nine Muses."

"I'm not so sure that's what he intended. I think he helped me realize my potential. Darrius was my only guide as my powers developed, and it was Darrius who warned that Stygian should be avoided because he posed a threat. Is it possible that Darrius was actually limiting the growth of my abilities?"

"Darrius's advice is not misguided. Stygian murders innocent people for their magic. Power is the main motivator for Cererians who convert to the ways of the Brethren. *You* are powerful. The Yfel would love to claim you as their prize."

"I suppose you're right, Great Mother." The earth spirit's words made sense, yet Hilly was still unsure.

Denali smiled, satisfied with Hilly's decision. "What has become of the shaman Jake?" Denali blurted.

"He visited me at Lord Yr Wyddfa's kingdom and urged me to leave with him," Hilly replied. "I told him I was meeting with you, so he left to join my brothers at The Nine Muses."

"Interesting. He has taken your brothers to your ancestral home in Manchester-By-The-Sea. I wonder if that means the Guardian boulder for Chance's crystal is located nearby."

Hilly arched an eyebrow. "I thought you knew everything that occurred in the world."

A small grin cracked across the icy angles of Denali's face. "As an earth spirit, I am quite aware of what will transpire but sometimes the details can be cloaked. The shaman is clever and has learned to conceal his thoughts against those who are more powerful than himself. It's a small irritant, but I will find out in due course."

Hilly rubbed her chin. "I find it interesting that the Prophecy provided for so many protection layers so others could not find and destroy the Guardians. But there are disadvantages to that strategy. Without Fen, the Guardians can't be unlocked. Without Jake, we can't locate the them."

"The construct of the Prophecy was deliberate," Denali explained. "We wanted to avoid another catastrophe."

"*Another* catastrophe?"

Denali stopped talking and peered into the blue waters of the nearby pool. When she spoke again, her voice was barely audible. "When the Cererians first arrived on this planet a millennium ago, they found it to be a peaceful world. The magical populations practiced their craft without prejudice and lived in harmony with the land and each other." She looked at Hilly. "But that tranquil life was soon shattered when Stygian inadvertently discovered he could consume a magician's power when their soul left their body after death."

"What happened?" Hilly pressed.

"I've said enough. It's up to you and your siblings to right this wrong. Your family, along with the shaman, will establish peace on this planet once again." Denali stood. "It's time for you to rejoin the others."

"But, Mother, I've just arrived. I thought we'd—"

"Silence!" Denali walked away from Hilly. "You must leave. And it must be now."

Hilly stared at Denali's back. Confused, she cried out, "Yr Wyddfa was more cordial when he bid me goodbye!"

Denali whirled. Ice-crystal tears cascaded down her cheeks and shattered on the floor. "You impertinent child!" she roared. "Your words are like daggers in my heart."

Hilly fell to her knees and raised her hands. "I beg forgiveness, mother. I meant no disrespect." The entity swiped the glittering remains of tears from her cheeks. "Mother, why are you crying?"

Denali marched several paces away.

"Mother?"

"Our time together grows short, daughter," Denali uttered as she gazed into the distance. She faced Hilly. "You must leave. Go now...please."

Hilly rose. "Have I angered you?"

"No."

"Tell me what I've done. I'll set it right."

Denali stepped forward and cradled Hilly's cheek. "You are everything I wanted in a child. There is nothing you could do that would make me prouder of who you've become, and what you will give humanity."

"Then let me stay. Tell me the stories of our world before the Cererians and their murderous chaos arrived."

Denali smiled wide. "We will meet again. Soon. But, you must rejoin your brothers and the shaman." Denali threw her arms wide and Hilly vanished.

Moments later Hilly dropped from the sky and rolled into a snowbank. She pushed into a sitting position and shook her head dislodging snowflakes and ice crystals. She was sitting on the slope where the opening to Denali's realm had first appeared.

Hilly sighed.

I look forward to seeing you again, Mother, she telepathically messaged to Denali.

Go forth, Firewalker. Make your mark on this world, Denali replied.

Chapter 8

The Plan

"Feeding your faces again?" Jake said as he burst into the dining room.

"Jake!" Chance shouted. He gripped the shaman in a bear hug and lifted him up.

Kai frowned and crossed his arms. "So, where'd you go? You left me alone over the Atlantic without saying a word."

Jake avoided Kai's stare as he circled the table checking out the plates of food. He picked up a few morsels of meat and popped them in his mouth. "Where'd you get the food?" he mumbled.

"You must be the missing shaman," a male voice greeted.

Jake glanced up.

"I'm Robert Downs," the Cererian said cheerfully. He extended a hand toward Jake. "But you may call me Bob."

Jake wiped his hands on his pants and took the man's hand. "Jake Pierson."

"I know. Darrius asked that I keep an eye on all of you." He glanced at his watch. "You're an hour overdue. I was beginning to think you may have gotten into trouble."

"Trouble? Me?" Jake grabbed a couple of rolls and slumped into a chair. He studied the man through narrowed eyes.

Bob smiled. "Darrius warned me about your antics." He poured a glass of water and sipped while eyeing Jake over the rim.

"Antics?" Jake glanced at Chance and Kai then shrugged. "I don't know what you mean."

"Mr. Pierson, I'm not here to be your babysitter. Please do what you like, but I take my role as an observer seriously. I've been entrusted with safeguarding the lives of Chance and Kai. Darrius advised me *you* would be ambivalent toward my protection but I'm at your disposal should you require it." Bob grinned wider, raised his glass, and added, "Cheers, Mr. Pierson."

"Here, here," Chance echoed, raising his glass.

Kai coughed a chuckle into his fist.

Jake juggled two rolls and peered at the Cererian.

Bob gazed back at the shaman with a serene smile.

After several moments, Jake slammed the rolls on the table, snatched his fork, and stabbed the ham slices on the platter in front of him. "Okay, Bob," he said. "You do what you've gotta do, and I'll do what I've gotta do." He paused. "Okay?"

"Right-o, Mr. Pierson," Bob replied.

"Jake. Call me Jake."

"Right-o, Jake."

"Now you're pissing me off."

"That was my intention."

Kai burst out laughing.

"Lighten up, Jake," Chance joked as he lobbed a dinner roll that bounced off Jake's head.

"Have your fun while you can," Jake warned.

"Ooh, I'm scared," Chance said as he held his trembling hands in the air.

Jake glared. *Do something about your brother,* he telepathically messaged Kai.

Chance is a big kid, Kai replied. *Ignore him.*

Bob's gaze darted between Jake and Kai. A wry smile popped onto his face.

"You're listening to our private conversation, aren't you, Bob?" Jake said accusingly.

"What conversation?" Chance asked. "Were you guys mind-talking about me? I don't appreciate you talking about me behind my back...right in front of me."

Bob calmly gulped his water and walked toward the dining room door. He turned and faced Jake. "I wasn't listening to your mental chit chat. That's not something I, or any other Cererian would do. But your faces—yours and Kai's—betrayed your cloaked dialogue."

"What did you say about me?" Chance demanded as he got in Jake's face. Jake shoved him away, leapt to his feet, and thrust his hands forward defensively.

Chance did likewise.

"Guys!" Kai yelled. "Settle down." Kai pushed between Jake and Chance and gently pulled his brother to the other side of the table. "Good grief, Chance. Sit down and eat." He pointed at Jake. "And you! Quit provoking him. You know it bothers him when we have mental conversations. He feels left out." Kai patted his brother's head. "It's not Chance's fault he's a weirdo."

"Hey!" Chance roared as swatted at Kai.

Kai poured three drinks of bourbon and handed one to Jake and placed one on the table in front of Chance. Then he sat in a chair between the two men. He slowly sipped his drink and closed his eyes. "Mmm, that sure is good."

Kai's eyes shot open. "So, where *did* you go, Jake?" he demanded. "Halfway across the ocean, you rocketed out of sight and left me on my own."

"Hmpf," Jake replied with a full mouth.

"I bet he went back to Mount Snowdon," Chance guessed.

"Really? Jake wouldn't go against Darrius's wishes, would he?" Kai wiggled his eyebrows and they both laughed.

"I saw Hilly," Jake mumbled between bites.

"What did she say?" Kai asked.

"Well, she's not here, is she?" Jake barked.

Kai shot a glance at Chance. "Did Yr Wyddfa prevent you from talking to her?"

"No. We spoke…through the veil. The laird didn't trust me to be in the same room as her. She wanted to see Denali. That's all." Jake chewed his food slowly and stared into space.

Chance poked Kai with his elbow, pointed at Jake, and shrugged. "So, you're good with this?" Chance asked.

Jake sneered. "Not really. But there's nothing I can do."

"Man, you still have your knickers in a twist," Chance provoked. "You've got to get over that atomic wedgie up your ass before you do something you'll regret."

"You mean like this?" Jake tipped the entire table onto Chance and stormed out of the dining room.

"What the fuck?" Chance shouted. He easily righted the table and surveyed the mess strewn all over the floor. "That was a waste of perfectly good food!"

"Damn, Chance," Kai said. "Jake's really mad."

"I believe the shaman has a lot on his mind," Bob mused. "Events are happening fast, and his work has ground to a halt. I'll have a chat with him."

"Be careful, Bob," Chance warned. "You're liable to have your head chewed off if you piss him off further." Chance picked food fragments from his clothes and popped them into his mouth.

After searching the foyer and living room, Bob found Jake in the study. The shaman stood in front of the window and gripped a bottle of Woodford Reserve in his fist. He stared at the calm, blue sea, while absently guzzling from the bottle.

"How may I assist you, Jake?" Bob said standing just inside the doorway with his fingertips pressed together in front of his chest.

"Go away!" Jake snapped. He tilted the bottle to his mouth and gulped.

"It's not easy," Bob said.

Jake tilted his head. "What's not easy?"

"The next stage of the Prophecy."

Jake sighed and gazed at the ocean.

Bob walked into the room and sat in a chair to the side of the shaman. He followed Jake's gaze.

Jake tightened the cap on the bottle and walked it back to the credenza. "What do you know?" he demanded.

"No more than you. But it can't be easy to move forward when you don't have all the elements to execute the plan."

Jake scrutinized the tiny Cererian who sat ramrod straight with his chin tilted upward. "Everyone is changing," Jake softly replied. "Hilly...Fen...me."

The Cererian nodded. "Yes. It's to be expected."

"Right now, I feel like a fly bumping into the window looking for a way out, only to have a gigantic swatter splatter me all over the place."

"Interesting analogy."

"That's how I feel. I can't reach Fen. I can't reach Hilly. And I need to get Chance to his Guardian boulder."

"You're not accustomed to being quiet with nothing to do."

"Nope. I need to keep going. I need a plan." Jake stared at Bob. "I don't expect you to understand." Jake marched toward the study door. "I'm going to get some fresh air down at the beach."

In a flash, Bob appeared in front of Jake and held his palms in front of his face. "You're not going outside. It's not safe."

Jake gritted his teeth and pushed against Bob, trying to shove him aside.

The Cererian grabbed Jake's arm and bent it downward. Jake retaliated by swinging at Bob with his free fist. Bob caught Jake's fist and squeezed...hard. Jake collapsed to the floor. "My hand! You're crushing my hand!"

Kai and Chance ran to the room.

"What the?" Chance uttered as Jake squirmed under Bob's grip.

"Your friend and I are having a discussion," Bob said, then he released the shaman. Jake cradled his reddened fist to his chest. "We had a difference of opinion about him going outside."

"I guess you won," Chance observed.

"As a reminder," Bob announced, "Nobody is allowed outside. The reinforced magic will keep you all safe *only* if you remain within The Nine Muses." The Cererian left the study and hurried for the staircase where he paused and added, "Please be in the study at five o'clock. I'll have some updates."

Jake slumped against the door. He wrapped his arms around his legs and laid his forehead on his knees. Chance made a face at Kai and shrugged.

"Rough day, Jake?" Chance asked as he patted his friend's shoulder.

"You have no idea." Jake whispered. "I feel like I've been castrated, and Bob threw my balls in my face."

"Ouch!" Chance said wincing. "Come on, get yer ass up!" Chance ordered as he thumped his hand against Jake's shoulder.

Jake didn't move.

"C'mon Jake. You can't sit there stewing in your misery."

Jake looked up at his friend and sighed. "I get the feeling you won't let me stay on the floor?"

"Nope," Chance replied. "You can grab my hand, or I'll pick you up and carry you like a baby."

Jake sighed again before gripping his friend's hand. Chance easily hefted him onto his feet, guided him to a chair, and gently pushed him back.

Kai stood nearby swirling bourbon in his glass.

"Nice of you to ask if we wanted a drink," Chance teased.

"I don't want to make assumptions," Kai joked. He poured two more glasses. "Here, you go, Chance. Here, Jake."

Jake accepted the glass. Chance clinked Jake's glass and gulped his drink. "Ah, much better."

Jake didn't touch his drink. Instead, he placed it on the end table and stared at the floor. He slumped further into the chair.

"The ocean is so calm," Kai observed. "Completely different from the nor'easter that lashed The Nine Muses seven months ago. Back then, vicious lightning, hailstones, and pelting rain welcomed us as we ran onto the beach to fight Stygian."

"Yeah," Chance agreed. "Now, the sun is shining, and the water's surface is like glass. So peaceful."

"It won't be peaceful for long," Jake whispered.

The brothers looked at Jake. He had quietly risen and moved between them at the window. He jutted his jaw and steeled his eyes.

"I know that look," Kai mused.

"Yep," Chance agreed. "We're either going to have a lot of fun or get into trouble. I wager it's the latter."

Jake put a hand on each of his friends' shoulders. "Chance, Kai, we have a lot of work to do. I have a plan."

Chapter 9

The Cererian Homecoming

Darrius peered through the circular window into Stygian's cell pod, an egg-shaped metal structure filled with compressed air. Anchored to the floor, in the middle of a room the size of a large closet, the pod was big enough to contain one person.

Darrius pressed his head against the glass and grimaced. Shackled by invisible restraints, Stygian hovered mid-air, his arms and legs stretched out to the side forming an X.

His head slumped on his chest.

It's difficult to see him in this manner, Darrius telepathically said to his friend, the Senator. *He may be the leader of the Yfel, but I know him as a kind soul.*

Your kind soul killed ten of my guards before we secured him and his Brethren soldiers, Balor and Cary, the Senator replied. *Forced slumber is the only way we can prevent them from conjuring magic and harming more innocent Cererians.*

The Senator appeared as an ethereal being comprised of pure energy, a misty shape swirling with hues of purple and blue. He was as tall as Darrius and possessed two arm-like appendages with two large black orbs as eyes, but the similarities ended there. An electrical spark continually pulsed in the middle of his form and pushed charged particles throughout his body.

Darrius studied Stygian. *I suppose it's the right thing to do. But how will you prevent his outbursts when he stands trial?*

My engineers assure me they can easily transport these pods into the Justice Hall and manipulate the controls so Stygian will not be able to cast spells as he provides testimony.

Do you have faith in your engineers?

Not entirely. But this is new to all of us. Dealing with individuals like Stygian is unique. We were sorely unprepared for his level of abilities. Now we must manage the unfortunate results of our precipitous undertakings.

Precipitous undertakings? Is that what we're calling the mission mandate? Darrius scowled. *I, too, am a result of your precipitous undertaking.*

Careful, Darrius. Your sharp words will sever our friendship.

I apologize. I'm frustrated by the changes I've witnessed here on Ceres. Hundreds of objectors protested our arrival when Benedict, Alden, and I teleported into the city. Seeing them reduce their energy so their forms turned black was disturbing. The symbolic protest stretched around the teleportation building like a black band.

Yes. Cererians are nervous. Disturbing news from Earth regarding the Yfel Brethren's killings has spread panic among our citizens. So intense is their fear that even benevolent Cererians like yourself are suspect.

Darrius sighed. *Fear is the only sickness that relies on the destruction of others as its cure. Is it true that the transforming chambers are being deactivated? Or that the mission mandate has been cancelled?*

A flurry of bright blue flashed within the Senator. *It was inevitable, Darrius. Our generals considered stopping the mission a millennium ago when the original incident occurred, when Stygian acquired the magic of a dying human magician. But, if you recall, I intervened because I felt the event was an unfortunate accident. But your friend continued to murder magicians out of greed and power. Stygian made a fool of me. I was disgraced.*

Darrius's eyes softened as he studied the Senator. *I'm sure Stygian didn't plan to harm you with his actions. But, with the information we now possess, it's clearly evident the nature of his host human influenced his decision to choose the murderous path of the Yfel.*

The Senator drifted closer to Stygian's pod. *I wish I could say I believed you.*

I have an important question, Senator. With the transforming chambers dismantled, there is no longer a method for Cererians like me and my comrades to return to our natural state. So we will never be able to revert to our native Cererian form?

Alas, that is true. The Senator moved away.

Senator, it is quite clear that Cererians who have transformed into a human body like me are no longer welcome in our homeland. What are we to do? Accept our fate on Earth?

I'm sorry, Darrius. Circumstances are beyond my control. Surely you see the reasoning behind the decision. Cererians are peaceful. We don't have a history of wars and hatred like the inhabitants of Earth. Though you morphed into a benevolent Cererian, your behavior is still at odds with the sensibilities of our world. You have opposing opinions, and you don't mind challenging others.

Darrius dropped his head. The Senator's last statement stung. His friend made no attempt to hide his harsh opinion. When he looked up, a somber gray hue emanated from the Senator.

Excuse my bluntness, Darrius. But ours is a logical world. Nothing is to be gained circumventing an issue. I admired your bravery when you were the first to volunteer for our mission to Earth, and I commend you now on your ability to embrace your new life on that planet.

So, am I being banished from my homeland?

Effective immediately after the trial.

I feel sorry for you, Senator.

Oh? Why should you feel sorry for me?

You will never understand the extraordinary riches of human emotions. My body allows me to feel the sadness associated with being unwanted. But your Cererian sensibility will never allow you to experience the joy of sharing a feast with others, or the sorrow when a comrade has taken his last breath, or the anger that arises when injustice is waged against the innocent.

We must agree to disagree, Darrius. You have been a good friend to me, and I will miss our conversations.

Then this is goodbye?

Yes. I will see you at the trial, but then we must part ways.

Darrius studied the Senator. Dull grays and browns blinked across the surface of his body. *This is not your decision, is it Senator?*

I follow orders, too, Darrius. Obedience is the Cererian way.

Darrius peered into Stygian's cell, recalling the moment the two of them had become friends—it had been when he and Stygian emerged from their birthing chambers simultaneously. From that moment onward, they were inseparable. Darrius had convinced Stygian to join him on the inaugural flight to Earth and to merge his Cererian life force with human DNA.

Now, they traveled a similar path: Stygian awaited trial and possible death, and Darrius faced banishment and possible death.

It disturbs me, Darrius, the Senator said.

What disturbs you?

The number of Cererians from the original mission who have elected to join the Yfel Brethren.

They can't control their urges. They can't control the inclinations of their human DNA.

Do you support the Brethren?

No, but I understand their situation. I have compassion for the struggle they encounter between their Cererian and human halves. That's another benefit of being partially human.

What is?

Knowing compassion.

In my opinion, it's a trait that weakens the individual.

It's a pity that our scientists didn't devote more time to studying the long-term effects of the human transformation process before requesting thousands of our soldiers to submit to the painful procedure.

The Senator flashed violet. *You've never complained before, Darrius. It doesn't suit you. Come, the trial will soon begin. I'll accompany you to your companions.*

"What will happen during the trial?" Alden asked Benedict. The two Cererians stood beside a black quartz wall adjacent to the front of the Justice Hall building.

"Protocol demands Stygian and the twins be tried separately," Benedict replied. "I suspect the room will be heavily fortified considering Stygian's power."

"I understand that they are currently held in suspended animation and are unable to communicate with anybody?"

"Yes," Benedict responded. "But since the rogue magician, Ryan, penetrated the prison and helped Aaron escape, I'm sure security will take steps to prevent another breach." Benedict gazed into the night sky, a black canvas punctuated with white stars. The planet, Earth, appeared as a large star on the horizon. "I forgot how beautiful it was here on Ceres. I have missed these views."

Alden followed his gaze. "Yes, the night sky is extraordinary. I grew up near the polar caps where it's more desolate. We lived underground and rarely ventured above ground. The shifting magnetic fields would disrupt our core energy if we lingered outside too long."

A group of native Cererians appeared nearby. Androgenous in appearance, the five individuals pulsed a rhythmic yellow-green glow. They regarded Benedict and Alden for a minute before they ventured closer.

You two have just returned from Earth, is that correct? one of them asked telepathically. Flashes of light appeared in his body as he spoke each word. He stared at Benedict and Alden through two black circles that swam in the middle of his head.

That is correct, Benedict replied. He dipped his head in greeting.

What is it like there? another asked.

It is extraordinary, Alden replied. *There are flora and fauna that are vastly different than those here on Ceres. And the inhabitants are kind.*

Not all of them are kind, Benedict interjected. *Some can be cruel and manipulative, like some Cererians.*

The native Cererians faced each other and conversed privately. Their colors brightened and dimmed before they faced Alden and Benedict. *We have been discussing your appearance,* the first one said. *We understand the process is complicated and is permanent.*

Benedict responded. *They have refined the process for fusing our life energy with a human body using harvested DNA. Because the genetic material was obtained from ancient graves, there were no documents to indicate how a person would appear.* Benedict gestured toward Alden. *As you can see, Alden and I are quite different from each other.*

The group of Cererians twinkled and flashed while Alden and Benedict chuckled.

They have placed the program on hold for the time being, Alden added. *They are not transforming any more candidates until we understand more about the impact of our presence on Earth.*

Are you here for the trial? One asked.

Yes. Benedict answered.

I've never met an Yfel Brethren, another noted. *I can't imagine murdering others to enhance my powers.*

How distasteful, yet another concurred.

The trial will be interesting, Benedict remarked.

Darrius and the Senator approached the group. The native Cererians bowed deeply. Their colors muted and paled as they did so. They quietly backed away and disappeared.

Alden and Benedict dipped their heads respectfully.

Senator, let me introduce you to my dear companions, Benedict and Alden, Darrius said as he gestured toward his friends.

It is an honor to meet you, the Senator responded. *Darrius has told me about your accomplishments with the shaman and the magicians.*

The honor is ours, Benedict and Alden responded in unison.

I must take my leave of you, the Senator announced. *I must prepare for the trial. Let's hope we have a positive outcome.*

Yes, they chorused.

Be well, the Senator said as he drifted into the Justice Hall.

Be well, Darrius called after him.

Once the Senator left them, Darrius turned to his friends. "Stygian is held in suspended animation, but I felt something odd when I visited his cell."

"Odd?" Alden inquired.

"I could see Stygian hanging in the middle of the cell pod, but there was something strange about the way he appeared. He seemed faint, almost transparent at times. When I looked directly at him, he appeared normal, but if I glanced away, he appeared transparent out of the corner of my eyes."

"Could the atmosphere in the pod be effecting his biology?" Alden asked.

"Perhaps," Darrius replied. "Though with Ryan's ability to thwart Cererian security forces, stay vigil."

"We should alert the Senator," Benedict advised.

"No!" Darrius shouted and then quickly added in a softer tone, "Listen carefully, we can't trust anybody, not even the Senator." Darrius quieted as another group of native Cererians drifted by and floated into the Justice Hall.

"Are we in danger?" Alden whispered as he eyed the individuals moving away.

"I don't know for sure," Darrius responded. "But be prepared to move fast once the trial has concluded."

"The trial may take days," Benedict remarked. "If we are in danger, we should leave now."

"We must stay," Darrius warned. "It will appear odd if we leave before we give testimony."

"Being vague is not like you, Darrius," Alden observed. "What's going on?"

Darrius faced his friends and cloaked their conversation. *Things are not as they appear. The Senator is no longer our ally. He is merely an actor—one of many—who performs at the direction of more powerful individuals.*

Cererians? Alden asked.

I'm not sure, Darrius replied.

Chapter 10

The Cererian Trial

The Cererian Justice Hall was an impressive structure.

Despite the dramatic effect of the glistening black quartz walls that rose five stories high and formed a pentagon, the spacious interior of the building was devoid of architectural ornamentation. A three-story rotunda dominated the middle of the space, while several short-walled enclosures had been constructed in several areas of the floor. These black quartz walls marked zones that served as separate judicial and witness areas, a viewing gallery for spectators, and in the center, a section where the accused would be held during the trial. Soaring high above the chambers, the rotunda's transparent curved ceiling provided a view of the inky Cererian night sky.

For a typical trial, which was rare in a peaceful society with no lawlessness, the viewing gallery possessed ample room for at least two hundred Cererians, but this was not a normal hearing. Word had spread about Stygian and his followers. Cererians, unfamiliar with senseless killings, flocked to the Justice Hall to catch a glimpse of the creatures accused of murdering hundreds of innocent souls. Because of the unusual nature of the trial, additional space was designated outside, and several widescreens were erected so thousands could witness the proceedings.

There were no attorneys. The accused spoke for themselves and were tried on their testimony and the accounts provided by any witnesses. Long ago, Ceres had evolved to the point that falsehoods were impossible.

Cererians couldn't lie if they tried. They could only speak the truth. But many remained skeptical of the "inter-breeds", which was what Cererians infused with human DNA were called. Many wondered if the inter-breeds would be able to maintain the truth and not distort the facts.

As spectators gathered, their heightened excitement pulsed hues of blues and greens throughout their ethereal bodies. Cererians crammed into the interior spaces and hovered above the top of the barrier walls, each jockeying for a better view of the prisoners on trial.

Within the space reserved for the accused, three cell pods levitated like a trio of enormous metallic eggs. Stygian occupied the one in the front, and the two flanking cells contained his soldiers, Cary and Balor. The Brethren were all in forced slumber.

Earlier, guards accompanied the pods from the prisoner housing area to the Justice Hall, entering through a door in the back of the building. They followed a corridor that snaked below the main floor before rising up to the main gallery via a large shaft.

The six guards—two per each cell pod—flashed the deep-red colors of the elite security squad known for their bravery, dedication, and superior powers. The soldiers drifted continuously around their respective pods, noting any changes of the prisoner within. A curious spectator hovered too far over the demarcation barrier between the viewing gallery and the prisoner zone, and the squad delivered a bolt of energy toward the hapless intruder, rendering them unconscious. The individual's internal energy faded to gray as he fell to the floor.

Darrius studied the cell pods from his bench in the witness zone. Stygian appeared as before: spread eagle with his head drooped to his chest. But there was one change. The trace of a smile appeared on his friend's face. Darrius looked away to clear his vision and then refocused on Stygian. There was no doubt. A corner of his friend's mouth bowed upward, producing a shallow dimple in his pale cheek.

"Looks uncomfortable," Benedict whispered to his colleagues. "It's obvious the holding structures were built without thought to varying sizes of the prisoners they would contain. I'm two feet taller than Stygian and would be bent over at a severe angle."

"Natural Cererians would easily fit in these cells," Darrius remarked. "They weren't constructed for humans."

"Shsh," Alden said. "The trial is beginning."

A melodic chime reverberated throughout the hall.

Three Cererian justices entered and took their places in the judicial section. They hovered side by side in a straight line and faced the prisoners.

A second chime sounded.

Silence filled the space.

At the third chime, the lead justice spoke telepathically to the assemblage,

I, Orion, lead member of the High Order of Truth, call this session to order. Guards, awaken the prisoners so they can see, hear, and speak, but do not activate their limbs.

The soldiers waved one appendage down the side of the pod, releasing a portion of the binding spell that held the prisoners' eyes and mouths in place.

Stygian's eyes flew open. Once he realized he could not move his body, his mouth twisted into a sneer, and he glared at the judges in front of him.

The twins, Balor and Cary, groaned and shut their eyes tightly against the agony of their cramping muscles.

Orion continued. *The accused are Stygian Chernobog, and the brothers Balor and Cary Atwood. The guards have enabled their hearing and speech.*

Orion turned first to his right and then left. *Also officiating are Mason and Luther, members of the High Order of Truth. Their names were selected at random and without prejudice.*

Orion floated to the barrier separating the judicial section from the witness area. *The witnesses are Darrius Dagda, Benedict, and Alden Stark.*

These Cererian brothers have made serious allegations against the accused. The sole purpose of this trial is to determine if crimes have been committed. Let me remind everyone that you are prevented from reading anyone's mind and you are not permitted to have private conversations.

Are there any questions?

Silence.

Then we shall proceed. Prisoners, the guards have enabled your hearing and speech.

Orion drifted to Balor's pod. *Balor Atwood, do you understand the charges against you?*

Balor's eyes twitched to his right, toward Stygian's pod, before he answered telepathically. *Yes, my lord.*

Orion then faced Stygian's cell pod. *Stygian Chernobog, do you understand the charges against you?*

Stygian narrowed his eyes and sneered.

Do you understand? Orion repeated.

"Yessss," Stygian hissed.

Please restrict your comments to telepathic replies, prisoner Stygian.

I don't recognize you as my leader, Stygian replied. *I loathe you and these proceedings.*

For the record, prisoner Stygian, Orion pressed. *Do you understand the charges against you?*

Stygian eyeballs vibrated furiously as he glared at Orion. *YES!,* he finally replied.

Orion proceeded to the cell pod to the left of Stygian. *Cary Atwood, do you understand the charges against you?*

Cary glanced toward Stygian's pod before replying, *Yes, my lord.*

Orion returned to the judicial area and rejoined the other justices. *We are ready to begin.*

Mason floated to the bench of witnesses. *Please stand, Darrius Dagda.*

Darrius rose and nodded at the judge.

You have indicated Stygian committed crimes against the humans on Earth. You claim he harmed others, a crime punishable by death since it goes against our cardinal rule of no harm to anyone.

That is correct, Darrius responded.

Face the accused, Mason said as he led Darrius to the center cell containing Stygian. Darrius locked eyes with his friend.

Repeat your allegation in front of the accused, Mason requested.

Stygian's pupils flared as he scowled at his old friend.

I, Darrius Dagda, witnessed the death of several humans at the hands of Stygian Chernobog. Once he killed each human, he consumed their magic and cast the bodies aside without honor.

How do you plead, Stygian? Mason asked the Yfel leader.

Stygian ignored Mason and glared at Darrius.

Stygian? Mason asked.

I am only guilty of being true to who I am. If that goes against your rules, then so be it. A sinister smile wavered on Stygian's face.

Are you pleading not guilty?

Yes.

Darrius returned to his bench while Mason faced the other judges. *Stygian has pleaded not guilty to the allegations against him.* Mason faced Stygian. We *will now hear your account, prisoner Stygian.*

The Yfel leader drew in a long, slow breath. *If anyone is guilty of a crime, it is all of you,* Stygian's eyes twitched from one justice to another. *It was your scientists who designed a plan to visit Earth and enlist the aid of young Cererians like myself. You claimed to have developed a process that allowed us to exist on the planet along with the inhabitants. I inquired about drawbacks, and I was guaranteed it was infallible. Nothing would go wrong. And furthermore, I was assured when my time was served, I would be restored to my original form.*

Darrius shifted nervously on the bench. His friend's words were true and he knew what was coming next.

Stygian's eyes darted to Darrius. *Darrius was there when I transformed into what you see today. He was there when the true nature of my body overtook my Cererian sensibilities.*

Is this true? Mason asked Darrius.

Yes, Darrius replied.

Go on, Stygian. Mason requested.

We befriended the local inhabitants and were invited to attend the funeral of a warrior, a magician with supernatural powers. As was customary for these people, his body was placed upon a funeral pyre. Once his relatives praised his accomplishments, they set fire to the wood. Their customs dictated friends and family to encircle the structure and bear witness to the deceased's ascension into the heavens. An ethereal, wispy fog drifted upward from the body as it burned. I was told it was his life force seeking the ether and it was an honor to bear witness on its journey.

When I observed the spectacle, a gust of wind pushed the life force toward me. Before I realized what had happened, I inadvertently inhaled the soul. I choked and convulsed. Others came to my aide, but I couldn't dislodge the spirit. Stygian paused.

Darrius sat tight-lipped as he listened to Stygian's testimony. His friend's words were true without embellishment. Darrius thought back to when the exploration party first arrived on Earth. Not long after their arrival, he realized his comrades' personalities were changing as the human DNA fought their Cererian sensibilities for control of their bodies. Changes were subtle at first. Some soldiers became more extroverted or introverted. Then their emotions escalated with some men becoming more peaceful while others exhibited rage.

Darrius had witnessed the transformation in Stygian. Known as a fierce but fair warrior on Ceres, when Stygian's energy was combined with human DNA, Darrius noticed his friend's temper shortened, and he resorted to physical violence even against his own soldiers.

Darrius stared at Stygian. *Is it his fault that he changed?* Darrius thought.

Go on, Stygian, Mason urged.

I collapsed. Darrius and the others took me back to my tent and nursed me. I was told a fever set upon me, and I began babbling in a language unknown to the men. Several days later, I awoke. I felt different...not physically...but emotionally. It was so long ago, but I remember to this day, that I felt as though I awoke with three personalities—my Cererian ego, my ever-changing human psyche, and something else, an energy that pulsed below the surface. I felt invincible...I felt powerful.

Stop there, Stygian, Mason directed. *I wish to ask Darrius a clarifying question.* Mason faced Darrius and asked, *Darrius, do you recall the account as Stygian has related?*

Darrius didn't hesitate. *Yes,* he answered.

Did Stygian appear different after the incident? Mason asked.

Darrius glanced at his friend and mulled over his answer.

Darrius? Mason urged.

Darrius faced the justice. *It was after Stygian awoke from the fever that I noticed a tremendous change, more so than before.*

How so? Mason asked.

He appeared obsessed with the magician population more than when we first arrived.

Please explain what you mean by 'obsessed.'

Our interaction with the planet's inhabitants had been limited, restricted to observing their customs and day-to-day activities, all of which had been approved by the village leaders. But after Stygian awoke from the fever he began spying on those who possessed high magic and followed them when they visited sacred spaces. Stygian would shape-shift into a creature and watch the magicians cast their spells.

Did Stygian ever interfere?

No.

Did Stygian practice their spells?

Not to my knowledge.

Spying on others is not becoming of an officer of his rank. Mason glanced at Stygian and then returned to Darrius.

I agree, Lord Mason, Darrius said. *However, he went beyond spying. He'd follow individuals to their homes and observe their habits.*

While that is unseemly behavior for an officer, it does not violate the terms of the original mission.

He observed their habits like a predator watching its prey. And when the time was right, he pounced.

Exactly what did he do?

He killed magicians and consumed their souls, and along with the souls, their magical powers. He quickly learned he was more powerful when he killed them and consumed their energy.

You witnessed this?

Yes.

Liar! Stygian yelled into everyone's heads.

Mason waved an appendage freezing the Yfel leader's ability to respond. *No outbursts of any kind are allowed. You were made aware of this rule, and it will not be tolerated.* Mason waved an appendage again. *You may now provide your account of the situation that Darrius has just described.*

Stygian's eyes vibrated with rage. He glared at Darrius and answered. *Darrius's account is accurate up to a point. Where our versions deviate, is my supposed killing of the magicians.*

Oh? Mason said, *Explain.*

I befriended many individuals within the population and, yes, I would go on exploration hikes with some of them where they would show me the medicinal properties of flora and fauna, which I reported to our generals. You can check the records and confirm those actions.

Do not tell me how to conduct the trial, Mason admonished. *I am aware of my responsibilities. Tread lightly, Stygian.*

Stygian scowled. *The situation Darrius mentions was an unfortunate mishap while I was out with a magician. While scaling the side of a cliff to show me a delicate orchid known for healing headaches, my friend fell and smashed his head. I ran to his side to help him, but he was near death. Darrius and other villagers happened upon us as the lad passed away.*

Did you consume his soul? Mason asked.

Stygian paused.

Did you consume his soul? Mason repeated. *Answer the question.*

I did...but it was by accident and without malice.

Mason faced Darrius. *How did you witness this scene, Darrius?*

While listening to Stygian's recount of the horrible incident, Darrius gripped his legs so tight that his fingernails punctured the fabric of his pants and blood seeped into the black linen. *When I and the villagers happened upon Stygian and the hapless magician, Stygian gripped the man's body closely. He grabbed his hair and had yanked his head back.*

Even though we were several yards away, we heard the snap of the young man's neck and witnessed Stygian place his mouth on the man's mouth while sucking in his life force.

Were there other occasions? Mason asked.

Once Stygian realized we had seen him, he vanished. Where he went, I do not know, but soon, other soldiers awakening to the demands of their human DNA left the camp and searched for Stygian, yearning to band with him. I didn't see him again until I, and other benevolent Cererians, were dispatched to protect the families of the chosen four, who he hunted with a vengeance. I witnessed him killing members of these families and saw him consume their magical essence.

Thank you, Darrius. Mason said.

Alden Stark, do you have testimony against Stygian? Mason asked.

Alden stood and replied. *Yes, my lord. I was present when Stygian and his soldiers attacked the Drury household in Amesbury, England. I witnessed him murdering the father, Chauncey. That is all, my lord.*

Alden took his seat.

Benedict, do you have testimony against Stygian? Mason asked.

Benedict cast a glance at Darrius and stood. *Yes, my lord. I was present at the magician's funeral, mentioned earlier. I, too, witnessed Stygian's unfortunate mishap with the deceased's soul.*

Unfortunate mishap? Mason said.

It is my opinion that Stygian did not act maliciously the first time. His actions afterward proved that he was taken by surprise.

Anything else? Mason asked.

I did not witness Stygian kill any other humans. Benedict sat and stared ahead avoiding Darrius's glare.

In regard to the trial for Stygian Chernobog, does anyone else have testimony? Mason asked the three witnesses.

No, they chorused.

Very well. We will adjourn to discuss the case against Stygian Chernobog. Guards, please silence our prisoners until our return.

Lord Mason? Darrius interrupted.

Yes?

What about the cases against Cary and Balor Atwood?

Our decision on Stygian's case will determine if charges remain against the Atwoods.

What does that mean? Darrius pressed.

If we find Stygian is not guilty, then it will follow that his soldiers are not guilty as well because they were only following their leader's orders. Now, if there are no more questions, we will adjourn. Mason joined the other justices.

A melodic chime sounded.

The justices drifted out of the Hall.

Darrius glanced at Stygian. The smirk had returned to his friend's face.

Carefully cloaking his words against eavesdropping, Darrius reached out to Benedict and Alden. *A deal has already been struck. Stygian will be found innocent of all charges. Be prepared to leave immediately.*

Chapter 11

Cererian Justice

Darrius, Alden, and Benedict gathered outside the Justice Hall. A comet streaked across the night sky. "I'd heard that a comet is a harbinger of bad tidings," Alden remarked as he watched it trail away.

"Depends," Darrius added. "In some cultures, it brings you luck or carries it away."

"It's simply a celestial body coursing through space slowly burning itself out," Benedict said.

"The members of the High Order of Truth have been deliberating for some time," Darrius observed. "This is unusual, even for this type of trial. The letter of the law cannot be bent. Cererian justice is black or white. You're either right or wrong."

"If Stygian forged a deal with the High Council, as you believe, then the delay may be a result of the participants agreeing to the details of the bargain." Alden said.

Before Darrius could respond, an attendant approached them.

It is time to return to the Justice Hall, the Cererian messaged before turning and floating into the building.

"Be prepared to teleport to The Nine Muses when I give the signal," Darrius warned.

"What's the signal?" Alden asked.

"You'll know," Darrius replied. "Just remember...on the count of three."

They strode into the Hall. As Darrius passed in front of Stygian's cell pod, he met his friend's gaze. Confidence and determination filled Stygian's eyes. Darrius lingered for a moment before reluctantly turning away and following Benedict and Alden to the witness section.

A melodic chime sounded, and the Hall quieted.

Orion, Mason, and Luther drifted into the judicial area and positioned themselves in a straight line facing the prisoners.

Orion floated forward. *I, Orion, lead member of the High Order of Truth will share the judgment against Stygian Chernobog.* He gestured toward the witness area. *After hearing testimony from our witnesses, we have arrived at the decision that Stygian Chernobog is not guilty of the crimes levied against him. Additionally, we also find that the twins, Balor and Cary Atwood, are not guilty of any crimes as they were following the orders of Stygian and also their original commander, Aaron Aningan, who is not able to provide testimony to the contrary.*

Darrius stood up. *This is an outrage!*

Protocol, Darrius, Orion reprimanded.

Darrius's lips thinned as he swallowed the other thoughts he yearned to scream at the assemblage. He clenched his fists and sat down.

I will continue, Orion said, *Cererians murdering magicians for their power is a serious issue and is not condoned. But we find that we, as a nation, bear responsibility for how these three, and the Yfel in general, came into being. We cannot shirk our responsibilities. Adequate research should have been completed before we sent the first expedition to Earth. Our scientists should have studied the effects of merging Cererian energy with human DNA for many years instead of a few months. The unfortunate results could not be foreseen but could have been avoided if we had taken the proper precautions. As such, we cannot hold our soldiers responsible for the actions of their leaders. Hence, the only fair decision that can be made is that Stygian and the twins committed no crime and are free to go. Guards, release the prisoners.*

Balor and Cary emerged from their cell pods and joined Stygian as he unfolded his tall frame from his cell. The Yfel leader rubbed his wrists and rolled his neck while staring at Darrius.

May I speak? Benedict asked.

Rise, Benedict, Orion replied.

How will the council address future cases? Releasing these soldiers allows others to murder with impunity. How do you explain your judgment to the inhabitants of Earth? How do you explain that, despite our mission of peace and non-interference, we intentionally release the Yfel to do whatever they will to the magical populations?

Benedict sat and folded his hands into his lap.

Orion faced Mason and Luther. A myriad of colors flashed throughout their bodies as they discussed the matter privately.

After several moments, Orion turned and faced Benedict.

We acknowledge your questions, and they have merit. The ruling on this trial stands as declared: not guilty. We cannot advise on future events, but we will deliver your concerns to the High Council for guidance on future cases. Are there any more questions?

I have one, Darrius announced.

He stood without being recognized. *If you will not rule on the Yfel's future conduct on Earth, then more lives will be lost. Lives that I, and Stygian, and all Cererians swore to protect. You have granted Stygian and his followers free rein to do as they please upon their return to Earth while you placate us with assurances that the matter will be addressed by the High Council.*

Your question, Darrius? Orion stated.

Do Stygian and the twins know they will be banished from Ceres after today? And do they know they will never be allowed to return to their natural Cererian form?

Stygian's eyes darted to Darrius. His eyebrows arched with surprise.

Silence! A stern voice demanded as a large Cererian glided forward. The three judicial members backed away and bowed as the Cererian drifted between them and Darrius.

Hello, Senator, Darrius greeted.

You surprise me, Darrius. The Senator moved forward until he was inches away. A fiery red punctuated by deep orange pulsed throughout him.

Oh?

I thought we had an understanding.

Darrius stood his ground, his hands clenched behind his back. He stuck out an index finger. Alden and Benedict noticed the small action.

You're embarrassing yourself in front of the entire assemblage, the Senator stated. The dignitary swiveled right and then left as he studied Benedict and Alden who were seated with their hands in their laps. *Your outbursts are inappropriate.*

Orion has not answered my question, Senator. Will you answer for him?

Impudence! The Senator bellowed. *How dare you talk to me with that tone.*

Darrius thrust a second finger outward. Benedict nodded at Alden.

Is this verdict your idea of the positive outcome you desired? Darrius pressed. *When Stygian, someone you described to me as "making a fool of you" and "disgracing you" is found innocent of murder?*

Darrius... The Senator warned, raising an appendage upward.

Darrius glanced at Stygian who scowled in the Senator's direction. *By the angered look on Stygian's face, it's apparent you haven't shared all the sordid details of the deal you've struck with the High Council. Perhaps you should let him in on your little secret.* Darrius thrust his third finger out.

Enraged, the Senator unleashed bolts of energy toward the witnesses.

Fortunately, Darrius, Benedict, and Alden had already vanished.

Chapter 12

The Labyrinth

Barefoot, Fen stepped slowly along the labyrinth's outer pathway. Over a millennium, the feet of countless worshippers had worn the red, hard-packed dirt smooth.

Distant drumming and chanting propelled her forward as she strolled the spiral of stones delineated by spokes of smaller rocks. She couldn't recall when she had started her but now, the setting sun threw long shadows over the distant red mountains and a chill settled in as the October night approached.

Although she walked by herself, she didn't feel lonely. On the contrary, she felt utterly at peace, enshrouded by a community of souls who accompanied her and eased her mind. When her toe hit a pebble, the skittering stone broke Fen's concentration. She bent down and inspected her foot.

When she stood, a young dark-haired woman with dark eyes stood in front of her.

Fen was not alarmed. "Hello. Who are you?"

The young girl smiled. "I am Miriam."

"I am..."

"You are Fenna Kemp."

"I'm sorry, I don't recall meeting you," Fen said. "Actually, I don't remember much."

"That's okay, Fen, you're safe here."

"Would you like to join me as I walk the labyrinth?" Fen invited.

"I am the labyrinth," Miriam replied.

Fen tilted her head. "How curious. How can that be?"

"Look around. I am all things that you see." Fen scanned the landscape. A screech captured her attention, and she glanced up. A bald eagle soared effortlessly in the azure sky. It cried again and flew east.

"Take my hand, Fen," Miriam requested.

Fen didn't hesitate. Miriam's skin was smooth and chilled like marble. "My dear, you're so cold," she said. "Here, let me warm you." Fen wrapped her arms around the young woman. "With the setting sun, you've become quite chilled." Fen closed her eyes and hummed an ancient healing tune.

"Fen," a male voice called.

Fen opened her eyes to total darkness. She stood atop a butte, and Miriam had vanished. Stars glittered in the sky as though diamonds had been scattered into the heavens.

"Fen," the male voice repeated.

"Hello, is someone there?"

Miriam sidled up to her and whispered in her ear. "The shaman calls out for you."

"The shaman?" Fen repeated, unsure of whom she referenced.

"He desires for you join him."

"And leave this place? It's so peaceful here. I'm content."

"Shall I tell him no?"

"Who is he? Do I know him?"

"He is Jake, the Keeper of the Word."

"I think I know him," Fen whispered.

"He's very powerful," Miriam added.

"Why does he wish to disturb me?"

"He needs you. Jake is powerful but impotent when it comes to opening the Guardian boulder."

The chanting and drumming intensified. Fen winced. "I feel faint," she whispered. A shockwave suddenly rocked the land. The vibration raced up the plateau and shook Fen so violently that she fell forward onto her hands and knees. Wave after wave of magnetic energy washed over her. "Please stop," she begged.

Silence.

When Fen opened her eyes, she squinted and held her hand up against the dazzling sunshine. She had returned to the labyrinth and was alone. Fen spied a lone figure standing atop the butte. Long black hair flowed in the breeze.

Miriam, she thought as she stared at the person. Glancing around, she realized that she had not moved much farther within the labyrinth. It seemed odd that she hadn't reached the center even though she'd been continuously walking for a full day.

"Miriam, is this a dream?" Fen said aloud.

SCREECH!

Fen whirled. A black dragon flew at her from the west. Its leathery wings were fifty feet wide, and its onyx scales glittered wet in the sunshine. It shrieked again and slowly descended toward her. The downdraft from its wings pummeled her, and she held her arm up against the blast.

"No!" she cried out. "You're not allowed in this place!"

The dragon settled on the ground just outside the labyrinth. The force of its landing jostled Fen, and she collapsed onto her knees. Defending herself, she raised her hands toward the dragon as it lumbered toward her, its mouth open. A fetid smell wafted.

Memories raced into Fen's mind: The Nine Muses, Hilly, Chance, Kai, and Jake. Yes, Jake. And the dragon on the beach.

Miriam appeared and whispered in Fen's ear. "Dispatch the creature."

Fen struggled to her feet and pushed her hands toward the beast, summoning her immense power. When a bright light engulfed her hands and arms, she pushed the pulsing energy toward the dragon. The plasma whipped forward and covered the creature like a fishing net.

The dragon vanished.

Night returned.

Fen had returned to the plateau and stared into the star-dusted sky. Miriam stood beside her.

"Nothing is ever as it seems," Miriam stated.

Fen turned and looked at her. "Everything is so odd here. Some memories return while others run away."

Miriam smiled. "Do you remember the shaman?"

"Yes...I think so."

"Good, then I'll take you to him."

"But I don't want to leave."

"You will never leave this place, Fen. You are home. Look around and tell me what you see."

Fen gazed toward the labyrinth. Hundreds of thousands of people stood side-by-side and gazed up at her. They sang a joyous, familiar tune from long ago. "My family?" she asked.

Miriam nodded. "Yes. They are the Healers. Like you." Miriam pointed toward the crowd. "Look closely. Do you recognize anyone?"

Fen followed Miriam's gesture. There, at the front stood a small dark-skinned man in a simple mundu. The edges brushed against his bare feet. His hands were pressed at heart center, and he bowed deeply.

"Prasad?" Fen gasped. "How is this possible?"

"He is a member of the Healers as you are."

Fen searched Miriam's eyes. "But he's Cererian."

"His lineage doesn't matter in this world," Miriam replied. "The Healers of the cosmos reside in this dimension."

"May I see him?"

"Be patient. We must first meet with the shaman."

"But if I can't leave, how will I meet with Jake?"

“Through the whispers of space and time,” Miriam replied. “I exist in this realm and all other worlds simultaneously. You reside in this spiritual place, and Jake stands in the physical realm. I will act as a conduit through which you will communicate.

Chapter 13

Bear Seamount

MIRIAM WALKED AHEAD OF Fen.

Having begun their journey in arid lands, the duo now meandered through a lush meadow blanketed with wildflowers. Colorful blooms stretched to the horizon in all directions.

The spiritual entity looked over her shoulder and smiled at Fen who followed obediently behind her.

"Where are we going?" Fen asked. "It seems like we've been walking for hours. That large waterfall in the distance is no closer than when we started."

Miriam giggled. "There is no time in this dimension." She curled a finger. "Come along. We're almost there."

They passed a patch of purple lupines that filled the air with sweet perfume. "We have arrived," Miriam declared, pointing into the distance. "Look."

Ahead of them loomed a tall transparent wall. Fluid and perpetual, the aquamarine space shimmered.

"I thought this was a waterfall," Fen remarked as she gazed up the sheer barrier that disappeared into the sky. Mesmerized, Fen poked the wall. Her finger penetrated the membrane. She licked her finger. "Sea water," she proclaimed. It's salty like the ocean."

Miriam giggled. "It *is* the ocean. The Atlantic Ocean."

Fen gazed at the watery partition. “How can this be? We’re standing on soil. How can the sea loom above us without crashing down?”

“Because we occupy two dimensions at the same time. Rise with me.” The pair floated upward in front of the great wall of water. As they rose, schools of rainbow-colored fish frantically darted away. With one beady eye trained on them, a giant right whale studied the women as they drifted by.

They stopped and hovered.

“There in the distance, do you see the great mountain?” Miriam asked as she pointed into the deep blue depths.

“Yes. I see it.”

“That ancient mountain is Bear Seamount.”

“Bear Seamount?”

“It is an underwater mountain. It’s over one-hundred-million years old and once knew what dry land felt like. When the great flood consumed the planet, Bear Seamount was submerged.” She peered lovingly into the shimmering water. “He is beautiful, is he not?”

“Yes,” Fen agreed. “But why are we here, Miriam?”

“To meet with the shaman, so you can discuss unlocking the Guardian boulder.”

“The Guardian exists on Bear Seamount?”

Miriam nodded.

“How will we breathe underwater?” Fen asked.

“It’s daunting, is it not? But not impossible.” Miriam waved her hand through the water. Channels appeared briefly where her fingers dragged through. “That is why I’m with you. I will be your connection between the physical world and this watery universe.”

“Why can’t I go back to the physical world?”

Miriam cupped Fen’s face. “Oh, precious one, you will never leave this realm. This is where you belong now...with the Healers.”

Fen stared into the churning blue-green water.

"Are you disappointed?" Miriam asked.

"Surprisingly, no. I feel peaceful and content here."

Miriam nodded. "Yes. The serenity you're experiencing is a result of the combined energy of the Healers."

"You said we were going to meet Jake. How do you know of him?"

"He appeared while you were in the labyrinth. He demanded to speak with you. But I sent him away."

"He came to this world to find me?"

"No. He stood outside this realm. But his powers sensed where you were. He's an arrogant shaman. He has much to learn if the Prophecy is to reach completion. Still, while you walked the pathway, I reached out to him and arranged this meeting so he can create his plan for Chance's Guardian boulder."

"Chance?" Fen asked. "Do I know this person?"

Miriam patted Fen's shoulder. "Your paths have crossed."

Fen's face darkened with worry. "I don't remember him. Why are my memories so muddled?"

"Don't worry, Fen. In time, you'll remember only that which is important."

"But I don't even recall what I should do with the Guardian boulder."

"Shh." Miriam held up a hand. "The shaman has messaged me. I need to forge a pathway between our worlds." Miriam swept her hands to the side, creating a long tunnel that spiraled in the water like a frothy whirlpool. The mile-long tubular corridor sliced through the ocean and stretched into the distance with one end jutting into the realm of the Healers and the other end in view of The Nine Muses.

Fen took a step toward the tunnel, but Miriam grabbed her arm. "No, Fen. You must stay here. The shaman will come to us."

A pinprick of a form appeared in the distance.

"Jake approaches," Miriam announced.

The dark shape grew larger as it neared. Fen could make out the figure of a man trotting toward them, his eyes fixed on her.

"Is this the shaman you spoke of?" Fen asked.

"Yes."

When Jake was six feet from the end of the tunnel, Miriam held up her hand. "Stop there, Shaman."

He halted and smiled at Fen. She smiled back.

"You summoned me, Miriam?" he said sarcastically.

"Careful with your tone, Shaman. You desired to speak with Fen and now you have that opportunity. If you continue to be belligerent, I'll close this tube and release the ocean's waters upon you."

Jake gazed around his cylindrical refuge from the sea. A hammerhead shark swam nearby, its eyes considering him as tasty prey. A school of mackerel scurried by shimmering like scattered silver coins in the current.

He stepped closer toward the end of the tube.

"Stop!" Miriam screamed. "I warn you Shaman."

"Okay...okay," Jake said holding his hands up in resignation.

"Please do as Miriam requests," Fen begged. "I wouldn't want anything to happen to you."

"Are you okay, Fen?" Jake asked. "Is she treating you well?"

"I'm perfectly fine. I feel like I've arrived home. I'm with my people—my family."

"I'm glad to hear that. The way you suddenly disappeared really upset your brothers."

"How I disappeared? Brothers?"

"You don't remember your brothers, Chance or Kai?" Jake frowned. "Miriam hasn't told you how you came to this place?"

"I've been sleeping—resting—contemplating. My memories are murky." Fen pressed her hand to her forehead.

"We were all in the lounge at the Amesbury cottage. Darrius, Benedict, Alden, Chance, Kai, and me. I sensed something approaching in the storm, and in the blink of an eye, you were gone. I assume it was Miriam who snatched you."

Fen faced Miriam. "Is this true?"

"Yes. It was critical that you be taken to the Land of the Healers before harm found you."

"But why erase my memories?"

"In time, the life you lived before will no longer be important to you. The work you do in this realm will be rewarding enough."

"What work is that?" Jake asked, his eyes narrowing.

Miriam's pupils expanded making her eyes appear solid black. "Do I question the work you do in the physical realm, Shaman?"

"That doesn't answer his question, Miriam," Fen said. She turned to Jake. "During my meditation, I was told I would be restoring emotional health to all the souls that pass through this dimension on their way to the Ether."

"Sounds lovely," Jake replied. "And what of your responsibilities to the Prophecy?"

"Do not test my patience, Shaman!" Miriam screamed as she raised a hand threateningly toward the water.

Fen gripped Miriam's arm and gently pulled it down. She peered into the entity's eyes. "Please, Miriam. Let me talk with Jake."

Tense moments passed before Miriam's eyes returned to normal. "As you wish, Fen."

"You asked to talk with me, Jake," Fen said. "What was it you wanted to discuss?"

Jake smirked. "About the Guardian boulder, of course. That is still your primary responsibility, right?"

Fen dropped her head and tapped her chin. "Hmm," she murmured. "Yes. I recall that. I can read the symbols carved on the Guardians."

"That's right. It appears your memories are coming back."

"Yes!" Fen shouted. "We were just in Wales. For Kai's crystal of air."

"That's right. Keep going, Fen," Jake urged.

"Your father!" she shouted. "Your father attacked us. And you swooped in and saved us."

"What's the last thing you remember?" Jake asked.

"Let's see. I was sitting on the couch in the lounge, and you said, 'They're coming.'"

"And here we are," Jake said.

Fen stared at the ground to collect her thoughts. "I can't recall that moment clearly. It must have happened too fast."

"You were gone in a split second," Jake said.

"Who did you bring with you to the cottage?" Fen asked Miriam.

"The one person you would trust," the entity responded. "Prasad came with me."

"What the fuck?" Jake blurted.

Fen's face flushed pink. "My Prasad? How could he leave the Land of the Healers?"

"As you have joined me on this journey, Prasad accompanied me to fetch you from the Amesbury cottage. In both instances, we traveled on the threads of magic woven between the two dimensions.

Tears welled in Fen's eyes. "It was a wonderful surprise to see Prasad with the throng of Healers this morning. I can't wait to see him again."

Jake eyed Miriam suspiciously. "What a coincidence. And all this time, I thought Prasad had gone to the ether himself. After all, he traded his life for Hilly's. How convenient that he's been waiting for Fen all this time."

"Be nice, Jake," Fen admonished. "When can I see him again?" she asked Miriam.

"Once you've acquired all the knowledge of the Healers, you'll be able to visit with Prasad as often as you desire.

Jake bit the inside of his cheek. "Sounds great, Fen," he cajoled.

"Finish your discussion with Fen, Shaman," Miriam insisted. "The sooner you're done, the sooner Fen can return home to the Land of the Healers."

"Oh, yes!" Fen agreed.

Jake sighed. "Fen, I understand Miriam has worked out a way for us to work together at the Guardian boulder."

"I have," Miriam responded.

Fen touched Miriam's arm and whispered, "Please let me talk with Jake directly."

Miriam nodded. "Of course." She grinned at Jake who was clenching his fists at his side.

"Miriam has shown me where the Guardian boulder is located."

"What?" Jake yelled. "That's not possible!"

"Who says?" Miriam shouted back.

"The Prophecy has forbidden it!"

"The Prophecy has no control over me." Miriam sneered at Jake. "In this dimension, I do what I want and say what I desire."

Fen's eyes darted between Miriam and Jake. She raised a hand toward each person dispelling her calming energy. But her actions backfired, and the healing energy rushed back into her head resulting in a migraine. She grabbed her temples and yelled, "Stop! I can't take your bickering, and I can't soothe your emotions. My healing powers aren't working properly in this dimension."

"That's an interesting development," Jake observed. "Why would that happen, Miriam?"

Miriam consoled Fen. "It's a transition," she chirped while patting Fen's shoulder. "Your body needs to adjust to this world. Give it more time."

"Oh," Fen muttered. She gazed at the ground, her forehead furrowing. When she looked up again, her eyes were clear and determined. "Jake, Miriam has found a way for me to remain in this world and open the

Guardian boulder. It's complicated, but she will bring our universes together at Bear Seamount in a manner like today."

"And once the Guardian is open and Chance's earth crystal is reunited, what will happen to you then?" Jake asked.

"She will come home with me," Miriam answered. "I will ensure she sees her beloved Prasad." Miriam lightly stroked Fen's hair like a mother comforting her child.

"Miriam, what if I need to talk with Jake or my brothers. Is there no way I can reach out to them?"

"It's best that you allow me to arrange the connections," Miriam responded.

"So, there *is* a way I can do it on my own?"

Miriam narrowed her eyes and her lips tightened. "We can discuss this later, Fen. It's time we leave." She turned to Jake. "Time for you to go as well, Shaman."

"We haven't finished talking about our plan," Jake protested.

"I'll contact you later," Miriam said tersely. "I suggest you run because I'm closing the tunnel on this end and the ocean will crush you."

Trapped in the confines of the connection tube, Jake flew toward the other end. The tunnel collapsed and sea water engulfed him just as he reached the exit. He launched into the air, soaring high above The Nine Muses.

Chance and Kai awaited Jake inside the study. They stood shoulder-to-shoulder in front of the window and searched the ocean and sky for any sign of their friend.

"I thought you said he was only going to be gone an hour?" Chance asked.

"That's what he told me," Kai replied. "You know how Jake gets distracted."

"I'm not that late," Jake barked.

Kai and Chance whirled. Jake slammed the door to the study and collapsed into a chair. He was drenched. Salt water dripped from his face and clothes. A puddle soon formed on the floor under the chair.

Speechless, Chance and Kai stared at their friend and then eyed each other. Kai left the study and soon returned with a fluffy beach towel. He tossed it at Jake. "Dry yourself off. That's an expensive leather chair you're leaking all over."

Jake snatched the towel and rubbed his hair half-heartedly, the hint of a sneer on his face.

"How did it go?" Chance asked.

"Great...just great," Jake seethed.

"Do we have a plan?" Chance pressed.

Jake dropped the towel on his chest and glared through blood-shot eyes.

"Tell me we have a plan," Chance said.

Jake looked away. "Not yet," he whispered. "I'm still working on it. I hit a snag."

Kai handed Jake a shot of bourbon. "You look like you could use this."

Jake gulped it and handed the empty glass back. "Thanks."

"Did you see Fen?" Kai asked.

"Yup," Jake replied.

Kai glanced at Chance and shrugged. "Did you and Fen speak?"

"Uh-huh." Jake leaned back in the chair, crossed his arms across his chest, and stared at the ceiling.

Kai leaned over Jake and peered into his eyes. "Help me understand. If you talked with Fen, then why don't you have a plan?"

Jake pushed Kai away and stood.

"What's that for?" Kai complained. "I'm on your side—remember?"

Jake poured a drink and swirled the bourbon in the glass before tossing it back and smacking his lips.

"Well?" Kai pressed. "What's the next step?"

"You can be a pest sometimes, you know that?" Jake grumbled.

"Yeah, yeah…so I've been told. About the plan…"

"Miriam kicked me out of her dimension. Okay?" Jake yelled. "Fen's her hostage, and she's using your sister as a pawn to play me…to play all of us."

"Who's Miriam?" Chance asked.

"Apparently, she's the queen of wherever Fen is right now," Kai replied

"Something's strange about Miriam," Jake mused. "I can't put my finger on it, but as far as spiritual entities go, she's one messed-up bitch."

Chance shared a knowing smile with Kai. "So Miriam stole your nuts and won't give them back until you do her bidding."

Kai and Chance laughed hard.

"Careful, Chance, or you'll be laughing through a fat lip," Jake threatened with his fist hovering under his friend's face.

"C'mon, Jake," Kai soothed. "We're trying to lighten the mood."

"I don't need your antics now," Jake barked. "I need to figure this out. Why would Miriam manipulate Fen? Why would she encourage your sister not to worry about her memory loss?"

"What memory loss?" Chance asked.

"She couldn't recall how she arrived in the realm of the Healers. I had to tell her about the Amesbury cottage and about the two of you."

"Fen didn't know about us?" Kai asked. "That's weird. Maybe she's been in that dimension too long."

"If Miriam gets her way, Fen will never leave," Jake added. "Fen said her work there is to lighten the emotional load of those traveling to the ether."

"That doesn't sound glamorous," Kai said. "Fen's power is so much greater than acting as a counselor to the dead."

"I know," Jake agreed. "That's why I'm suspicious. I'll play Miriam's game for now, until I find out what's really going on."

"So, our plan is to wait?" Chance asked.

"Yep," Jake replied. "We wait for Miriam's next move."

Chapter 14

Complications

JAKE BURST OUT OF the French doors leading to the back porch and slumped into a chaise lounge. Overhead, fragrant vines twisted along the pergola, shading his eyes from the afternoon sun. *Something's up,* he thought. *Who the hell is this Miriam anyway?*

"Relaxing in this beautiful weather?" a familiar voice asked.

Jake jerked to a sitting position. "Darrius!" Benedict and Alden were standing behind his friend. "When did you guys get back?"

"Just now," Darrius replied.

Jake eased back into the chaise and draped his arm across his face. "And how was the trial? Is Stygian dancing at the end of a rope or whatever the Cererian death penalty is?"

Darrius glanced at his associates. "The trial had an unexpected outcome."

Jake lifted his arm. "Oh?" He studied the Cererians' serious faces. "Hm," Jake mused. "Appears your day was worse than mine. What happened?"

"Stygian and the twins were released," Darrius uttered.

"Released? As in not guilty of killing magicians and free to do as they please released?"

"Yes. Apparently, the murdering habits of the Yfel are viewed as an unfortunate result of combining Cererian energy with human DNA. Cererian leaders bear the responsibility of not conducting adequate research before instructing their soldiers to undergo the transformation process. Hence, Stygian and his followers were found not guilty."

"Damn," Jake hissed.

"What the fuck!" Chance shouted as he and Kai appeared on the patio. "Stygian was set free?"

"Yes," Darrius responded. "I'm extremely disappointed."

"Are your judges out of their Cererian minds?" Chance said. "He's free to hunt us, and they don't give a fuck."

"Not exactly," Alden replied. "They understand the situation and will take our concerns to the High Council for guidance."

"Well now I feel safe. How about you, Kai? Do you feel secure knowing judges are working on a solution."

"Not exactly," Kai replied grimacing. "But it does seem like the Cererian judges have released the beast and are now trying to figure out how to build a cage to contain it."

"This day keeps getting better..." Jake said.

"What do you mean?" Darrius asked.

"I just met with Miriam and Fen about the Guardian boulder," he replied.

"Who's Miriam?' Darrius asked.

"I have no fucking clue. The bitch is really powerful and doesn't exist in this world at all." He turned toward Chance and Kai. "It was Miriam and another being who stole Fen from the Amesbury cottage."

"Another being?" Alden asked.

"Miriam said Prasad accompanied her, so Fen would willingly leave the cottage, but I have my doubts."

"It couldn't have been Prasad," Darrius affirmed. "He's dead."

"Ah, but that's where it gets interesting...Miriam claims Prasad lives in the realm of the Healers. It's the universe where she took Fen."

"I've never heard of the realm of the Healers," Alden said.

"Neither have I," Benedict added.

"Where is this place?" Darrius asked.

Jake spread his arms. "It's here, there, and everywhere, according to Miriam, but it's in a universe that no human or Cererian can enter."

"But Fen is there, and she's human," Kai noted.

"Exactly!" Jake said, jabbing his finger into the air.

"And there's another little detail I unearthed," Jake announced. "Miriam is dismissive of Fen's memory loss. Fen told me her memory had been murky since she arrived in that place, but Miriam assured Fen it was just part of the process of being in the Land of the Healers. I think Fen has been mesmerized by Miriam."

"Were you able to work out a plan for having Fen accompany you at the Guardian boulder?" Darrius asked.

"Nope," Jake replied. "Miriam will 'contact me to confirm the details.' Since Fen can't enter our physical world, and we can't go to the Land of the Healers, Miriam will create a special dimension where we can meet and work together."

Darrius sighed. "It appears we've both run into complications. I don't say this very often, but I need a drink." Darrius strode into the house. Jake looked at Chance and Kai before dashing after Darrius.

The men found the Cererian in the study pouring four glasses of bourbon.

"Déjà vu," Chance said. "Almost eight months ago, we shared a drink here." He snatched a glass from the bar. Jake and Kai took their drinks as well.

Darrius stood in front of the picture window and stared at the calm ocean as he slowly sipped. The three men joined him.

Benedict, Alden, and Bob soon entered the room.

"What's going on?" Bob asked. "I understand from Benedict you were outside the house. I gave you strict instructions not to go outside."

"Lighten up, Bob," Jake responded. "We had the best Cererian bodyguards at our side if that prick, Stygian, had shown his face."

"Darrius, I'm not pleased by this behavior," Bob complained. "How can we have order if these...these magicians won't follow instructions."

Darrius faced Bob and gulped his drink.

Bob's eyebrows arched. "You're drinking alcohol?"

"It's a tradition in this house," Darrius replied. "Kai, please pour me another. I think you'll find, Bob, that I, and the Kemps, and Jake won't fit snugly into your orderly methods. I suggest you reassess your procedures so they encourage cooperation instead of alienation."

Darrius turned toward the ocean, hesitated for a moment, and then faced Bob again. "And you really need to work on your sanctimonious attitude. These men will save this world and are deserving of your respect."

"But—" Bob started.

"But nothing," Darrius interrupted. "You're a good observer but you have a lot to learn about humans. Your education begins now. Apologize to these fine men."

Bob glanced at the Kemps and Jake with wide eyes before lowering his gaze. "I sincerely apologize if my actions have negatively impacted any of you. It was not my intention to upset you." He peeked at Darrius. "I hope we can start anew."

Jake traded glances with Kai and Chance. "Yep, I'm good," he remarked as he held his glass aloft. "To Bob," he toasted.

"To Bob," the others chorused.

Darrius abruptly changed the subject. "Alden and Benedict, I need you to make inquiries about an entity known as Miriam and find out what you can about the Land of the Healers."

"Yes, Darrius." Benedict and Alden rushed out of the study.

"Bob," Darrius continued. "Request additional observers to help fortify The Nine Muses. Stygian will come here, and we must prepare for his attack."

"Yes, Darrius," Bob replied, scurrying out of the room.

"What do we do in the meantime, Darrius?" Jake asked. "I can't take Chance and Kai to the Guardian until we know Fen will be with us."

"I know you'll find this hard but try to relax until we have some answers."

"That's your best idea?" Jake smirked. "Time for another drink." He grabbed the decanter and poured a double for himself.

Darrius wiggled his glass. Jake frowned as he poured a double for the Cererian.

"I'm your ally, Jake," Darrius said as he watched Jake go to the window. "If something's bothering you, spit it out. I'm not a mind reader."

"Oh, really?" Jake mocked. He grimaced at the bitterness of his own words.

The friends stood shoulder to shoulder, saying nothing.

Then Jake quietly uttered, "I don't blame you for anything, Darrius. A few days ago, everything made sense and now—now it's a shit show!"

"Hm," Darrius replied. "To use your words, I, too, feel that I'm stepping in feces and have no way of cleaning my shoes."

The two men exchanged glances before breaking into laughter.

"Yep, that sums it up," Jake said. "Darrius, I'm frustrated. I can't talk to Hilly. I can't talk to Fen. And a freakin' entity nobody knows is making me jump through hoops for her own entertainment."

"Watching Stygian be released without penalty crushed my belief in my Cererian mission," Darrius added. "I feel abandoned by my people."

"We're fucked," Jake surmised.

"Unless we get answers..." Darrius added.

Bob entered the study and cleared his throat. "Darrius, I've contacted Ceres. They have refused your request to provide additional soldiers at this time."

Darrius huffed. "I'm not surprised. I made enemies today."

"Enemies?" Jake asked.

“I didn’t leave Ceres on a good note.” Darrius sighed. “We are truly on our own for whatever the Yfel throw at us.”

“And the longer we delay uniting Chance’s crystal with the Guardian boulder, the more susceptible we are to be thwarted in our efforts with Fen’s crystal,” Jake added.

Jake snatched the bourbon and slumped beside Kai on the couch. Without asking, he filled their glasses. “Cheers!” he shouted before tossing the drink back. “We are truly fucked.”

Alden and Benedict strode into the study.

“You have news?” Darrius asked.

“We do,” Benedict answered. He glanced at the men sitting on the couch. “Perhaps we should discuss this in private, Darrius.”

“No,” he responded. “Whatever you need to say, share it with all of us.”

“Very well. Alden and I asked many of our colleagues—the ones who will still talk to us—about the entity that goes by the name of Miriam. They’ve never heard of her or the Land of the Healers. We also reached out to the supernatural community...” Benedict paused and glanced at Alden.

“I contacted Yr Wyddfa,” Alden blurted.

“What?” Darrius demanded. “Without my permission?”

“I apologize for the lapse in protocol, Darrius, but time was of the essence.”

“And did he provide any information?”

“Like us, he is forbidden by the Prophecy to reveal any of the Word. But he did offer guidance.” Alden faced Jake. “Yr Wyddfa said you hold the key to Miriam’s true identity.”

Jake’s brow furrowed. “What the fuck? I hold the key?”

“Damn, Jake,” Chance stated. “Is this a sister you didn’t know you had?”

Jake bit his lip as he thought about the possibilities. “I don’t know anybody that powerful except—” Jake stopped in mid-sentence. He glanced up at Darrius. “Except my dad.”

"Ryan has Fen?" Chance yelled jumping to his feet. "We need to get her back."

"I thought you killed your dad." Kai said

"I said I didn't know *if* I killed him. We battered each other pretty bad."

"Ryan has disguised himself as this entity, Miriam, and tricked Fen into believing she is the Land of the Healers?" Darrius surmised.

"Apparently," Jake replied.

"And it was Ryan who entered the Amesbury cottage and snatched her away?" Alden asked.

"Apparently." Jake grimaced and shook his head. He shivered recalling that Miriam stood beside him on the butte.

"And Ryan has sequestered himself into a realm that we can't enter?" Chance asked.

"Miria—er, my dad said no human nor Cererian could enter."

"You're able to jump into many different dimensions," Kai observed. "Why can't you jump into this one."

Jake searched Kai's face and then looked at the Cererians. "When I went to Wyoming, I knew Fen was there...somewhere. That's when the entity came to me. She appeared first in the middle of the sacred circle and then beside me on the butte. Nothing seemed familiar about her, and she was a shadow—a phantom—so I took her at her word that nobody could enter her realm."

"So, you never tried," Kai confirmed.

"No, I never tried. I took her at her word. Fuckin' Ryan!"

"What does this mean?" Chance asked. "If Ryan has Fen, then it's over. We failed."

"We haven't!" Jake shouted. "I'll get her back, I promise!" Jake vanished.

"Crap, where did he go?" Chance asked.

"He's gone to get Fen," Kai answered. "But where?"

"He mentioned Wyoming," Chance said. "Fen was born in Lowell, so it must be somewhere near that town."

"We should try to help him," Kai added.

"No!" Darrius shouted as he held up his hand. "Nobody else leaves The Nine Muses."

"What do we do in the meantime?" Chance asked.

"We wait," Darrius responded. "Our next move lies in the shaman's hands."

Chapter 15

Stygian

"Lord Stygian, how can we serve you?" Balor fell to his knees and pressed his forehead to the ground. His brother, Cary, dropped beside him and lowered his head onto the dirt.

Stygian stared at the tops of the soldiers' heads, lost in thought. The pre-trial agreement with the Senator annoyed him. Their discussion had guaranteed his freedom, but at what cost? He may have been released from his physical shackles, but he was still a captive, controlled by others, expecting him to jump when instructed or murder when commanded. Darrius's words at the conclusion of the trial also bothered him. What else was the Senator keeping from him?

Have I been betrayed? he wondered.

Days earlier, the Senator entered the holding facility where Stygian and the twins were held awaiting trial. Once the high-ranking official dismissed the guards, the Senator drifted in front of Stygian's cell pod and quietly observed him. Restraining magic prevented the Yfel leader from speaking or moving, but his eyes worked perfectly fine, so he summoned all his hate and contempt into his glare at the dignitary.

The Senator wasted no time. *I have a proposition, Stygian. You and your soldiers will readily agree to the terms of this proposal, and, in return, each of you will be found not guilty.*

Waving one of his appendages, the Senator released a portion of the restraining magic so Stygian could move his head.

Nod if you understand, he demanded. *Then I will allow you to telepathically respond.*

Reluctantly, Stygian obeyed his tormentor and slowly nodded.

The Senator once again waved an appendage. *You may now converse.*

At first Stygian remained silent, his eyes vibrating with anger as he gathered his thoughts and measured his response—a delayed reply would anger the Senator, but it would also prove that he was in no hurry to strike a bargain.

The Senator shifted nervously.

Stygian narrowed his eyes at the slight movement and a hint of a smirk flitted across his face. *Such a sweet-smelling deal doesn't come without roots planted in manure.* He grinned confidently. *What would compel a high-ranking Cererian, like yourself, to approach the leader of the Yfel Brethren with such an offer?*

Bursts of red flashed throughout the Senator's ethereal body. *Careful Stygian. I have the power to order your execution right here, without a trial. The Yfel's deeds on Earth have become messy, but your skills have value. In exchange for your expertise, you and your soldiers will be released, without fear of retribution—but only if you agree to this deal immediately.*

What expertise? Stygian asked, the smirk curling deeper in the corner of his mouth.

You know what I mean, the Senator replied gruffly.

A grin spread wide across Stygian's face popping twin dimples. The Senator's impatience pleased him. *I possess many skills. Exactly which one do you want?*

I crave the same thing you do—Freedom. We have an opportunity to help each other. You and your soldiers yearn for freedom to continue your murderous ways, and I have a desire to be free of my adversaries.

Stygian squinted. *Adversaries?*

Yes, the Senator responded. *I have a few meddlesome individuals that must be eliminated.*

Cererians? Stygian asked.

Would that bother you?

Stygian considered the offer. He held the winning hand in this insane game of wits and relished watching the Senator squirm while he mulled over his response. Being restrained, unable to move, in this metallic cell was pushing him to the edge of insanity, but his ego prevented him from quickly jumping at the Senator's deal. Best to let the dignitary hang on the end of the rope a little while longer.

Well? the Senator pressed as he anxiously drifted back and forth in front of the cell pod.

It appears we can help each other, Stygian declared. *In exchange for our release, we will assist you in finding your own freedom from certain individuals. However, our skills are specialized and unique, possessed by no other being.* He paused and reflected on his next statement. *So, I have an amendment to your proposal, so the terms are fair to both parties.*

Sparks of orange and yellow swirled within the Senator's body. *A counteroffer? How dare you, Stygian!*

Then there is no deal! Stygian squeezed his eyes shut, so the Senator wouldn't be able to detect any of his emotions, but the Yfel leader knew the Senator had already swallowed the hook, now he just needed to reel the dignitary in. And, to do so, demanded patience.

An awkward silence descended into the room.

The Senator had ceased pacing and lingered in front of Stygian's pod. *Open your eyes!* the Senator demanded. *I want to see with who I'm striking a deal.*

Stygian slowly opened his eyes and peered at the dignitary.

What do you want, Stygian?

In exchange for our services, my soldiers and I will never face persecution of any kind here on Ceres or Earth and will be able to execute our skills using any method we determine is warranted without penalty of death or confinement. You must guarantee that the Yfel will be able to conduct its business without interference.

The Senator pondered Stygian's counter proposal with a flurry of blue pulses that rushed through his body.

Agreed, he announced.

Stygian stared down at his soldiers posturing at his feet. That morning's deliberation with the Senator remained on his mind, and he felt great. Actually, he felt extraordinary and that momentary feeling of hopelessness in the cell pod had given way to exultation as he stood supreme and powerful over his men.

Skills, indeed, he thought. An icy smirk slowly grew on his face as he recalled the smell of fear he inhaled from the smug dignitary. Even after several hours, the pungent taste remained in his mouth, and he licked his lips savoring the flavor.

"Rise and face me," he ordered.

Balor and Cary jumped to their feet and stood rigidly at attention as their leader slowly circled them. Stygian regarded their muscular chests and thick arms and legs. Standing side-by-side, the twins appeared like an impenetrable barrier of flesh and bone. *Perfect pair of soldiers,* he thought.

Although taller than the twins, Stygian was lean and sinewy with white-blond hair and eyelashes. When he unearthed the details of his host body, he wasn't surprised to learn his body was born from DNA harvested from a Nordic warrior. What had disturbed him, though, was learning the warrior's tomb was discovered outside the gates of an ancient village and was void of any funerary objects or tributes, except for a simple silver medallion placed upon the dead man's chest. The medal had been engraved with a rune indicating the man had died dishonorably.

He would never know the deed that doomed the individual to a solitary existence in the afterlife, but Stygian no longer cared. He embraced the union of his Cererian and human personalities with great fervor. Over the millennium he had killed thousands of magicians and consumed their supernatural abilities. Men, women, children—it made no difference when it came to quenching his thirst for blood and magic.

He was invincible and no one could defeat him.

Until he met Oma.

The statuesque, raven-haired daughter of a chieftain caught his attention at a summer solstice celebration almost a thousand years earlier. Hundreds of villagers had gathered to enjoy the harvest and support their athletes in friendly competition between the clans.

While exploring the area with his followers, Stygian happened upon the festival and quickly made his way through the crowds chatting amicably and offering food they had pillaged from other towns. He possessed the impressive ability to put people at ease and win their trust, so he could eventually steal their magic. He and his men were wolves in sheep's clothing, and, as they made their way through the flock, they assessed who would be their next victims.

Stygian reached the edge of a large clearing and gazed across. People stood a hundred feet away and formed lines across the back and down each side of the field. Directly in front of him stood a circular wooden object propped on a tripod.

His mind raced. *What were the people doing? What was this thing in front of him?*

He shielded his eyes from the glaring sun while scanning the other side.

A raven-haired woman drew back the string of her longbow, the arrow pointed directly at him, and she glared.

Her eyes. He couldn't stop staring at her emerald-green eyes.

She blinked and lowered the bow.

"Move!" a spectator yelled.

But Stygian couldn't move. It was as though his feet had sprung roots and had plunged deep into the earth. His heart pounded, and his lips went dry.

Without hesitation, the archer raised her bow, pulled back the string, and released the arrow in a quick, fluid movement. The arrow thudded between Stygian's feet.

Then the archer hurried across the field toward the Cererian.

His eyes darted first to the right and then to the left, willing himself to move, but his legs wouldn't obey.

The tall, magnificent woman approached him. Long, black tresses streamed behind her as she rushed toward him in aubergine leggings, a black skirt and a lavender cotton shirt covered by a leather vest with shoulders caps. Even if a herd of horses were bearing down on him, the Cererian was frozen and couldn't move.

"You're in the field of play, Stranger," she grumbled as she stopped in front of him, her eyes even with his. Her lips thinned as she regarded him. Then she bent down, plucked the arrow from the ground and placed it into the sheath on her back. "If you don't move, I'll make sure the next arrow pierces your heart."

Stygian opened his mouth several times but only a hoarse squeak tumbled out.

"Are you ill?" the archer asked as she looked him over head to toe. "You're not from this region. From where do you hail?"

Sweat trickled down his forehead, and he swiped his eyes. *Is this beauty an enchantress? Has she bewitched me?* He drew in a long breath. The fresh scent of lupines filled his nostrils. "I'm...I'm..." he stuttered. "I'm known as

Stygian." He folded his arm awkwardly across his midsection and bowed. "And your name?"

"I'm Oma," she replied. "I'm the chieftain's daughter, and the best archer in this area...lucky for you." A generous smile erased the suspicious glare from her eyes. "Come with me, Stygian." She held out her hand. Delicate long, white fingers curled in invitation.

Stygian sighed as the memory of Oma caressed his brain. That long ago encounter led to seven days of utter bliss for the Cererian, an emotion he had never experienced. For one week, he devoted his life to the dark-haired warrior who stole his heart. He sent his soldiers away and abandoned his mission to kill magicians. Oma cast her spell, and Stygian gladly surrendered.

But his soul had suffered. It was being ripped out of his body by his abstinence. Fighting the natural urges to kill magicians and feed on their powers pushed him to the brink of insanity. And visions of murdering Oma sickened him...terrified him.

After seven days, he needed to feed. But not on Oma, nor any of her villagers.

Like a coward, he fled from her bed and ran into the night never to return to his beloved.

A year later Stygian discovered how much power Oma really wielded. He would learn of the Firewalkers. They were unique individuals possessing great power over fire, the sun, and some believed, the universe. Oma was the daughter of a tenth-generation Firewalker.

He never saw her again.

But he knew she was pregnant with his child, and, over the millennium, he kept track of the Firewalker bloodlines, lineage stained with Cererian blood.

He watched and waited, aware that one day the Cererian Prophecy would demand he reconnect with a Firewalker.

He'd waited for Hilly Kemp.

Stygian had attempted to contact Hilly several times, but his efforts to reach her were misinterpreted as were his attempt to seize her body. Darrius had tricked Hilly at The Nine Muses, convincing her that he was evil and intended harm.

Darrius turned Hilly against him and taught her how to fight him.

Stygian drew in a deep breath, squared his shoulders, and jutted his chin.

"My lord?" Balor asked, yanking Stygian from his musings.

Stygian shook his head. "Did you say, something Balor?"

"Yes, my Lord. What would you want us to do?"

Stygian smiled. "We go to Earth, my soldiers. We are free to be ourselves, and so we shall return to the planet that has been so kind to us over the years."

Balor turned to his brother and nodded. "We are ready to serve you, Lord Stygian," they shouted in unison as they bowed.

"Where will we meet?" Cary asked.

"We will meet at a lovely place I like to call home. The Nine Muses," Stygian replied with a merciless smirk. "I have such fond memories of that place."

Balor and Cary exchanged confused glances.

Stygian glanced around Ceres, taking one last look at the structures, the inhabitants, and the bleak night. "Let's away, men," he ordered.

One by one, the Cererians disappeared.

Chapter 16

The Circle of Calm

Miriam spirited Fen back to the Land of the Healers. She hoped Jake had succumbed to the crushing ocean waves she unleashed on him but knew better.

I'll deal with the shaman later, she mused.

She gripped Fen's hand and led her into the labyrinth.

"Why am I here, Miriam?" Fen asked. The entity dropped Fen's hand, soared into the sky, and vanished from view.

Fen watched her disappear and frowned. *She brought me back here. But from where? Why can't I remember anything?*

She gazed around. Red rocks and dirt stretched in every direction as far as she could see. The labyrinth sat in the middle of a russet world devoid of anything except the nearby butte that shimmered in the noonday heat.

"I'm going to explore," Fen whispered to herself. Following the spiraling pathway from the center, she eventually came to the outer wall of the structure. Constructed of stacked rocks, the barrier was just over eight inches high. She lifted one foot to step over the outer wall, but an unseen force pulled her back onto the pathway.

Odd, she thought.

Bracing her hands on the top of the wall, she attempted to swing her leg over the edge, but her foot wouldn't budge as though it was tethered to an invisible anchor.

Why can't I leave the labyrinth?

Fen sighed and abandoned her efforts to climb over the perimeter. Instead, she walked quickly on the curved path following the spiral. After several unfettered steps, she stopped. *If I stay within the labyrinth, I'm free to go anywhere. But I can't go beyond the wall.*

She pivoted and stepped quickly for six paces. On the seventh step, she swung her leg onto the boundary wall. But the moment her foot went beyond the barrier, her leg was yanked back onto the path, snatched by invisible hands.

Very strange, she thought.

A grunt caught Fen's attention, and she glanced up. A stocky form approached. As the shape ambled toward her, Fen detected four legs.

With each lumbering step, the creature kicked up dust and gravel.

"Hello!" she called out.

Snort! The animal snuffed as it lumbered forward.

Anxious to meet the beast, Fen tried to climb over the wall again, but her foot was whipped back into the labyrinth.

I should be upset, she thought. *But I feel peaceful when I'm in this space. Why?*

The animal stopped beyond the outer barrier.

A white bison, Fen thought. *Why is it here?*

The beast shook its massive head. Clouds of red dust showered the area, then it snorted and stomped a hoof.

Fen studied the beast. A large buffalo, pure white, except for the bits of red soil embedded in its fur, stared at her with friendly, pale-blue eyes.

Some cultures believe these beasts are sacred creatures, she remembered. *The bringers of hope and good things to come.*

"Hi there," she greeted as she reached across the perimeter as far as she could hoping to touch the animal.

Come to me, a guttural voice penetrated her mind.

Fen squinted at the buffalo. "Did you speak to me in my brain?"

Come to me, Guardian of Peace. Speak to me using your mind's voice, your gift of telepathy.

"Telepathy? Who is this Guardian of Peace you mention? My name is Fen...Fen... I can't seem to remember my last name."

You've been bewitched by the entity Miriam. Come to me, and you'll be free of her control. The shaggy beast stomped its hoof.

"I can't move," she answered. "Every time I try to step outside the lines, I'm forced back."

The animal snorted loudly. Billowing clouds of red dust blew over the labyrinth wall and gusted onto the inner pathways. After three huffs, the outer perimeter was covered completely with red soil.

The bison easily stepped over the rocks. *Cover your face, Guardian,* it warned. *With each layer of magical dust I blow from my dimension into yours, the spell will be broken.*

"Dimension?" Fen asked as she shielded her face with her hands.

The buffalo stomped and snorted several times. A barrage of dirt hit Fen's legs and filled the air. Coughing, she removed her hands and fanned the red-tinged cloud from her face.

Gently, the bison nudged her thigh with his scraggly head. *Grip my fur, and I will lead you out of this prison.*

"Prison? This is no prison. I like it here," Fen replied. "It's peaceful."

Yet you could not leave when you wanted to. Not all prisons are made of metal cages. Some are constructed from false wishes and desires.

Fen glanced around the labyrinth. Now that Miriam's mesmerizing spell had been broken, her mind was clearing. Memories returned: The Nine Muses, her and Kai unlocking the Welsh Guardian boulder, the Amesbury cottage with her siblings and Jake—and Miriam.

Miriam. Where is Miriam? she thought as she looked around nervously. A shiver raced up her spine, and she anxiously gripped the shaggy mane of the buffalo. *Please take me from this place,* she messaged.

Good. You've found your mind's voice once again. Hold tight, Guardian of Peace. Freedom is still far away. The massive bison stepped backward ensuring it stayed on the path of red dirt it had spread across the labyrinth like a freedom runway.

With each step, Fen remembered more of the past like her Revelation at The Nine Muses, holding hands with Prasad, and more. The animal continued to backup, gently pulling Fen from her forced confinement. When they took the last step onto the red soil outside the perimeter wall, the labyrinth disappeared and something new shimmered into existence. The Big Horn Medicine Wheel.

Chanting and drumming drifted from far away.

What happened? she asked the shaggy beast.

You have been removed from your prison. Your ancestors will soon be here to welcome you home.

My ancestors? Where am I? Miriam told me I was in the Land of the Healers.

You stand by the Circle of Calm, the white bison explained. *This sacred medicine wheel will protect you. The entity who called herself Miriam was an imposter.*

An imposter?

"Yes, an imposter," a female voice answered.

Fen turned toward the medicine wheel. A dark-haired woman walked toward her from the center of the sacred circle. A generous smile graced her smooth, tanned face. She wore a black cotton shift and necklaces strung with multi-colored stones and shells. A pendant dangled low, near her belly. It was a dreamcatcher festooned with white feathers and blue beads.

Fen's eyes widened. "I have a pendant like yours! She withdrew the necklace she had tucked inside her shirt for protection.

"Yes," the woman answered. "It is the mark of the Calm. I am called Galena."

"I am Fen...Fen Kemp," Fen offered. "Goodness, I remember my *full* name."

"And this is Bodhi. He is your spirit animal," Galena gently caressed the fluffy face of the bison. "His name means hope, something you were in desperate need of. He was the only one who could find and free you from your prison."

"My memories are returning, but I'm still a unsure of what happened," Fen replied. "I was walking on the labyrinth and Bodhi appeared."

"We searched many days for you." Dizziness took hold of Fen. She grabbed her head and stared at the ground, trying to steady herself.

"It's so foggy," she whispered as if talking loudly might prompt the vertigo to return. "I was sitting on the couch in England and a woman called my name. Miriam rushed toward me. I threw my hands up in defense but then I recognized someone beside her." Tears welled in Fen's eyes. "She had brought Prasad." She dropped her head and wept. "That wasn't Prasad, was it?"

Galena gently rubbed Fen's shoulder. "I've heard of the great healer, Prasad."

Fen looked up and wiped her eyes. "You have?"

"Yes. He once lived in the Circle of Calm. But he is in the ether now." Galena glanced upward. She held her hands toward the clouds and offered a silent prayer.

"The imposter tricked you into leaving the safety of the cottage."

"Who is the imposter? And will she try to take me again?"

"I will tell you soon. First, you must meet your family. Come, walk with me." Galena reached for Fen's hand, but Fen pulled back, unsure if she should trust another entity making promises.

"Have all your memories returned?" Galena gently prodded. "Do you recall Miriam and the place she kept you prisoner?"

"I remember very little of my time with Miriam. But I recall everything about my family and anything that happened before."

"Then the veil of confusion is departing. Do not fear me, Fen. Search your heart. What does your intuition tell you?"

Fen closed her eyes and breathed deeply several times. Finally free of Miriam's mesmerizing magic, she allowed the natural energy swirling around her to mix with her personal aura. An immediate tranquility descended upon her. When she opened her eyes, doubt was replaced with confidence.

Fen reached for Galena's hand. "I'm ready."

The entity's eyes sparkled. "I'll lead you to your ancestors. They're anxiously awaiting your arrival."

Fen glanced at the white bison. "What about Bodhi? If Miriam is free, she might try to hurt him."

"Don't worry about Bodhi," Galena assured. "Nobody can harm him. He's protected these lands and the sacred circle for a millennium." Galena raised her hands to heart center and bowed toward the shaggy bison. Fen also bowed toward the great beast.

Bodhi snorted, stomped his hoof, and vanished.

"Where did he go?" Fen asked.

"He's there," Galena replied. She threw her arms wide. "Bodhi is everywhere. Now, please, it is time to meet your family."

Galena snapped her fingers and they appeared in another land, one marked by lush vegetation, fields of wildflowers, and pristine streams. Men and women strolled the grounds.

Fen stared in awe. "Where are we?"

"We are within the Circle of Calm," Galena answered. "This is where you will find your family."

"My original family?"

Galena nodded. "They have been waiting for you."

Chapter 17

The Imposter

Growling, Miriam clenched her fists so hard that her nails punctured deep into her palms. Blood dripped to the ground, each drop hitting the dirt in a cloud of steam.

Blackness filled her eyes as she glared at the red soil scattered across the labyrinth, the maze which had served as Fen's prison for the last few days.

"Galena stole Fen," she hissed. She snapped her fingers.

A second later she appeared in another dimension just outside the outer wall of the Big Horn Medicine Wheel, a sacred structure that occupied the same space as the labyrinth in Miriam's universe.

She stared at the center cairn and sniffed the air. *I can smell the healer*, Miriam thought. *Galena took Fen through the portal.*

A loud snort snatched Miriam's attention. She whirled to find the white bison ambling toward her. Dust and gravel scattered with each of his lumbering steps.

"Meddlesome spirit!" Miriam shouted. "You had no right to take Fen from my labyrinth. You'll pay for your disrespect."

Unperturbed, Bodhi plodded forward, stopping a few feet from Miriam. The beast lowered his head until the tips of his enormous horns arced toward the entity's midsection.

"Ha!" Miriam scoffed. "You're no match for me!"

Snorting, the buffalo dragged one hoof along the ground, flinging dirt clods behind him. He bellowed and pawed the ground with his other hoof, digging a small drench and throwing the clumps of dirt well into the distance.

An electric blue cloud pulsed around his head as bolts of electricity snaked between the horn tips, snapping and hissing like an angry asp.

Miriam sneered. Raising her hands toward the creature, she yelled, "You can't hurt me, bison! You have no idea who you're dealing—"

Bodhi roared and rushed forward, cutting Miriam off as he plowed into her stomach. The magic shooting from her fingertips glanced off Bodhi's body, his supernatural fur deflecting the entity's spell. One of his curved horns punctured Miriam's side and protruded from her back, inches from her spine.

With Miriam firmly impaled on his horn, Bodhi tossed his head and flipped her twenty feet into the air. When she plummeted to earth, she rolled onto her back. Black fluid poured from the gaping wound soaking the ground beneath her.

"I'll kill you!" Miriam screamed as she struggled to stand.

Before she could get far, Bodhi trampled her to the ground and straddled her. With his nose inches from her face, he snorted multiple times. Each huff grew with intensity until miniature vortices swirled around them, weaving and bobbing until the cyclones united as a small tornado born of dust and gravel.

Bodhi backed away.

Now the size of a house, the twister moved over Miriam sucking her into its swirling winds and carrying her away.

Bodhi ambled along the outer wall of the medicine wheel, stopping occasionally to check the structure for any damage Miriam may have caused. Satisfied that the sacred circle was intact, the buffalo vanished.

Miriam plunged to earth hundreds of miles away.

The force of her fall created a small crater and sent shockwaves rippling across the desert.

She lay motionless.

One arm wrapped around her body like a fleshy cummerbund while the other bent upward, each finger twisted in a different direction. Her torso and legs were so mangled, the flesh resembled ground meat embedded with bits of white bone.

She groaned.

Her moaning intensified until Miriam howled like a wounded animal.

"Fucking bison!" she screamed as she willed her shattered body upright.

Agonizing pain rolled through her. Between gasps, she spat out the words of a conjuring. With each phrase, the broken bones followed the orders of the spell and snapped back into place, grinding and scraping as cartilage fused together. Holding her hands in front of her, she squinted at each finger, commanding them to straighten and pop back into place. Then she yanked her head to one side, snapping her shattered neck into proper alignment.

Half of Miriam's face was missing. What remained was a pulverized blob of raw meat with a dark hole where the eye had once rested. The orb lay on her battered cheek, held in place by a thin rope of connective tissue, which prevented the eye from falling onto the ground. She reached up and shoved it back into the socket, twisting and turning until she could see clearly.

She stood and whispered more magic. A wispy cloud manifested and shrouded her from head to toe. Flashes of static charges popped within the mist as Miriam completed her transformation spell.

After several moments, the enchanted mist dissipated.

The entity methodically peeled the remaining skin off her face and body until her body glistened in red, pulsing gore. She snatched clumps of hair from her head and tossed the matted mess to the ground. Naked, bloody, and bald, Miriam stood in the sunshine, her muscles and sinew wet and raw.

Slowly, filaments of new skin zigzagged across her body. Threads of tissue raced up and down her arms, legs, and torso, intersecting and overlapping with other layers until a new blanket of human skin formed.

Her naked body gleamed white and clean.

But it was no longer Miriam...it was Ryan Pierson.

Jake had quietly observed the battle between the white bison and Miriam. The butte on which he stood was far above the sacred circle and afforded him a front row seat without being detected. Once Miriam had been whisked away by the supernatural tornado and the white buffalo had vanished into thin air, Jake stood.

"Damn," he said aloud.

He eyed the horizon where he'd seen the tornado take Miriam and then looked back to the medicine wheel where the red soil was stained black by the fluids, which had leaked from the entity's wounds.

Interesting, he mused. *That buffalo is more powerful than Miriam.*

Jake shuddered recalling Darrius's speculation that Miriam may be his father, Ryan. It was clear she was a powerful and dangerous imposter, but in their encounters, Jake couldn't detect much about her. She was a shadow, a creature without substance.

If it was Dad, I'd know it, wouldn't I?

Jake had to figure it out quickly.

Miriam had been swept away, but how far? Did she land in some distant dimension, or was she still within this physical world?

Jake stared at the medicine wheel. He knew Fen was there...somewhere.

Has that buffalo taken control of Fen?

Jake launched into the air and landed deftly on the outside of the sacred circle. Opening his senses, he probed the surrounding area. Fen's life markers pulsed a steady energy.

Fen's here, he thought. *But where?*

He walked clockwise around the outer wall scrutinizing the area for any sign of his friend. Besides the occasional life force energy given off by Fen, there were no other signs anyone or anything had visited, including the white bison. It was as though the beast had never been present.

Jake arrived back where he started. *Where's that bison? I bet if I enter the wheel, he'll show up.* A wicked grin spread across his face.

Crossing the threshold of the medicine wheel and penetrating its sacred power was not his first option, but if he was to find Fen, he needed to enter the circle. He calculated the risk of invoking the rage of the mysterious bison. But the only way to discover if the creature would appear was to climb over the perimeter wall.

Jake carefully stepped over the outer circle of small rocks and tread slowly along one gravelly spoke until he reached the stones that faced east.

Nothing. The air was still.

He walked clockwise to the next line of rocks spoking out from the central cairn and stopped.

Silence.

He repeated this methodical walk to each line of stones until he returned to where he started.

Then he narrowed his eyes on the cairn in the middle of the structure. *I'm going in,* he thought as he headed straight for the ancient pile of stones in the center. When he reached the rocks, a light breeze scattered gravel at his feet.

Jake gazed upward. Billowing thunderheads filled the sky stretching back toward the western horizon. Lightning stabbed the desert in the distance.

I got someone's attention, Jake thought.

Holding his hands out to either side, palms forward, he announced, "I am Jake Pierson, shaman, and Keeper of the Word. I have entered this sacred space with respect and honor. I mean no harm."

A menacing growl came from above. Jake glanced up to find a jet-black cyclone rotating in the sky above his head. Lightning flickered from cloud to cloud but didn't strike the ground. He momentarily thought about Miriam being swept away by a magical tornado. But no buffalo had appeared, so he continued with his greeting.

"I'm here for Fen Kemp, Guardian of Peace. I only wish to talk with her." He paused and listened. The storm grumbled but the lightning flashes ceased.

"I'm a friend," he added.

"I know of you, Jake Pierson," a female spoke.

Jake whirled. "What the—"

Except for the shift color, the woman standing before him was Miriam.

"Miriam?" he asked.

The woman chuckled and shook her head. "I am known as Galena."

Recognizing the name, Jake bowed and brought his hands together at heart center. "Galena, I am honored by your presence."

"You know of me?" The entity smiled gently.

He raised his head. "Yes, the Sentinel boulder shared stories about the sacred sisters who protect this world and all who live in it. I thought the tales were myths."

She nodded. "The Sentinel boulder is the one who bound you to the Word. A wise spirit is he. My sisters and I have existed for millions of years since the planet was formed. This reverent space is known as the Circle of Calm." The entity stepped closer.

"You say you've come to talk with Fen?"

"Yes," he replied.

"There has been another."

Jake frowned. "Another?"

Galena approached Jake until she was inches away. With her shoulders squared and her arms relaxed at her side, the entity exuded power and confidence. "Miriam is not who she said she is."

"What do you know about her?" Jake probed.

"Nothing is ever as it appears," Galena said as she gripped Jake's hand.

Jake gasped. His heart hammered and beads of sweat popped out on his forehead. Images exploded in his brain. The scenes flickered fast—Fen, Miriam, the Amesbury cottage, the dimensional battle with his father. Intense light, a multitude of colors, and faces strobed too fast, and Jake closed his eyes against the pressure building behind his eyes.

Finally, Galena released his hand.

Jake bent forward and groaned. Nauseous, he pinched his side to distract himself from vomiting. Instead, he collapsed with dry heaves. After several minutes, he willed himself to stand.

"What the—" He caught himself before he cursed. "What was that?"

"I shared glimpses of the imposter, the one who goes by the name of Miriam. The trickster had ensnared Fen in a hypnotic existence and used her to lure you and the others into a web."

"Miriam told me Fen was resting in the Land of the Healers."

"The imposter lied to force Fen to submit to his bidding."

"*His* bidding?"

"Miriam wore a fraudster's skin, a shadow covering that made her appear as a female earth spirit. Miriam cloaked her true identity, which was your father, Ryan Pierson."

Jake bit his lip so hard, blood trickled down his chin. *How is he so powerful?* he thought.

Miriam tilted her head. "He has transformed into a creature with supernatural strengths."

"You read my mind without permission?"

"Your thoughts scattered into the air like seeds on the wind."

Jake scrutinized Galena. The small woman with long dark hair had a slight build but her arms were strong and sinewy. Although she appeared as the mirror image of Miriam, her eyes were light blue instead of dark.

"Why should I trust anything you have to say?" Jake asked. "You look and act like Miriam."

"You're not trusting your instincts, Shaman," she replied. The entity known as Miriam was an imposter and she—he fooled you. Perhaps you were too willing to believe instead of using your skills to know for sure."

Jake's face flushed red. Galena's words wounded his pride. But it was true, he had been too willing to trust Miriam even though he couldn't detect her energy source. Plus, Miriam had Fen. He'd do anything for Fen.

Galena studied Jake's face. "You're puzzled by this conundrum, Shaman. Miriam tricked you and now you're faced with the same dilemma with me. You must dig deep and explore your feelings."

"Perhaps if I was able to see Fen. What you say and what you do are different things."

Galena glanced toward the outer ring of the sacred circle. Jake followed her gaze and saw the white buffalo chewing his cud placidly.

Galena nodded at the beast, and the bison slowly entered the medicine wheel. Just off his shoulder and hidden by his immense size walked Fen. She gripped his shaggy fur with one hand as they walked toward the center cairn.

Jake started toward her.

"No, Shaman," Galena scolded as she gripped his arm. "Do not leave this sacred spot. Fen shall come to you."

Jake obeyed. Instead, he released all his senses to scan the figure walking toward him. He needed to ensure it was Fen and not another ruse. So far, his instincts verified that a human, a magical person, ambled toward him. In addition, the figure released the unique scent shared by all the Kemps.

But Jake wasn't ready to believe. He needed to touch her and connect with her cells to confirm she was Fen.

The great beast stopped six feet away. Fen stared between Galena and Jake, her forehead was furrowed with confusion. Then Fen squinted and leaned forward looking directly into Jake's eyes. Her calm, emotionless face broke into a generous smile as big tears rolled down her cheeks.

"Jake is that really you?" her voice cracked.

Jake looked to Galena who nodded approval for him to speak. "It's really me, Fen."

"Galena, may I be permitted to join you and Jake?" Fen asked.

Galena nodded and the great beast ambled forward leading Fen as she gripped tightly to his hair. When the bison reached Galena, she tousled the thick tufts of fur between his horns. "This is Bodhi, Fen's spirit animal. He's always by her side in this physical plane."

"Thank you for bringing Fen to me, Bodhi," Jake said bowing toward the animal. "May I hug her?" Jake asked Galena.

The entity nodded.

Jake rushed forward and grabbed Fen in a bear hug. He buried his face into her hair and whispered, "I thought I'd lost you." The moment he touched her skin, he knew she was real.

"I've always been here," she replied as they parted.

"Fen has little memory of her ordeal with Miriam," Galena explained. "The entity mesmerized her, keeping her thoughts foggy, and preventing her from remembering anything."

"Fen has an important role to fulfill," Jake insisted as he held Fen's hand afraid to let her go.

"I'm aware of the Prophecy, Shaman," Galena responded.

"Do you approve of Fen coming with me so she can unlock the Guardian boulder?"

Galena gently smiled. “You don’t understand, Shaman. Fen is safe if she is with Bodhi. Bodhi is an entity of the Circle of Calm and cannot leave this space.”

“But I can protect her while she’s with me,” Jake insisted.

Galena stepped forward and reached for his face. He jerked as she cupped his chin and lightly brushed his cheek with her thumb. “You still have so much to learn. Fen will not leave this realm, but she will complete her duty to the Guardian boulder and unite her crystal with its Guardian.”

“She still needs to locate her family gemstone. How will she do that if she is not allowed to leave the Circle of Calm?”

“Because she already possesses her family crystal.”

“I do?” Fen asked

“Yes,” Galena replied. “The Guardian boulder in Wales gifted you a protection necklace.”

“Yes, this.” Fen withdrew the diminutive dreamcatcher pendant with white feathers and bluestone chips.”

“That’s it,” Galena replied. “That’s why your family tried to bring you here as soon as possible, but Miriam beat us to it. Fortunately for us, she didn’t realize you already possessed the precious jewel.”

“But I sensed it was really Fen’s people approaching the cottage,” Jake protested.

“See how powerful your father has become?” she replied. “He not only fooled you, but he tricked Fen as well. So, you see, Fen will not leave the safety of this land. But we can arrange to have her meet you within the confines of our protected dominion, one that Ryan cannot penetrate.”

“This sounds awfully familiar,” Jake mocked. “My father told me the same thing when he controlled Fen. What’s odd is that he knew where the Guardian boulder was located and that’s privileged information.”

“He’s more formidable than anyone believed. If he knows the location of the Guardian boulders then he has tapped into the sacred text of the

Prophecy. That is most troubling. Ryan's transformation is occurring at an alarming rate."

"I wish I'd killed him in Wales," Jake mused.

"I'm not sure you could," Galena noted.

Jake looked at her with determination. "I'll find a way, or he'll continue to hunt all of us."

"You've been hunted since you were eight, when the Sentinel Boulder graced you with the Word," Galena replied. "He wouldn't have entrusted this important responsibility to you if he wasn't convinced you could shoulder the burden."

"Jake, I have faith in you," Fen whispered as she clenched his hand. "I can feel the emotions racing through your mind. Would you allow me to provide healing energy so you can think more clearly?"

Jake's eyes watered. "Please, Fen. Anything you can give me. I've been so confused since I left England."

Fen hummed. As she sang the ancient melody, Jake closed his eyes and swayed back and forth to the lyrical tune, his thoughts gently retreating away.

Jake awoke with a start.

He sat on the ground with his back against the central cairn and his legs drawn up against his chest. He struggled into a standing position. "Fen? Galena?"

He was alone, except for Bodhi. The white buffalo stood nearby and snorted at Jake's outburst. Red dust coated Jake, and he fanned the air.

"Thanks!" he chaffed. "Where is everyone?" Jake patted the dirt from his clothes.

Bodhi grumbled and snorted.

Shaman, take a lock of Bodhi's hair. Galena's gentle voice drifted through Jake's brain. *It will protect you from Ryan and will be your connection to Fen. When you need her, hold the lock of hair and call out to her.*

Bodhi ambled forward until his withers were even with Jake's face. The beast's enormous size was intimidating, and Jake backed away as it approached.

The bison snorted impatiently.

"Okay, okay." Jake plunged his hand into the thick hair around Bodhi's shoulders and twisted a lock of fur around one finger. In one movement, he yanked it out. *Is this enough?* Jake asked holding up the hair.

Yes, Galena messaged. *Blessings be with you, Shaman.*

Bodhi snorted and disappeared, leaving Jake alone within the medicine wheel.

Since Fen's emotional healing, Jake's confidence soared, and he was resolute about the future. He gripped the hair in his fist and telepathically messaged Fen, *Thank you, Fen, for your healing. I'll work on a plan with your brothers and contact you soon.* Jake reverently stepped along the lines of the wheel until he could easily get over the outer wall.

He gazed around the medicine wheel one more time and disappeared.

Chapter 18

Homecoming

"THIS IS WHERE YOU were subdued by the Firewalker witch?" Balor asked, sweeping his arms out to either side. The Cererians stood on the beach below The Nine Muses. Seawater swirled around his boots and sank deep into the sodden sand.

Stygian glared at Balor's head and envisioned it exploding. His capture at the hands of Hilly was still a shock and embarrassment, but he was also somewhat proud. Hilly had outsmarted him. Only someone born of his blood could outwit him, and she had played the game exceptionally well.

Except she had died in the process.

If Prasad hadn't intervened, and traded his life for Hilly's, the Firewalker line would have ended, and the Cererian Prophecy would have disintegrated.

Stygian sighed. *I'm glad Prasad interceded.*

He dismissed his impulse to kill the soldier and pointed toward the horizon. "I swooped in from that direction, disguised as a monstrous storm, a nor'easter I believe the humans call it."

Cary kicked at a small lump lodged in the sand and held it up to the sun. Hues of red and orange radiated from the nugget.

"Sea glass," Stygian observed. "Grains of sand fused into colorful glass. A result of the intense energy that exploded here eight months ago." Stygian plucked the glass from Cary's hand and held it up. "A thing of beauty born from destruction."

"Will we attack soon?" Balor asked.

"Patience, soldier," Stygian replied. "Your former commander, Aaron, was headstrong and impetuous. I'll teach you that calculated and properly timed actions will result in success."

Stygian faced The Nine Muses perched on the cliff above them. "No doubt, Darrius and his friends have secured the structure with their protective conjuring. The last time I visited, their magic prevented me from penetrating the outer seals."

"But you were able to enter the Firewalker's mind," Balor insisted. "You told us you were able to do that several times."

"That's true," Stygian replied. "But Hilly is not here. I sense that only her brothers are in the building along with Darrius and his team. I don't even feel the shaman, Jake." He slapped Balor on the shoulder and the soldier tensed. "I like your eagerness, Balor. But right now, you and Cary will investigate the area and look for holes in their magical grid. Be as thorough with your inspection as possible, even if you must move a few walls."

Balor studied Stygian's face.

"Yes, Balor, do as much damage as you can inflict," Stygian directed. "Keep everyone busy while I search for the Firewalker."

"Yes, sir!" Balor barked as he bolted away. "Cary, come with me. We have work to do."

One by one, the two soldiers teleported from the beach to a location closer to The Nine Muses. Stygian peered into the western sky and closed his eyes. *Where are you, Hilly?* Slowly moving his head back and forth he sniffed the air using his keen senses to find her. After several moments, he sighed.

Ah, there you are.

Then he also disappeared from the beach.

"Where the hell is Jake?" Chance barked as he paced in the study.

Eyes closed, Kai sat in a chair with his heels resting on the windowsill. When he didn't respond, Chance marched to him and leaned close to one ear.

"I said where the hell is Jake!"

Kai jerked to his feet and whirled ready to fight. Chance grabbed Kai's hands before he unleashed a bolt of energy. "Easy, Kai, it's just me. Jeez, I didn't realize you had fallen asleep. We were just talking seconds ago."

Kai shook his head. "I didn't realize I'd fallen asleep either. I was staring at the waves rolling in from the ocean and you were droning on about something...I guess I nodded off."

"Was I that boring?"

"You have your moments." Kai said, punching his brother's arm. "Where are the others?"

"You mean the Cererian boys?" Chance joked. "They're checking protection spells for the one-thousandth time."

"I don't blame them being cautious," Kai replied. "Darrius was really bothered by Stygian's release."

"He worked hard to bring Stygian to justice. Then his own people abandoned him. It doesn't take a genius to figure out that Stygian will come looking for all of us."

"Damn, I don't even want to think about another battle on this beach."

"Where would you prefer the battle take place?" Chance joked.

The brothers chuckled nervously.

"Good to see you two are in great spirits," Darrius said as he entered the study. "Is Jake back yet?"

"Not yet," Chance replied. "He's been gone an hour. I'm worried."

"Stygian and his soldiers were detected on the beach," Benedict announced as he joined Darrius.

"Shit," Kai said. "Get ready for round two."

"Easy, Kai," Darrius soothed. "There won't be a battle today. I'm not surprised by the Yfel's presence. Stygian won't try anything just yet. Although he can't penetrate the magic surrounding this house, he'll be able to sense the bodies contained within the home."

"Then he already knows Hilly, Fen, and Jake aren't here." Kai remarked.

"Jake and Hilly are the stronger magicians out of all of us," Chance observed. "If I was Stygian, I'd attack the weaker ones to get them out of the way." Chance stared out the window and lightly tapped the triskele pin stuck in his collar. "But as long as I'm wearing this, Stygian won't be able to do a thing to me." Chance turned to Kai. "That leaves you baby brother."

"Um...I don't think so," Kai complained. "You're not throwing me to the wolves because you have special jewelry." Kai grabbed at the pin.

"Get off of me!" Chance shouted as he shoved Kai against the wall.

Kai grimaced and charged his brother, but Darrius caught his arm. "This is not helping anything, Kai. You're letting your emotions rule your head. Please sit down." Turning to Chance, Darrius continued, "And you, stop antagonizing your brother. Just because you wear that pin doesn't make you invincible. Remember that."

Pouting, the brothers sat in opposite chairs.

"I know Stygian better than any of you," Darrius explained. "He's a very patient, calculating individual. When he attacks, he'll want that moment to be worth his while. That means he'll wait for Hilly and Jake."

"Gee, I feel special," Chance pouted.

"Yeah, me too," Kai agreed.

WHAM!

The house shuddered as though a fist had punched down onto the roof.

"What the hell?" Chance exclaimed, racing into the foyer followed by the others.

Dust drifted down from the ceiling.

Benedict pointed upward. "The twins are prowling on the roof testing our protection magic."

"If they continue assaulting The Nine Muses," Darrius mused. "We'll be busy reinforcing the conjuring all night."

"Perhaps that's Stygian's plan," Alden observed. "If we're kept busy shoring up weaknesses exposed by their concussive bolts, then we won't have time to do anything else."

"Yes," Darrius agreed. "And it allows Stygian the opportunity to teleport in search of Hilly, Fen, and Jake while the twins keep us busy."

"Nobody will find Hilly and Fen," Jake said.

Kai jerked. "Damn, I'll never get used to you popping in like that. It's a good thing the Cererian protection magic around the house doesn't stop you from getting in."

Jake grinned. "The protection magic is for Cererians, and I'm not Cererian the last time I checked."

The walls shuddered again. Several portraits crashed to the floor. "There go the ancestors," Kai quipped.

"How long have they been rearranging the house?" Jake asked.

"Not long," Darrius replied. "Although, I suspect Stygian has ordered the twins to do whatever damage they can while he searches for Fen and Hilly."

"Like I said, he won't be able to find them," Jake replied. "Both of them are under the protection of earth spirits. I don't care how strong Stygian is, his powers don't compare to theirs. Hilly's with Denali and Fen's with—with Galena."

"Galena?" Chance inquired. "Who the hell is Galena?"

"A new person at this weird-ass party," Jake replied.

"Did you meet with Miriam?" Chance asked. "Did you get things sorted?"

"Yes and no," Jake replied. "This new entity is called Galena. She confirmed my dad was disguised as Miriam and had mesmerized Fen.

"And I did meet with Fen. She's okay. Her memories are returning, and she's now in a place called the Circle of Calm, the place she should have been taken originally. Galena, who is the spitting image of Miriam, is a sacred sister who's in charge of this new universe where Fen resides. I must now deal with her. Oh, and I met her magical bison, Bodhi."

Chance and Kai exchanged puzzled looks and then burst out laughing.

"Bodhi the bison?" Kai snorted.

"A Miriam look-alike?" Chance spat through chuckles.

"The Circle of Calm?" they chorused before they burst into full laughter.

Jake sighed and strode back into the study and collapsed into a chair facing the ocean.

"The brothers are just letting off some nervous energy," Darrius said as he joined Jake. "The constant pounding on the house is unnerving."

On cue, a tremendous shudder shook the area above the study causing glasses to fall off the shelf and shatter on the floor. The two men regarded the mess and then resumed staring out the window.

"Kai and Chance can make all the jokes they need to feel sane," Jake offered. "Because now I have some answers, and I can move forward with a plan."

"Great news," Darrius responded.

"But the tricky part is my dad. He doesn't know I'm aware of his true identity—at least I don't think he does. I was cloaked when Bodhi kicked my dad's ass with a supernatural tornado that pulled him far away. So, I have two choices: continue with the ruse of Miriam in the hopes of capturing him or work with Galena and Fen to secure the crystal in the Guardian boulder and hope my dad won't interfere."

"Ryan sounds incredibly powerful," Darrius observed. "If you don't deal with him now, and on your terms, he'll find you later but then he might have all the advantages."

"Ryan also knows the whereabouts of the Guardian boulders," Jake mentioned. "Nobody should have access to this information except me. Galena said his knowledge of the sacred sites indicates just how powerful he's become. He can use this information to lead Stygian and the twins directly to us or keep us all to himself."

"That is troubling," Darrius said. He rested his chin on the tips of his fingers and stared out the window. "What do your instincts tell you?"

"I need to deal with Dad. But spending my time chasing him through the universe might be counter-productive, so I want to expedite our trip to the Guardian boulder."

"Sorry to interrupt," Kai said as he and Chance walked into the study. "We were eavesdropping. I understand your dad could cause us a lot of grief. You can rely on Chance and me to help you in any way we can."

"We will?" Chance said, glancing at his brother.

"We will," Kai emphasized. "You've done so much for our family. It's only fair that we support you when you need us."

"Sure," Chance chimed in. "How can we help?"

Jake slowly turned and looked at the eager brothers. He sighed and returned gazing at the serene ocean. "This is a solo encounter, guys. I appreciate your enthusiasm, but going another round with my dad is going to take some clever maneuvering through different dimensions."

Benedict rushed into the study. "Darrius, Stygian is no longer on the property."

"Stygian is wasting his time," Jake muttered.

"And the twins have already destroyed the garage and are working on the pergola in the back yard." Benedict rushed away when a crash thundered in a distant room.

Unfazed by the commotion, Darrius continued gazing out the window.

"You're not disturbed by this information?" Jake asked.

"No," Darrius replied. "Stygian did far worse when he visited The Nine Muses eight months ago. The house will stand despite what Balor and Cary lob at it."

A tree flew past the large window.

"Did you see that?" Kai asked as he rushed to the window. "Damn, they've already dismantled the pergola and are breaking up the flagstones."

"They are dangerously close to the Omphalos Stone. It's the last remaining portal to Ceres," Alden announced as he quietly entered the room.

"I don't care," Darrius muttered. "We have no need of it."

"What about our parents?" Chance argued. "When you sent them to Ceres for their safety, you promised we would be reunited. Without that portal, they can't come back."

Darrius sighed and left the room. He strolled to the patio doors and watched Balor assault the flagstone floor with a blur of punches.

"Darrius?" Chance called out as he and Kai joined him. "What about Mom and Dad?"

"They're no longer alive," the Cererian replied impassively.

"What?" Kai whispered. "Dead?"

"What happened?" Chance demanded. "Why are we just hearing about this?"

Darrius stared outside. Balor stopped pulverizing the flagstones and glanced up. Unblinking, the two Cererians studied each other for several moments before Balor sneered and grabbed the iron frame around the fire pit. Tortured metal screeched as he wrenched it away from the cement holding it to the ground.

Darrius faced the Kemps. "I found out minutes before Stygian's trial. The Senator had informed me that I, and my colleagues, were exiled from Ceres and mentioned that your parents were no longer alive."

"What exactly did he say?" Kai asked. "Did he say what happened?"

Darrius sighed. “His exact words were ‘This mess on Earth must be cleared up. I’ve already taken care of any links to Ceres, including the Kemps. They have been terminated. Now it’s time for you to do your job.’”

Chance wrapped his arm around Kai and drew him close. The two brothers held on to each other and stared at the floor.

CRASH!

“Cary ripped the porte cochere away from the roof,” Alden announced. “We’ll need to reinforce the protection magic around the house.”

“I’ll head upstairs,” Bob said as he disappeared.

“I’ll check the rear. You focus on the front,” Benedict added.

“Balor found the Omphalos Stone,” Darrius announced. He watched as the Yfel soldier plucked it from the ground and presented it to Darrius like a present before pulverizing the ancient stone between his hands.

Chapter 19

Bound by Blood

Hilly leaned against a boulder under the snowy overhang where Denali had deposited her.

Denali's in a mood, she thought. *Why did she kick me out moments after I arrived?*

A shiver raced down Hilly's spine, and she stood, fists clenched.

Using her psychic abilities, she explored the area with her mind: skimming over glaciers, plunging deep into crevasses, and soaring high into the clear azure sky.

She sensed nobody.

But that feeling remained. The hairs prickled on the back of her neck warning her of something ominous.

Unexpectedly, a tremendous warmth spread throughout her cells beginning in her abdomen and flooding up into her chest. She flushed as her heart pounded in her ears. She gasped as the sensation wound around her brain like a seductive caress.

She knew this feeling, having first experienced it eight months earlier when she arrived at The Nine Muses for the reading of her parents' will.

Hilly, his voice drifted through her brain like a gentle breeze.

Stygian. Hilly crouched low under the icy overhang and surveyed her surroundings. Anticipating a battle, she held her hands in front of her, fingers splayed, ready to dispel bolts of magic.

I'm not here to fight.

Hilly eased at Stygian's tone. But he'd tricked her before at The Nine Muses when he attempted to enter her body.

What do you want? she replied.

I only want to talk.

Hilly's heart hammered, and she swooned. His hypnotic voice plucked gently at her sensibilities. She gasped, surprised at the warm sensation returning to her lower belly. *Denali will kill you,* she warned.

I have no doubt. But your earth mother will surely allow me to speak to my kin.

Despite the frigid temperature, beads of sweat trickled down Hilly's face, and a fire flared in her abdomen.

I will grant you five minutes, she responded.

Face to face, Stygian insisted.

Hilly panted. The sensation pulsed in her body, the tempo growing faster and faster with each passing second. From her body's reaction, she knew Stygian was getting closer. Her hands throbbed. When she looked at them, her palms glowed blood red and waves of intense heat rose from her fingers. Hilly plunged her hands into a nearby snowbank. Steam billowed upward.

A clap of thunder startled her.

An avalanche of snow and ice roared down Denali's slopes. Boulders bounced along the ground while sheets of tightly packed snow dislodged and slid downward like a thick blanket of ice.

You will not see my daughter! Denali yelled into Hilly and Stygian's brains.

A figure stood no more than a hundred yards from Hilly and struggled in the middle of the plunging snowpack.

Stygian! Hilly thought.

Boulders rained down on the Yfel leader, but he easily deflected them away.

I come in peace, Denali! he messaged the great earth spirit.

A thunderous growl shook the ground as if the mountain itself was ripping apart. A maelstrom swirled in the sky, growing larger with each rotation until the entire mountaintop had been consumed by menacing thunderheads and a monstrous blizzard. Damp snowflakes the size of dinner plates swirled wrapping everything in a damp frosty blanket.

A blast of frigid air slammed Stygian in the chest and propelled the Cererian backward. Another barrage of boulders cascaded from above and glanced off his body as he struggled to stand. After he batted the last boulder away, the Cererian stood, defiant, covered from head to toe in an icy blanket of snow.

Great earth mother, Denali, Stygian messaged. *I will do no harm to your earth child, Hilly. Grant me five minutes with her or strike me dead now.*

Hilly's eyes widened. Stygian wouldn't purposely invoke the wrath of Denali unless he truly meant no harm.

Mother, she implored Denali, *please allow me five minutes with him.*

Are you sure, my child? Denali asked. *He has tried to harm you in the past.*

I'm sure, Great Mother. Hilly stood outside the overhang staring at Stygian. She swiped away a single tear that had formed in the corner of her eye. *He wouldn't dare try anything in your kingdom.*

Granted, Denali replied.

Immediately, the cyclone sucked upward into itself and retreated over the high ridges. A clear blue sky soon returned to the entire region.

Covered in a thick mantle of soggy snow, the tall Cererian appeared like an abominable snowman amid deflected boulders littering the ground around his feet. He shook himself and chunks of slushy snow fell to the ground.

When he met Hilly's gaze, a tentative smile flickered on his lips as she slowly approached him and stopped a few yards away.

"You have five minutes," she declared.

"Denali has quite a punch," he joked.

"You have five minutes," Hilly reminded him. "Denali won't give you a second chance."

"Direct. I like that." Stygian took a step forward.

"Stop!" Hilly said, holding up her hand. "Tell me what you want from there."

"I see your hands are still red," he observed. Hilly swung her hands behind her back. "It's because of our shared blood. You're not the only one who feels the stirring when we're in close proximity. We are bound by blood, and it boils when we're near each other."

Hilly blushed and looked away. "What do you want? You now have four minutes."

"I want to forge an alliance. You and me."

"You're kidding! The Yfel murdered my family, kidnapped and tortured me, and now you want to be associates?" Hilly whirled to leave. "You're wasting my time."

"Please!" Stygian shouted. "I'm serious. The Cererian Prophecy is nearing completion."

Hilly stopped and hung her head. "Yes, I'm aware."

"Perhaps you're not aware of the final days..."

"I know what will happen."

"Then you understand why I'm here. Darrius and I have been friends since we emerged from our Cererian birthing chambers. Unfortunate circumstances have severed the close bond we once shared."

"You have three minutes," Hilly cautioned.

"I'm not a powerful warrior. I'm a coward who traded my friend's life for my freedom."

"What do you mean?" Hilly pressed.

"In exchange for my freedom, and that of my soldiers, I agreed to assassinate Darrius, Alden, and Benedict, in addition to other Cererians as dictated to me. I am nothing more than someone's leashed cur."

"Go on..." Hilly urged. Her face softened. "What do you want of me?"

"I'm a dead man no matter what occurs, so I want to join forces with you, my only descendant, to vanquish those who would do harm to my friends, or the colleagues of my friends. Together, no one will be able to touch us."

"I don't want control of the world, Stygian."

"That's not what I'm proposing. I want my last days to be spent doing something honorable, not as a puppet dancing on a string."

"You want my help killing the Cererian you struck a deal with?"

"Yes, and in return, I'll help you kill Ryan Pierson. Your shaman friend will not be able to kill his father by himself. Ryan has evolved into an all-powerful being. But you and I, together, will be strong enough to destroy him."

"Why don't you and your soldiers dispatch this Cererian who controls you?"

Stygian dropped his head and sighed. Slowly, he opened his coat and pulled up his shirt. An inflamed area the size of a fist glowed blood red on Stygian's left breast, above his heart. The angry mass pulsed rhythmically in time with the Cererian's heartbeat.

"What's that?!" she cried.

"I'm being monitored at all times, Hilly. I took a chance coming here...talking with you." He turned to leave. "This was a mistake."

"Wait!" Hilly shouted. She crept forward and slowly held her palm toward the throbbing mass of tissue and closed her eyes.

"What are you doing?" Stygian asked.

Hilly didn't respond. Connected with the pulsating tumor, she propelled herself through space and time and soared through dimensions searching for its master. A few moments later, she dropped her hand. "I'll help you," she whispered.

"What did you see?"

"I saw the individual who yanks the reins on your bit. As we speak, he's already coercing others to assassinate you and your soldiers. I don't know him, but his energy is black and empty."

"He's known as the Senator," Stygian offered.

The Cererian's time is up, Denali thundered through the valley.

Please, Mother, Hilly implored. *I sense Stygian is honorable. I need more time.* Hilly faced Stygian. "How do I know I can trust you?"

"Search your heart, Firewalker. Would I harm my own blood?"

The Cererian Prophecy is clear, Denali stated. *I will not interfere with your destiny. Do what you will as you travel the pathway to your future.*

"Is Denali allowing us to leave?" Stygian asked.

"Yes," Hilly nodded.

"You seem sad," he noted.

Hilly managed a weak smile as she gazed around. "I'll miss these slopes."

Stygian nodded. "But you'll save the world." He grasped Hilly's hand, which had cooled considerably. "Come on, Firewalker, let's make sure the shaman completes his mission."

Unseen by the others, Jake discreetly teleported from the study and reappeared on the beach far from The Nine Muses. As he neared a group of boulders, Hilly strolled out from behind her hiding place.

"I got your message," he said rushing to her. He lifted her up and swung her around. "I've missed you."

He placed her on the sand gently and stood back to look at her. "What's wrong? I can tell something's wrong."

"It's probably me," Stygian announced as he appeared from around a large rock.

"Stygian!" Jake yelled as he withdrew his battle blades, Cathal and Cadmar.

Hilly ran between the men and held up her hands. "Stop! Listen to me, Jake!"

Jake waved his weapons at the Cererian. "Give me a reason, Stygian."

"Jake, we're here for a good reason," she insisted.

"We?" Jake asked.

"I encouraged Stygian to come with me and talk with you."

"What about?" Jake lowered his weapons but kept a wary eye on the Cererian.

"We have a proposition." Hilly glanced at Stygian. "Due to unusual circumstances, Stygian and I are joining forces."

"What?" Jake yelled. "Do you realize how many people, your family included, that monster has killed?"

"Jake," Hilly spoke softly, barely audible. "Please listen. After you hear what we have to say, you can do as you wish but give us a chance. We realize how strong your father has become."

"How do you know?" Jake demanded.

"It doesn't matter how we know, let's just say we're aware it may be difficult for you to deal with your father *and* help Chance and Fen find their Guardian boulders. As such, we are willing to help you."

"But why now?" Jake sneered at Stygian. "Why unite with this son of a bitch now?"

The Cererian stepped forward. "Because I need Hilly's help with a delicate matter."

Hilly glanced at Stygian and rolled her eyes. "What he means is, if I help him with his problem, he'll help us with Ryan."

Jake scoffed. "And what kind of a problem can the great Stygian have that he would need additional help from you?"

Hilly began to speak but Stygian held up his hand. "Please, Hilly. Let me explain. I can't share specifics, Shaman, but Hilly is helping me remove a Cererian thorn from my side."

Jake rubbed the stubble on his chin. "That must be some mighty important thorn that you need Hilly's powers to deal with him."

"He is," Stygian nodded.

"You agreed to this, Hilly?" Jake asked.

"Yes," she replied.

"How will you take care of my dad?"

"Don't worry about the details," Hilly responded. "Rest assured that we'll take care of Ryan so you can focus on getting everyone to the Guardian boulders."

"Why should I trust him?" Jake said stabbing his finger in Stygian's direction.

"Because I do," Hilly answered softly. "I have complete faith in him."

Hilly placed a hand on Jake's chest over his heart. "I know this is hard for you but let us deal with Ryan. Right now, we need to divide in order to conquer."

"My dad's crafty, Hilly. He'll run you straight to hell and back again. Shit, he might even be able to split himself into two Ryans for all I know."

"Really?" Hilly asked. "Can he be in two places at once?"

"My dad has become so strong. I no longer know what he's capable of."

"Where can we find him?" Stygian asked.

"A place I'm beginning to think is the center of the world. The Bighorn Medicine Wheel. You'll stand on the butte above the sacred circle and keep your psychic senses peeled for a dark-haired woman by the name of Miriam."

"A dark-haired woman?!" Hilly exclaimed.

"Yeah, dad thinks he's fooled me into believing he's some spiritual guide for Fen. I've since learned that Fen is protected by the sacred sister, Galena, and the white buffalo Bodhi."

Hilly shook her head. "Nothing is ever as it seems."

"You can say that again," Jake agreed. "By the way, you'll need me to draw Dad out. If he senses your energy, he won't show."

"How do you propose we handle that?" Stygian asked.

"I'll reach out to Miriam. Er...Dad, and request a meeting. He's expecting me to contact him, so he won't be suspicious. You and Hilly need to cloak your whereabouts and when he shows up, I zip out of the picture, and you two take over. Find his heart and destroy it."

"His heart?" Hilly asked.

"Yeah," Jake replied. "It won't be easy. It's not where you think it is. Locate that lump of coal that keeps him alive and pulverize it." Jake narrowed his eyes. "Expect the unexpected at all times with Ryan."

Stygian joined Hilly and quietly slipped his arm around her waist. "Don't worry, Shaman, I'll see that no harm befalls Hilly. I promise."

Jake eyed the Cererian's action. "Promises from you are like throwing seeds in the wind," Jake grabbed Hilly's hand and led her several paces away. "Listen, Hilly, watch your back at all times."

"I can handle myself, Jake," she replied calmly.

"I know." He peeked at the Cererian watching them. "But remember that Stygian's even more powerful since he killed Aaron and consumed his supernatural powers. He's well aware that if he keeps one of us from fulfilling our duties to the Prophecy, then this world will never know peace again."

Hilly gripped Jake's hand and peered into his eyes. "I promise I'll stand with you and my siblings in the end."

She turned abruptly and joined Stygian. "Jake, reach out to me when you've made contact with your dad." A generous smile filled her face. "And thanks for trusting us to take care of this matter." She raised her hand and waved.

Instantly, she and Stygian vanished.

Chapter 20

A Constantly Changing Plan

"JAKE!" KAI CALLED OUT while running through the house.

"Mr. Pierson!" Alden and Benedict cried in unison.

"Did you find him yet?" Darrius asked as the men met in the foyer.

"Nope," Kai responded. "I left him in the study for a few seconds and when I returned, he'd disappeared."

"Did the Yfel snatch him?" Chance pondered.

"Not Jake," Kai said and then added, "Shit, I hope they didn't get Jake."

"What's all the fuss?" Jake asked as he walked up to the group of men.

Five angry faces stared back at him.

"We've been hunting for you for thirty minutes," Darrius snapped. "Kai said you simply disappeared. Where have you been?"

Jake swirled the bourbon in his glass and sipped it. "I had a pressing engagement." He glanced at Kai. "Sorry, brother, it was urgent. I didn't have time to say anything."

"Shit," Kai responded. "That wasn't cool. I thought you got snatched by the Yfel."

"You shouldn't have left without notice," Darrius admonished.

Jake gulped his drink. "Darrius, a quick word..." The shaman whirled and headed to the study.

Chance and Kai exchanged puzzled glances.

Darrius gestured for Alden and Benedict to remain in the foyer as he followed after Jake who stood by the study door. When Darrius entered, Jake shut the door.

"I met with Hilly," he announced. "And Stygian..."

"What? Are you crazy?!"

Jake held up his hands. "Easy, Darrius. Everything is okay. Hilly reached out to me and insisted I come alone. It wasn't until I met her on the beach that Stygian popped out of nowhere."

"He could have killed you—killed both of you."

"I doubt he could do anything to Hilly, and I definitely would have given him a bloody fight." Jake sighed. "They've joined forces."

"That's nonsense!" Darrius stormed to the window and glared at Balor who was lobbing hunks of concrete into the ocean.

"It's true. Hilly wanted to meet with me personally so she could explain."

Darrius shook his head. "I don't understand."

"Apparently, Stygian is being coerced by some Cererian and asked for Hilly's help in getting rid of this person. In exchange, he'll help her find and destroy my dad."

"Which Cererian?" Darrius asked.

"He wouldn't share the details."

"How will they deal with your dad?"

"They feel the two of them have a better chance of killing Dad together than I do alone. Their plan will allow me to focus on guiding Chance and Fen to their Guardian boulders without looking over my shoulder for Dad. Setting my pride aside, I must admit combining their powers will be the far superior option in destroying Ryan."

Darrius watched Balor toss the remains of the pergola off the cliff. "What about Balor and Cary? Do they know Stygian is off on a new adventure?"

Jake huffed. "You know your friend better than I, Darrius. I didn't talk to him about his soldiers, but I imagine Stygian wants the boys occupied so he and Hilly can do their work uninterrupted. So, to answer your question, Cary and Balor will continue to pound away on the house."

Another tremendous shudder sent more dust drifting from the ceiling.

Darrius silently walked to the liquor cabinet and poured himself a drink. After gulping it, he turned to Jake. "My return to The Nine Muses has been most interesting. Nothing is unfolding as I planned."

"Plan?" Jake stated. "What's a goddamned plan? I'm flying by the seat of my pants every waking hour. Things are changing so fast, a goddamned program wouldn't help me keep track."

Darrius shook his head. "I miss the days when I had four neophyte warriors asking me about their future. As we approach the end of The Cererian Prophecy, there seems to be more questions than answers."

"Do you really think we'll reach the end of the Prophecy?" Jake asked as he poured himself another drink.

"I wager your already know the answer." Darrius pushed his empty glass toward Jake who filled it with bourbon.

They clinked glasses and then sat in silence as Balor stomped around outside.

Darrius broke the silence. "I sense you'll be leaving again."

Jake smirked. "Yep. I'll be arranging a meeting with Miri—my dad...and meet him on the Wyoming butte. Hilly and Stygian will be cloaked there. When Dad shows his face, I'll teleport away, and they'll take care of Ryan—hopefully.

"In preparation of their success, I need to get things in order with Chance and his Guardian boulder, which won't be easy because the bloody thing is underwater."

"How can I assist you?" Darrius asked.

"Right now, I need Balor and Cary kept busy. If Alden, Benedict, and Bob can keep the twins occupied, I could use your help with the first Guardian boulder. I'll message you when I'm returning from Wyoming. Have Chance and Kai ready to go."

"One small problem," Darrius noted.

"What's that?"

"Chance and Kai can't breathe underwater."

Jake grinned. "That's true. But I've got a solution. I just hope they're not claustrophobic."

Chapter 21

The Lure

"WHAT A HOT AND desolate place," Stygian complained as he gazed around the reddish landscape. "Where is that shaman of yours?"

"Don't worry, Jake will be here," Hilly replied.

The duo stood atop the mesa within sight of the medicine wheel on the valley floor below. Hilly knelt and leaned forward so she could scrutinize each rocky cairn within the sacred circle. "Even if we see a dark-haired woman, we can't reveal ourselves to her yet."

"I thought you were going to be cloaked until I arrived," Jake said when he materialized in front of them.

"You're late," Stygian grumbled.

"Don't mind him," Hilly said as she gave Jake a quick hug. "He's been grumpy lately."

Jake glanced at the Cererian. "Sorry it took a while to get the meeting set up, but keep in mind we have to play by Dad's rules."

"That's okay," Hilly said. "What time did Ryan say he would meet you?"

"About an hour from now, so I suggest you cloak yourselves."

"We've eliminated our energy markers already," Hilly explained. "We're mere shadows to most magical souls."

"Miria—er, Dad is not like most magical people," Jake replied.

"Argh!" Stygian yelled. Clutching his chest, he fell to his knees and wheezed.

"What's wrong?" Hilly cried as she ran to his side.

Stygian shoved her away, a little too aggressively, and she tumbled close to the edge of the plateau. Clumps of red dirt crumbled and cascaded down the mountainside.

"What the hell was that for?" she demanded when she recovered her footing. She marched to the Cererian who was on all fours in visible distress.

Stygian had ripped his shirt open. The red, glowing mass on his chest pulsated as tiny explosions popped and hissed. A putrid smell of charred meat wafted.

"What the fuck is that?" Jake yelled, pointing at Stygian's chest.

"He's cooking you alive!" Hilly screamed as she pushed her hands toward Stygian's chest.

The Cererian grabbed her shoulder and flung her to the side. "Stay away! He's punishing me—I'm not completing my mission...fast enough."

"Who's punishing you?" Jake insisted.

"Jake, please..." Hilly said as she watched the Cererian grimace and gasp. "That monstrosity on Stygian is his controller, an attachment that's manipulated by the Cererian we told you about."

Stygian closed his eyes and mouthed inaudible words. Soon, his torture eased, and he rolled onto his side and panted.

"I've never seen a Cererian show such pain," Jake observed. "That Cererian thorn in your side must be incredibly powerful to bring someone like you to your knees."

Stygian glared at Jake and then closed his eyes. Still on his side, he drew his knees toward his chest and hugged himself. He appeared childlike and not like the omnipotent leader of murderous soldiers.

"Is there anything I can do?" Hilly offered.

Stygian pushed himself up to a sitting position.

"Perhaps we should have traveled to Ceres first," Hilly said.

Stygian shook his head. "No, we're doing the right thing by finding Ryan first."

Hilly tilted her head. "Does the Senator know where you are? I mean, can he always see and hear where you're at?"

"No," Stygian responded shaking his head. "But he does have expectations."

"What are those?" Hilly pressed.

"He expects me to inform him of my progress daily. Apparently, I forgot to update him, so he sent me a little reminder." Stygian rubbed his chest.

"Was that what you were doing when you closed your eyes and mumbled something?" Hilly asked.

Stygian gazed at Hilly with weary eyes. For a moment he appeared like an exhausted teenager who had partied hard all night. It was difficult for her to remember that he was over a thousand years old.

"No, you saw me cursing under my breath," he replied as a weak smile drifted across his face. "I mentally conversed with the Senator as he applied pressure to the controller."

"Damn," Jake said as he stepped closer to inspect the attachment. "That Senator is a son of a bitch. That controller looks alive, like it's a part of you."

"It is part of me. It's connected to my body and lives off my blood." Stygian drew in a long, deep breath and stood. "It's none of your concern, Shaman. We have a job to do."

"Fine," Jake replied. "You and Hilly need to disappear and remove all traces of your existence here. Then we wait for the dark-haired bitch to visit."

Hilly joined Stygian. "We'll wait for your signal."

"What's the signal?" Stygian asked.

"When I withdraw Cathal and Cadmar, you and Hilly will take over."

"You said you would teleport right away, Jake," Hilly confirmed. "If you reveal your weapons, you might make matters worse and get in our way."

"I know what I said, Hilly. Don't worry about me. I'll stay out of your way. Now, go—and don't forget to find Ryan's heart and destroy it." Jake dismissed them with a wave of his hand.

Jake grabbed a comfortable seat on the ground near the edge of the cliff and dangled his legs over the side. He absently swung his feet back and forth as he peered into the distance toward the Big Horn Medicine Wheel. It had been about an hour since Hilly and Stygian cloaked their presence. Jake stared until his eyes ached.

There was no sign of anybody, not even the white bison, Bodhi.

Sweat rolled down his face and arms, and he leaned back onto his hands and closed his eyes against the bright light of the noonday sun.

Where is that motherfucker? he thought.

"I'm right here."

Jake launched upward and swiveled midair to see Miriam had appeared beside him on the mesa. Jake landed with his fists clenched and growled softly.

"I couldn't help myself," Miriam said as she pushed loose hairs behind her right ear. "You seemed so peaceful, your face so serene." She strode toward him until mere inches separated them. "You mentioned you wanted to meet about Fen."

"Yes. Where is she?"

"Fen is with Prasad and didn't want to be interrupted." Miriam turned and walked several steps back. "So, you tell me what you want, and I'll relay that information to her."

"I'd rather talk to Fen," Jake responded.

"You will talk to *me* and only me, Shaman!" Miriam screamed and rushed at Jake.

Jake held his hands forward, stopping her from bowling him over, but he didn't step back. He and the entity glared at each other.

Miriam fumed for a few seconds and then turned and walked away. Her voice was calm when she continued speaking. "Besides, I'm the one that will need to make the arrangements to get Fen to Bear Seamount. Or have you forgotten that?"

"I haven't forgotten a damned thing," Jake seethed.

"Good, so what do you want to tell me—um, Fen?"

Miriam stood about ten feet away. As Jake gazed at her, his mind drifted to Ryan, and the memories they once shared: a loving father to a little boy, learning his father defected to the Yfel, and then his interdimensional battle with Ryan in Wales.

"Shaman?" Miriam asked, breaking Jake from his daydream.

Slowly, Jake walked toward Miriam, stopped and then leaned forward toward her ear. "What I have to say is..." he whispered. He stopped and licked his lips. Miriam grew antsy.

With an icy smirk on his face, Jake tilted his head to one side and then the other, which caused Miriam to shift uneasily.

"Tell me, Shaman," she demanded.

"What I have to say is—go to hell, Dad!" Jake withdrew Cathal and Cadmar and brandished them in front of the entity. At the exact moment, Hilly and Stygian materialized on either side of Miriam and grasped the being's arms.

Jake slashed at his father and vanished.

Jake materialized inside the study of The Nine Muses and collapsed to the floor. Cathal and Cadmar tumbled beside him. Jake had messaged Darrius seconds before he teleported, and the Cererian was ready and waiting for his friend.

After Jake fell to the floor, blood slowly spread along the floor and seeped into the carpet. "Are you injured?" Darrius asked anxiously as he rolled his friend back and forth looking for a wound.

Jake didn't answer. He stared up at the ceiling, his breathing labored.

"Jake, I don't see a wound. Where's all this blood coming from?"

Jake lifted his right hand, which clutched something. "I got him, Darrius," Jake wheezed.

Darrius inspected the item in Jake's hand: a severed hand and forearm. "Who's this?" Darrius asked as he pulled it from Jake's grasp.

A faint smile drifted on Jake's face. "Dad."

Darrius dropped the mutilated appendage to the floor. "Where's the rest of him?"

"I can only imagine," Jake grinned. "Hilly and Stygian are dealing with the bastard now."

The moment Jake vanished, Miriam transformed into Ryan and seized Hilly's throat with his remaining arm. His fingers dug deep and crushed her windpipe and her eyes bulged.

Stygian punched Ryan in the back with such force, his fingers protruded out the front side, above the navel.

Still impaled on Stygian's arm, Ryan released Hilly, swiveled toward the Cererian, and jabbed his arm through Stygian's chest, just missing the controller attachment.

Hilly launched into the air and landed on Ryan's chest. Locking both legs around his waist, she anchored one arm around his throat and punched her fist through his chest.

Latched together, the three combatants struggled against one another. A clap of thunder rocked the mesa and the trio disappeared.

Chapter 22

A Development

JAKE SOAKED IN THE bathtub, reliving the moment he surprised his father with the appearance of Hilly and Stygian. Humming, he tapped his toes on the porcelain popping tiny soap bubbles. It had been some time since he felt relaxed and in control, and he wallowed in the euphoric feeling.

Darrius poured the deep purple contents of a small bottle into the water.

"What's that?" Jake asked.

"One of Prasad's concoctions," Darrius answered. "A mood-lifting potion. I figured you wouldn't mind me adding this to the bath."

"I'll take anything you have." Jake sank into the water until the suds licked his chin.

A purple haze drifted in the bathroom as Darrius poured additional potions of all blends into the water. "Prasad would be happy to know he's still impacting the world even after his death."

Bang. Bang. Bang.

The loud knock shook the bathroom door.

"Is his highness ready for visitors?"

Jake grinned at Chance's voice.

"We come bearing gifts," Kai added.

Darrius tossed a towel at Jake who caught it midair. "You should put a towel over your body—cover the Word. The sacred text should not be on display when they come in."

"Come on, Darrius. Kai's seen this before and Chance won't tell anyone."

"It's not proper for those holy words to be on exhibit. Please cover your tattoos."

"This is gonna look really weird," Jake said as he arranged the towel across his chest and abdomen.

"It doesn't matter. Hide them, or I won't open the door."

Bang. Bang.

"Hey, is anybody in there?" Chance yelled.

"Okay, I'm ready." Jake's body was covered except his arms and legs, which rested on the edge of the tub.

Darrius nodded and opened the door.

"Ewie, you smell purty, Mr. Pierson," Chance mocked as he and Kai pushed into the bathroom.

Kai pushed a glass of bourbon into Jake's outstretched hand. "What's with the towel?" he asked as he sat down on the commode.

"I'm feeling a little modest," he lied.

"Bullshit!" Chance snatched the towel and flung it into the sink.

Jake slid beneath the water with just his eyes above the swirling suds.

"Hey, what's with those tats, Jake?" Chance said as he leaned over the tub.

"Please," Darrius said as he grabbed Chance's arm and pulled him away gently. "A little decorum, Chance."

"What's the big deal?" Chance whined. "I was asking him about his ink."

"Um, big brother," Kai added. "This is something you shouldn't be looking at."

Jake blew bubbles and resurfaced. "Forget it, Darrius. Let him look. I'm exhausted and don't care anymore."

"What's the big deal, guys?" Chance looked at everyone, his eyes pleading for an answer.

Darrius sighed. "You're right, Jake. It doesn't matter anymore. At least, it doesn't matter with present company."

"Damn, I'm so confused," Chance whined.

"What else is new," Kai joked. "I'll tell you later, big brother. Now, back to Jake. How ya doin'?"

"Not bad. Not bad at all," Jake replied, a sheepish grin on his face.

"I heard you got a parting shot at your dad," Chance said.

"Yep. It just sorta happened. The plan was for me to whip out Cathal and Cadmar to signal Hilly and Stygian." Jake sipped his drink and closed his eyes. "I guess I got a little overzealous."

"Whatcha gonna do with that arm?" Chance asked.

"Probably burn it," Jake said without hesitation. "I don't want any evidence of him lying around. Hell, with the power he wields, he might even be able to reanimate from that damned thing."

"What if Hilly and Stygian don't kill him?" Kai asked.

Jake narrowed his eyes. "They'll kill him. Hell, they've probably yanked out his heart already. But that's no longer *my* problem." He pointed at Chance. "You and I have an appointment with a Guardian boulder. That's all I care about."

"Me too," Kai whined.

Jake nodded. "Yeah, you too, Kai."

"What's the next step?" Chance asked.

"I've already messaged Galena about meeting us." Jake shifted and sat up. Waves lapped back and forth within the bathtub.

"Is she the new Miriam?" Chance asked.

"Galena is a one of the sacred sisters," Jake answered solemnly. "Show a little respect."

"That's hard for me to do in a bathroom," Chance joked.

Jake ignored his friend's behavior. "Since Fen is restricted to the dimension she shares with Galena and the bison, Bodhi, Galena will arrange to have our separate realms meet along the lines of the Guardian boulder. And that's *not* even the tricky part."

"It's not?" Kai asked, raising an eyebrow.

"Nope. Breathing underwater will be far more difficult." Jake slipped below the water. A series of bubbles floated to the surface. After several minutes he popped to the surface gasping for air and wearing a crown of soap bubbles. "It won't be easy, but it's doable."

"I've got a bad feeling," Chance said, his voice wavering. "I'm a strong swimmer, but I don't like being underwater for very long."

"I'm with you, big brother," Kai added. "I can swim really well, but if you're looking at a long time underwater, I'm not your man."

"Fen's the Kemp who can breathe underwater," Chance added. "She has that talent. The rest of us are land dwellers."

"Okay, okay," Jake said, holding up his hands. "Take it easy, guys. I wouldn't throw you out into the ocean and not have a plan."

Jake stood. Suds trailed down his abdomen and his legs. "Please throw me a towel...a dry one." Darrius tossed a large white one.

"Thanks, Darrius."

Jake methodically dried himself as he continued with his plan. "I'll construct an underwater corridor that you'll be able to stand up in—barely. It'll be tight, but at least you'll be able to breathe. The tube will stretch from the beach to the Guardian boulder, which is somewhere in the Atlantic Ocean."

"What about the twins?" Darrius asked. "They'll notice something going on."

"Good point," Jake replied. "That's where Alden, Benedict, and Bob come in. They need to create a diversion to ensure Balor and Cary are in front of the house when we all teleport to the beach. If you take Chance with you, Kai and I can take care of ourselves."

"Wait a minute," Chance uttered. "I've been to the beach before, so I should be able to flick there. What part of the beach are we talking about?"

"The stretch on the far side of the boulder wall," Jake replied.

"Where Hilly died," Kai whispered.

"Don't worry about me, Darrius," Chance said. "I've been there so I can flick there by myself."

"Great!" Jake exclaimed. "I'll share more details about the day and time when I hear back from Galena."

Knock. Knock.

All heads swirled at the rapping on the bathroom door.

Chance opened the door.

"There's been a development," Alden announced. "The arm Jake brought back with him is gone. It vanished leaving tattered pieces of cloth behind."

Jake's eyes widened. "Shit!"

"What does that mean, Jake?" Kai asked.

"It means Ryan isn't dead yet and has recalled his arm. I'm worried that Hilly and Stygian are having more of a fight than what they anticipated. I should join them."

Jake wrapped the towel around his hips and climbed out of the tub. "I need to get dressed and grab Cathal and Cadmar."

Darrius placed his hand on Jake's chest and stopped him. "Hilly and Stygian are capable of handling Ryan. You need to focus on completing your own mission."

The two men stared at each other for several tense moments.

Then Jake grabbed Darrius's wrist and pulled his arm away. "You're right, Darrius. But that won't stop me from thinking of Hilly and Stygian. I wish there was a way of contacting them, but when they're flipping in and out of dimensions at such a rapid pace, there's no way of knowing where they are."

"Alden, would you have Bob prepare dinner?" Darrius requested. "I have a feeling our situation in The Nine Muses will be changing rapidly."

"Definitely," Alden replied as he disappeared.

"Okay, guys, everyone out!" Jake shouted with renewed energy. "I've got things to do and plans to arrange."

Chapter 23

Battling a Shadow Man

Seconds after Jake escaped with the severed arm, the entity transformed back into Ryan and teleported into a pitch-black dimension, dragging Hilly and Stygian with him, their arms still impaled through his body. The trio tumbled endlessly through the darkness, their bodies locked together while Stygian and Hilly clawed through Ryan's internal organs desperately probing for his heart. Destroying the very center of Ryan's existence was the only way to kill the magician.

Ryan seethed.

Being surprised by Hilly and Stygian was inconceivable. Even worse was losing an arm to his son, Jake. That act was inexcusable.

Fury fueled by embarrassment governed his every move as he lashed out at his attackers. Supreme magic—powers he reserved for extreme situations—surged forward. After entering the dark dimension, Ryan released a silence grid—magical energy that prevented anyone from speaking or telepathically messaging. The translucent web coated their entwined bodies and soaked into their skin, quietly severing ties with the rest of the world.

Ryan considered his next moves. *I'll kill the Firewalker and Cererian and then find my boy and make him pay.* The thought made Ryan smile, despite the vicious assaults by Hilly and Stygian. As long as his heart continued to beat, it didn't matter how badly they mutilated his body since it regenerated as quickly as they ripped things apart.

Ryan and Stygian locked eyes. For a moment, the magician detected a glimmer of doubt in the Cererian's face. *Have I surpassed Stygian's powers?* he thought.

Stygian had once been Ryan's mentor, enticing him into the Yfel Brethren with promises of immense power in exchange for betraying his friends and family. Once Ryan sold his soul to the Cererian, he found it easy to erase the pain of betrayal through perfecting his technique of hunting, killing, and feasting.

Stygian was a thorough teacher.

But despite being forbidden from killing Cererians, Ryan couldn't resist the persistent urge to be better than Stygian, to exceed the Cererian's capabilities and, one day, lead the Yfel Brethren. To reach that goal, Ryan needed to feed on Cererians. He discovered a perverse method for hunting younger Cererians. He'd lure them away from their comrades, murder them, and discard their bodies without honor.

Each kill produced an ecstasy akin to making lustful love.

And Ryan was addicted.

His body swirled with the astonishing powers of twenty Cererians and over two-hundred magicians. The intensity of the magic originally disoriented him. Then, as he continued to flex his magical muscles, he delighted in his ever-evolving abilities like interdimensional travel, shape-shifting, and the ability to dim his body, so it appeared like a shadow—a person who is physically present but appears as a spirit. This shadowing talent is how he originally met with Jake as Miriam. He shape-shifted into a woman and wore a shadow veil, which prevented Jake from being able to psychically scan his body.

Now, Ryan skillfully battled his opponents with only one arm. In addition to maneuvering ten times swifter than Hilly and Stygian, Ryan deployed constant concussion waves, eruptions that originated deep within his core. The shockwaves rippled through Hilly and Stygian, momentarily confusing them. But they held fast to Ryan's squirming body.

After several attempts, Ryan was able to reclaim his missing arm, psychically locating the appendage in The Nine Muses and willing it "home" to the hole in the side of his body. The appendage, arriving as the petite arm of Miriam, quickly transformed into Ryan's muscular male arm once it reattached.

Becoming whole renewed the fire in Ryan's soul, and he catapulted the group into an underwater dimension of deep blue viscous fluid that severely restricted all movements. Though the combatants still pummeled one another, each maneuver appeared slow and tedious, taking four times as long to complete.

The warriors fought in slow-motion. Their grimaces stretched into minutes.

Now fully armed, Ryan reached for Hilly's throat with both hands and squeezed hard, so hard that his fingers penetrated the muscles on either side of her neck.

Hilly gasped from his tightening grip, which allowed a flood of blue ooze to fill her open mouth. Unable to telepathically reach Stygian, she signaled the Cererian for help, but he was too focused on searching for Ryan's heart and didn't notice her movements.

Fighting unconsciousness, Hilly tugged on Ryan's wrist with her free hand. But the magician squeezed even tighter. Reluctantly, Hilly withdrew her impaled arm from Ryan's torso and used both hands to dislodge the magician's chokehold as she unleashed bolts of energy toward his arms.

Ryan saw his chance to divide his opponents.

He released Hilly and shoved her backward into the gelatinous void. An icy smirk spread across his face as the Firewatcher witch slowly floated away, her energy bolts harmlessly deflected into the surrounding gelatin. Alone with the Cererian, Ryan grabbed Stygian's head with both hands and hurtled them into another dimension—a world filled with planets of all sizes and colors.

Once in the cosmos universe, Stygian noticed Hilly was no longer with them. The Cererian threw his weight into Ryan. Now that his movements were no longer impeded by the thick goo from the previous world, he rabbit-punched the magician about the head and face with his free fist, while digging deeper into his organs for the elusive heart with his other.

Ryan commanded his fingers to morph into daggers, which he thrust toward Stygian's eyes. Darting just in time, Stygian pushed the magician backward, gripped Ryan's throat, and crushed his thumb onto the Adam's apple.

Ryan released a wave of searing-hot energy throughout his body. Stygian snatched his hand away from the magician's neck, which felt like molten lava. Wisps of smoke drifted from the Cererian's fingertips, now charred and blistered from that brief encounter. The scorching magic sizzled the hairs on Stygian's impaled arm, causing his shirt to catch fire. Using his elemental powers, Stygian quickly blew the flames out with an icy mist then thrust his second hand into the magician's body.

Ryan plunged his index fingers into Stygian's ears penetrating almost to his brain. With the two men locked together, Ryan began spinning. Faster and faster the duo twirled until they appeared as a vibrating blur.

Suddenly, Hilly tumbled into their realm and landed several planets away. She quickly flew toward the spinning men and watched the blurred mass, calculating the precise moment of her attack. Thrusting her arms forward, she surprised Ryan from behind and penetrated deep into his back. Her left hand knocked against a solid object with ridges, and she instinctively gripped it. About the size of a walnut and rock hard, the nugget throbbed in her fist.

She had found Ryan's heart and squeezed.

Ryan's eyes widened, his fingers yanked away from Stygian's head, and the spinning ceased.

Stygian met Hilly's gaze, her eyes beaming and triumphant.

Quickly gathering his wits, Stygian plunged both arms through the front of the magician and located Hilly's hand with the beating organ. Wrapping his hand around hers, they applied pressure while their free hands shredded Ryan's internal organs.

Ryan howled like an enraged animal.

The magician released a bolt of energy that raced up his opponents' arms and exploded directly in their brains. Dazed, Hilly and Stygian slumped against the magician they cradled between them. Quickly, Ryan deployed another surge of searing heat, which set his body on fire.

Hilly winced and loosened her grip on Ryan's heart.

Stygian blew cooling air against the blistering temperatures and continued his assault.

Although slightly charred, Hilly relocated Ryan's heart and joined Stygian in crushing it. Infuriated, the magician gyrated and twisted like an angry python clutched between the two warriors.

But Hilly and Stygian held fast.

Abruptly, Ryan arched his back, bending backward so severely that his head nearly touched his backsides. The action pried Hilly's arms from his body.

In that instant of being free from her, Ryan zipped into another dimension, pulling Stygian with him.

The duo entered a hot, arid realm with four suns blazing in the sky where temperatures topped five-hundred degrees. The brightness blinded the pale-skinned Cererian, and blisters appeared along his arms and face. Stygian gritted his teeth from the pain.

Ryan wasn't affected by the heat of this world—a universe he created—and he delighted in watching the Cererian suffer. Upon arrival, Stygian's clothes spontaneously combusted and he was forced to withdraw his arms from Ryan's body so he could battle the flames consuming his clothes. With the Cererian preoccupied, Ryan maneuvered away in preparation to teleport to another realm.

Then a searing pain exploded in his back.

Hilly had followed Stygian's energy markers to the scorched universe. She surprised the magician by plunging her arms into his body up to her elbows so he wouldn't be able to dislodge her. She gripped his beating heart with both of her hands and squeezed the hard lump of tissue.

As a Firewalker witch, the fiery universe had no impact on her body, and she grimaced with concentration as she crushed the organ held tightly between her palms.

Ryan thrashed violently in her embrace.

After extinguishing the flames on his body, Stygian joined Hilly and thrust his arms through Ryan's chest and downward to meet her hands that held the heart nestled in the hip bone. They crushed the pulsating organ together and tore Ryan's body apart.

Shrieking, Ryan flailed and twisted but was growing weaker. The magician stopped squirming and fell limp between his combatant's arms.

Hilly and Stygian stopped. Then, with renewed enthusiasm, they continued pounding the magician and shredding his body.

Unresponsive during their assault, Ryan feigned weakness while concentrating all his powers on his inner core.

While Stygian ripped his kidneys and liver to pieces, Hilly tore the heart apart. But Ryan reanimated the organs as fast as they destroyed them.

Hilly shook her head and mouthed to Stygian, *"I can't destroy it."*

A low guttural laugh echoed in their heads.

Ryan raised his head and met Stygian's gaze. Slowly the magician faded from sight. Hilly's eyes widened.

"No," she mouthed.

Stygian withdrew his arms from Ryan's body and wrapped them around both the magician and Hilly in a tight bear-hug. Instantaneously, he teleported all three of them out of the arid realm.

When they reappeared, they stood atop the butte above the Bighorn Medicine Wheel.

Stygian still had his arms tightly wrapped around everybody.

Galena, stood quietly nearby.

When Ryan saw her, he threw his head back and screamed, "No!"

Galena touched Stygian's arm. "You can release the magician. He won't be able to leave." She raised her hands toward Ryan, palms forward and fingers splayed, and mouthed inaudible words as Hilly and Stygian stepped away.

"No!" Ryan shouted as he collapsed to the ground. He contorted and groaned as Galena continued her conjuring.

A black mass appeared in the sky.

"What's that?" Hilly asked as she looked upward.

"I'm not sure," Stygian replied shielding his eyes from the sun's glare.

Ryan shrieked, rolling side to side while holding his belly.

The black mass grew closer.

Caw. Caw. Caw.

"Crows," Hilly whispered.

The murder of crows descended upon Ryan covering him as he writhed. Galena continued her spell, swaying as soundless words tumbled from her lips.

A strangled cry escaped Ryan's lips and then he grew silent.

The crows launched into the air and flew west.

Ryan Pierson was gone.

Chapter 24

Preparations

"Ryan's gone," Jake whispered.

"How do you know?" Darrius asked.

"Hilly messaged me. She and Stygian witnessed Galena's magic. Apparently, she summoned a murder of crows that devoured him, including his heart, and then flew away."

"Galena was involved?" Darrius tapped his fingertips together in front of his chest. "How odd for an earth spirit—and one of such power—to interfere with the dealings of humans."

"I don't have the full story, but Hilly believes Stygian prearranged something with Galena. Stygian teleported them away from one of Ryan's universes and into a world where Galena could intervene. It was atop the butte above the Bighorn Medicine Wheel."

"Search your heart," Darrius requested. "I can't believe a magician with his exceptional abilities could be defeated by a murder of crows."

Jake closed his eyes. Several moments passed before he opened them and declared, "I don't sense my dad anywhere. It feels like a void...like something's missing. Still, you have a point. I thought I'd be the first to know when Dad died. I always imagined I'd somehow feel lighter...happier. But I don't feel anything."

"I hope Ryan is truly gone." Darrius said. "That'll be one less problem to worry about."

"When I talk to Hilly again, I'll ask for more details." Jake replied. "They're on their way to Ceres to take care of Stygian's little problem."

"Battling a Cererian is not so little. I'm curious who they'll be hunting, although, I have a good guess."

Alden entered the study. "Sorry for interrupting, but dinner is ready. I've already alerted Chance and Kai."

"Thanks, Alden," Darrius said. He looked back from the door. "Jake? Are you coming?"

"In a little while, Darrius."

"Is everything okay?"

"Yeah. I'm just thinking about our trip to the Guardian boulder."

"You're leaving tomorrow morning, correct?"

"That's right. I've already talked to Chance and Kai, but I'd like to go over the details one more time. The trip will be tricky."

"Okay. Don't be too late. You know how much Chance can eat." A smile flickered on Darrius's face before he turned and left the study.

Jake poured a drink. *I hope Dad is gone,* he thought. *But Darrius is right. Why would Galena get involved?* He gulped the drink, placed the glass on the counter, and left the study.

"Great that you could join us, Jake!" Chance bellowed as he shoveled mashed potatoes into his mouth. He chomped his food and wiggled his eyebrows at Jake. "You're lucky there's food still here," he added in a muffled voice as food bits flew out of his mouth.

"Darrius told us Ryan is gone," Kai said. "I'm glad to hear Hilly is okay."

"Actually, I don't know if she is okay," Jake corrected as he slumped into a chair and nibbled on a dinner roll. "We didn't talk too long." He stared at the bun after each bite.

"Something bothering you?" Kai asked.

"He's preoccupied with the trip to the Guardian boulder, aren't you?" Darrius noted.

Jake popped the rest of the roll into his mouth and jumped to his feet. "That's right, Darrius. We have a ton of work to do tomorrow, gentlemen, and I need to ensure you understand your individual roles."

"Yeah, yeah," Chance complained. "You've told me a hundred times already. Can't we take a break?"

Jake walked quickly to Chance and stuck his finger in Chance's face. "Okay, Mr. Know-it-all, tell me what you'll be doing tomorrow."

Chance stopped chewing mid-bite. A piece of ham dangled from the corner of his mouth. "Um...um..."

"Exactly!" Jake yelled. He swiveled and marched to Kai's chair. "And you? What will you be doing?"

"Well, I'm going to...I'm going to follow your directions, Jake!" Kai said triumphantly.

"You guys are hopeless," Jake exclaimed as he plopped into his seat.

"But we're willing," Kai added with a twinkle in his eyes.

Chapter 25

A Cererian Betrayal

HILLY AND STYGIAN STOOD together near the top of Ahuna Mons, a three-mile-high mountain on the outskirts of the Cererian city of Alaka. After surviving the extreme heat of Ryan's multi-sun universe, Stygian welcomed the frigid air.

A ferocious wind swept through his long, blond hair as he lifted his face and breathed deep in the thin altitude. His human body would soon suffer the effects of exposure to these elements, but his Cererian energy craved the harshness of home.

Hilly hugged herself in the gale and fought hard to remain erect on their mountainous perch. *Are you happy to be home?* she telepathically messaged.

Stygian nodded. *I'd forgotten how beautiful the outer regions were.* He lifted his hand and inspected it. His fingertips had healed with no remnants of the char or blisters from Ryan's heat wave.

Come, we should leave. He gently gripped Hilly's hand and the duo vanished.

When they reappeared, they were outside the Justice Hall, the same building where he stood trial. They moved beside a black quartz wall that bordered the pathway to the main entrance. The dark hours had descended upon Ceres and very few Cererians lingered in this section of the city.

This is where the Senator asked that I meet him, Stygian remarked.

Is there any way for us to get inside undetected? Hilly asked.

The building is impenetrable. Teleporting in is not an option.

Hilly abruptly jerked Stygian to the side and pulled him further behind the wall as two Cererians drifted by.

Members of the elite security squad, Stygian observed.

Each guard had two arm-like appendages hanging on either side of their round, ethereal body comprised of energy that flashed deep red and gold, colors of their defender rank. They moved further down the path and entered a pear-shaped chamber illuminated by an electric blue light. Once they were inside, the blue turned a deeper violet color.

A coupling pod, Stygian noted.

What's that? Hilly asked.

Stygian smirked. *It's a safe place for having sex.*

Out in the open...in public?

Cererians aren't uncomfortable displaying natural urges.

This may sound weird, Hilly started, *but how do you tell the sexes apart?*

Stygian chuckled. *It's not strange. Cererians carry both male and female sex organs. Intersexed, I believe you call it on Earth. We're androgynous except for the intensity of our natural energy. It's that natural energy that sexually attracts individuals to each other. The frequency and sequence of colors one Cererian pulses to another is a sign of their preferences. If they find a willing partner, they seek out a coupling pod. The sex organs reside in the appendages.*

Hilly stared at the coupling pod and blushed. *I feel like a voyeur.*

It's natural on Ceres and nothing to be embarrassed about.

Did that change for you when you became human?

Stygian studied Hilly's face and smiled gently. *Yes, it did. I was so naïve about the workings of a human male body. When I became aroused for the first time, I was scared my body was dying, so I sought Darrius's advice.*

Hilly held her hand to her mouth and stifled a giggle.

After Darrius finished laughing, he patiently told me about human sex. A broad grin spread across Stygian's face. *I've learned a lot more about human lovemaking since that first incident.*

Natural Cererians appear much different than I imagined, Hilly observed.

I, too, once appeared like that. Stygian's eyes saddened.

Are you okay? Hilly asked.

A bittersweet memory.

Oh?

I remember the day Darrius and I agreed to be part of the exploration team to Earth. We were very excited—and quite proud. Our leaders told us we would arrive on Earth in human bodies, a difficult undertaking that would involve combining our Cererian energy with the DNA from a human host. I was terrified and wanted to leave the program. But Darrius convinced me it was the right thing to do for Ceres and Earth.

The Cererian grew silent, and his eyes misted.

Hilly quietly observed him. Less than an hour earlier, they had almost lost their lives battling Ryan. Now, Stygian appeared fragile.

Stygian drew in a deep breath. Any vulnerability vanished as he gritted his teeth and steeled his eyes.

We'll stick to the original plan, Hilly, he said changing the subject. *I'll bring you as my prisoner with your hands manacled behind your back.*

It's risky, but I think it will work, she replied.

It's important the Senator believes he's in control the entire time. Don't be too cocky, or he might get suspicious.

Don't worry, Stygian, I'll behave myself until the right moment. Hilly winked.

The moment he removes the controlling device from my chest is your signal to pounce. I'll ensure the manacles are loose around your wrists. Then you can easily slip out of them and take care of the Senator.

Why don't you kill him? You have good reason with all that he's put you through.

Cererians don't kill Cererians, Stygian replied.

You killed Aaron, Hilly pointed out.

He tortured you. He had to be punished.

Stygian glanced away, lost in his thoughts. Killing Aaron had been spontaneous, a gut reaction to the Cererian's brutal treatment of Hilly. Aaron's execution hadn't been planned, nor was the subsequent consuming of Aaron's tremendous powers. Moments after the incident, Stygian regretted his actions. Anguish consumed him. He had been taught to never kill another Cererian and, yet he did.

Is everything okay? Hilly asked.

Stygian nodded slowly. Suddenly he grabbed his chest and fell to his knees. He swallowed the cry begging to emerge.

Is it the Senator? Hilly messaged as she knelt beside the Cererian. *Is he summoning you?*

Stygian nodded. *He demands my presence now. Are you sure you want to do this?*

Hilly helped the Cererian to his feet. *I'm ready. Everything will be fine.*

Turn around, Stygian demanded.

When she did, the Cererian pulled her arms back and bound her wrists together with restraints crafted from supernatural sources: two translucent loops encircled her wrists in a figure eight. The manacles could be loosened or tightened by a Cererian's thoughts.

Too tight? he asked.

Nope, she replied. *They're perfect.*

Stygian touched Hilly's elbow and guided her down the passageway toward the Justice Hall entrance. As they approached the ramp that led up to the doorway, two guards flashed crimson and confronted them.

State your business! the first one ordered.

I am Stygian Chernobourg. The Senator has requested a meeting with me.

The guard turned toward his companion. A myriad of bright colors flashed as they conversed with each other.

After several moments the guard faced Stygian. *All is in order. Follow me.*

Stygian stepped forward, pulling Hilly behind him.

Vile creature, the second guard seethed as Hilly passed. She frowned at the soldier's off-hand comment.

Pay him no mind, Stygian assured as he guided her into the building.

They halted underneath a three-story rotunda.

Hilly glanced upward and gasped at the transparent domed ceiling that revealed the star-studded night sky.

This way! the first guard barked as he floated down a side corridor that led to the back of the building.

Stygian pulled Hilly close and looked at her. *Remember the plan,* he messaged.

No talking! the second guard ordered as he shoved Hilly with one of his appendages.

The group assembled in front of black quartz double doors that soared twenty feet high. Slowly the doors swung inward, revealing a cavernous room. The curved walls spiraled upward to a flat, transparent ceiling. The space was void of any objects, except four black quartz urns standing about four-foot high. Each round vessel had been positioned on the floor in the center of the room. Four feet separated each urn, and each had been carefully arranged so they faced the elemental directions of north, east, south, and west.

A very large Cererian hovered in the middle of the elemental space. Almost twice the size of any other natural Cererian, the individual slowly flashed hues of blue.

Our lord! the two guards said in unison when they entered the chamber. Deep crimson and gold flashed throughout the soldiers' bodies as they led Stygian and Hilly to the center of the room.

Stygian, the Cererian greeted. *How nice to see you again.*

You summoned me, Senator, Stygian replied curtly.

And I see you've brought the infamous Firewalker witch, the Senator added while ignoring Stygian's tone.

Stygian led Hilly closer to the Senator.

Guards, you may leave us, the Senator commanded. He watched the soldiers leave and then waved an appendage, the action prompting the massive doors to quietly shut.

You never disappoint me, Stygian. The Senator floated directly in front of the Yfel leader who lowered his eyes as the dignitary approached. The Senator glided beside Hilly. *You've brought me such a fine gift.*

She stared at him with eyes that burned with rage. As the dignitary drifted around her back, he commented, *Nice restraints, Stygian, but they need to be a little tighter, don't you agree? You know how crafty Firewalkers can be.*

The Senator moved an appendage and the supernatural manacles clamped harder around Hilly's wrists. She grimaced and groaned.

Stygian jerked to help her, but quickly checked his movement. He had to remain subservient to the Senator and not interfere.

There, there, Firewalker, the Senator purred. *A little pinching is the least of your worries. Isn't that right, Stygian?*

Hilly glanced at her friend, but he turned away.

I've done my part, Senator, Stygian said. *Now, I want what's due to me. It's time you remove the controller from my chest.*

Cloaking her thoughts from the Senator, Hilly reached out to Stygian. *You're sticking to the plan, right? Loosen these shackles so I can kill him.*

Stygian glanced at Hilly before walking toward the doors. *Remember our agreement, Senator. I deliver the Firewalker, and you release me from my commitments.*

Yes, yes...all in good time. The Senator drifted to the center of the four urns. Once he reached the midpoint of their elemental alignment, additional energy swirled within his body. *We have additional details to work out.*

Additional details? Stygian screamed at the dignitary.

Careful, Stygian, or I'll find a reason to execute you alongside the Firewalker.

Hilly messaged Stygian again. *Loosen my restraints. My hands are going numb.*

Stygian's eyes darted between Hilly and the Senator. *We had a deal, Senator. Here's the witch, as promised. Now, remove this fucking device!*

The Senator raised an appendage, and Stygian collapsed to the floor clutching his chest. Rolling back and forth on his back, he grunted from the intense pain. Puffs of smoke drifted upward.

You're burning him! Hilly cried out.

The Senator shifted his attention to Hilly. *Ah, the girl loves you, Stygian, despite your betrayal. Get off the floor and join me. We have much to discuss.*

Stygian gasped and struggled to stand. He staggered toward the urns. When he reached them, he stared at the floor and wheezed.

The Senator pulsed a series of blues and purples. *There. We're all together again. Now, let's have a chat, shall we? Firewalker, are you aware your friend bargained a new deal with me and you were his collateral?*

Hilly glanced at Stygian who avoided her stare.

The Senator continued. *And those lovely restraints surrounding your wrists can only be controlled by me.* Hilly's eyes widened. *That's right. I gave him those priceless gems to dupe you into believing his scheme to kill me.*

"Tell me that's not true, Stygian!" Hilly screamed.

Stygian stared at the ground and panted.

But let's not get ahead ourselves. He's probably told you I'm coercing him to kill other Cererians like your friends Darrius, Alden, and Benedict. A flurry of yellow sparks fluttered through the Senator's body as a faint chuckle drifted through their brains.

That was not my doing, Firewalker. That was Stygian's plan. He yearned for vengeance, and he begged for my help to achieve it. I agreed I would turn a blind eye to his wickedness, if he brought me the one prize for which I yearned—you. He quickly agreed.

Tears welled in Hilly's eyes. She glanced at Stygian who stared at the floor, his bottom lip trembling. "You bastard!" she yelled at him.

Stygian flinched as though her words were sharpened knives.

Of course, I needed to protect my investments, the Senator added. *So, I installed the controller on Stygian's chest. Now I have my cherished prize and still have my faithful helper.* Another low chuckle echoed through their brains as pulses of bright yellow fluttered through the Senator's body.

Hilly lowered her head and took a small step sideways toward Stygian.

The Senator continued, *With our annual celebration in two moons, it will be a delight to show you off, Firewalker, just before you are vaporized. And Stygian will be right at my feet eager to do anything I ask.*

The air thickened.

Stygian's ears popped as the pressure slowly dipped. The Senator droned on. *My people are extremely curious about the evolution of magical creatures on Earth. Many consider you to be a mutant, so it was imperative to bring you here so we can dissect you and see how you developed.*

Hilly took another step towards Stygian. Their hands bumped, and their little fingers twisted together. A wall of heat instantly swirled in Hilly's abdomen and raced up her spine. Stygian cast a side glance toward Hilly and found her peering at him. "NOW" she mouthed.

"Powers of the north, the east, the south, and the west, I summon you now," Hilly whispered under her breath. She glanced upward at the transparent ceiling. A brilliant light shot out of her eyes, mouth, and fingertips.

The glass ceiling exploded and showered the floor with jagged shards. Stygian and the Senator deployed protection magic to avoid being impaled by the glass slivers spraying the room.

Stygian, stop your witch! the Senator screamed.

Her hands were still bound, but Hilly rose upward as she continued her silent conjuring. A concussive shockwave detonated from her core and exploded outward. The waves of energy rippled out and down blowing the massive quartz doors off the walls and catapulting the Senator and Stygian against a far wall.

Hilly hovered ten feet in the air with a brilliant ball of white light enshrouding her.

Stygian shielded his eyes from the intense glare.

Guards! the Senator shrieked.

The two Cererian soldiers quickly moved into the room and raised their appendages toward Hilly. Before they could deploy bolts of energy, another explosion erupted from Hilly's body. Searing temperatures raced toward the Cererian guards and vaporized them.

Kill her, Stygian! the Senator commanded.

Stygian rose from the floor and calmly walked under Hilly who hovered above him naked, her clothes having been burned off. The manacles had melted, and she pointed at Stygian while glaring at him with coal-black eyes.

"You betrayed me!" she accused.

Yes...yes...Stygian is to blame, the Senator babbled as he drifted toward his elemental altar. *Kill him, and you do us both a favor.*

Hilly scowled at the Senator. *I'll deal with you soon,* she said, jabbing her finger in his direction. *Stay away from your elemental platform.* A beam of white light shot from her finger, knocking the Senator against the wall again.

She snapped her attention back to Stygian. "As for you," she growled aloud. "There are actions that can never be forgiven."

The Cererian didn't move.

Hilly slowly descended to the floor and faced him. He grimaced at the intense heat radiating from her but held her gaze. She reached forward and ripped his shirt open. The controller on his chest pulsed an angry red. She grasped the burning mass.

Stygian moaned, almost whimpered, as her fingers closed around the outer edges.

Hilly yanked it from his body. Holding the throbbing controller in her right hand, she cauterized the bleeding wound with her left. The smell of burnt skin filled the room.

Stygian bit his lip and clenched his fists but didn't move. Instead, he closed his eyes against the agony of Hilly's actions.

Abruptly, she darted to the Senator, moving so fast she appeared as a blur, and slammed the controller directly into the middle of his ethereal body. The contraption penetrated his gelatinous exterior and rested in the middle of his large form.

Hilly plunged her other hand into the Senator's body and released her full fury. Intense heat boiled in her abdomen like molten lava, and the expanding force shot through her fingers directly into the Cererian dignitary.

His screams echoed in her head as she delivered bolt after bolt of fire lasers into his body. Within seconds the Senator's body went black, his energy charred and depleted.

Hilly withdrew her arms. A tarry ooze dripped from her fingers and a disgustingly pungent smell drifted. She stared at the Cererian, her lips twisted in a sneer.

Then she whirled toward Stygian.

He had slumped to the floor on his knees. His head hung to his chest.

By the time Hilly reached him, the heat from her body had dissipated and emerald green replaced her black, soulless eyes. Sweat coursed down her naked body, the skin having been darkened by the extreme temperatures.

"Look at me," she ordered.

Stygian stared at the floor, his shoulders slumped.

"Look at me," she repeated as she gently cupped his chin and tilted it upward.

With drowsy eyes he gazed back at her. Slowly, a smile crept across his face. "Well done, Hilly," he whispered in a hoarse voice. "Well done."

She knelt in front of him and placed her palm on his injured chest. He flinched but didn't pull away. Speaking in a foreign tongue, she conjured magic. Gradually, the wound scabbed over until a protective crust covered the damaged area.

"It's time to go home," she whispered.

Unexpectedly, he wrapped his arms around her pulling her tight against him. She buried her face in his neck and hugged him back.

Joined together, they vanished from Ceres.

Chapter 26

Crow Magic

"I DON'T UNDERSTAND WHY you got involved." Fen said. There was no malice in her voice, only curiosity like that of a student toward a teacher.

Galena sat on a smooth rock in the middle of a placid pool and meditated. Eyes closed and hands resting in her lap, the sacred sister dangled her bare feet in the cool water. "My motives are not for you to understand," she replied.

"But Ryan is not dead. You allowed the crows to scatter him in all directions of the compass. His energy still lives on."

Galena opened her eyes and smiled. "Yes, you are correct. Do you sense him now?"

"Yes. I can peer through his eyes, which are dangling in an Amazonian tree canopy, and I can feel the cool water through his fingertips protruding from the mud of an Alaskan marsh. But I don't understand." Fen sighed and gazed across the red landscape.

"All energy is sacred," Galena said as she joined Fen, linking her arm through hers.

"What about the souls he devoured?" Fen asked. "Since he was not killed, how will they escape and find peace in the ether?"

Galena waved her hand across the sky. Immediately the brightness of day transformed into inky night. She swept her hand again. A filter spread across their field of vision opening a window to the heavens. "See? The spirits of the fallen are home and have found rest."

She drew Fen closer as the two peered into the ether that swirled all around them. Phantoms drifted by undisturbed by the appearance of the two women. The shadows of humans, creatures, trees, and all living things including Cererians moved freely about unencumbered and unfettered by their earthly restraints.

"We are one," Fen whispered.

"Yes," Galena replied. "Living here on Earth or in the ether, we are all the same—pure energy."

"But how is that possible? How did the souls inside Ryan find their way?"

"Crow magic," Galena responded. "Ryan's powers were too great for Stygian. The Cererian realized he and Hilly wouldn't be successful in killing the magician as he originally thought, so he reached out to me during his battle and requested my help."

"But Ryan deployed silencing magic," Fen noted. "How was Stygian able to circumvent that spell and reach you?"

A warm smile brightened the sacred sister's face. "Because as I stood in this universe with you, I was also observing the battle in the realm of the four suns that Ryan created. Stygian didn't need to say a word, I gazed upon his face and knew what was needed."

"How does crow magic work?" Fen asked.

"Crows are the protectors of the departed. They carefully guide souls to the ether. But Ryan presented an unusual situation. Since he had evolved into a hideous creature who could not be destroyed. The magic I wove allowed the corvids to pull the magician apart while harvesting the spirits he held inside. Each bird flew away with a piece of the magician in its bill and carried the souls of the departed within the protection of their feathers."

Galena gazed upward and pointed. "Look there. There is a group of young Cererians that are finally free of their prison inside Ryan."

The two women watched the heavens. Like fireflies, phantoms flitted about, shining their eternal light for all to see.

"Thank you for rescuing me from Miriam/Ryan," Fen uttered, her eyes still fixed on the night sky.

"Your memories have returned?" Galena asked.

"I recall painful times, but I also remember wonderful moments, especially those spent with my family. But my time with them is growing short."

"Is this worrisome?"

Fen reflected on Galena's question. "Worrisome? No. But there are regrets."

Galena turned and studied Fen. "Regrets live in the past. Now is the time to focus on the present." A quick smile crinkled her eyes. "Come, Fen. We need to plan your trip to Bear Seamount." She gripped Fen's hand and led her away from the pool.

She arced her hand across the sky and the heavens disappeared. The two women now stood in the middle of the Big Horn Medicine Wheel by the central cairn.

"Are we in the physical world?" Fen asked, gazing at the butte where she had often seen Jake standing.

"We are in a parallel universe," Galena explained. "You will never be able to enter the physical plane again."

"Why?"

Galena smiled gently. "Because you're a shadow of your former self. Your energy has split from your physical body so you can take your rightful place as a Healer in this land. You span many universes at the same time. You can see, hear, and touch in those worlds simultaneously. You can feel all energies—living and deceased. They brush against you like ripples in a pool of water."

"It has begun," Fen whispered. "The Senator has been killed, and Hilly and Stygian have returned to Earth."

Galena nodded. "Yes. The wheel is in motion. Our time grows short, Fen. The shaman is anxious to meet with you."

Kai and Chance gathered around Jake as he scribbled a drawing on a napkin.

"That makes no fuckin' sense!" Chance moaned.

"What exactly is *that* supposed to represent?" Kai asked, pointing at a symbol.

Darrius leaned against the door of the study, his arms across his chest, and a bemused look upon his face.

"Guys, you're not paying attention," Jake grumbled. "Let me explain it again." He jabbed his felt tip marker at the X on the drawing. "This is where we meet...okay?"

Kai and Chance nodded. "On the beach, right?" Chance asked.

Jake rolled his eyes. "Yes, for the one-hundredth time, we're meeting on the beach. That's where I'll create a tube that will take us to the Guardian boulder in the Atlantic."

"Like a straw." Chance said.

Jake squinted at his friend. "A straw? Can you fit in a straw?"

"No, but a straw is like a tube, and—"

"Enough!" Jake yelled. He threw the marker and stormed out of the study.

Darrius watched him pass and then followed him.

Jake stopped in the living room and stared out the window. Only the stone pillars remained from the destroyed porte cochere. The Yfel soldier, Cary, had thrown his energy into the destruction of a nearby outbuilding.

Darrius sidled up beside his friend and gazed out.

"Hilly messaged me," Jake said somberly.

"She reached out to me as well," Darrius added. "The Senator is dead."

"Is that the fellow she was helping Stygian with?"

"Yes. He was quite important on Ceres. His death will not go unnoticed."

"What will the Cererians do?" Jake asked.

"Now that Stygian is no longer under their control? I'm not sure." Darrius paused. "But I wager they may try to interfere with the completion of the Prophecy."

Jake rubbed the stubble on his chin. "They'll probably try to enlist the aid of Cary or Balor, two people who might have the ability, or desire, to assassinate him."

"Hopefully, Stygian is maintaining contact with his soldiers lest their heads get turned by a more attractive offer from the Cererian government. But Stygian's problem is not our concern. Our immediate focus should be getting Chance to his Guardian boulder."

Jake sighed. "You're right. I'll try to explain the plan to those knuckleheads one more time."

Chapter 27

Breathing Underwater

Everyone assembled in the foyer.

Alden, Benedict, and Bob listened attentively as Jake explained their roles.

"It's critical that you keep the twins busy near the front of The Nine Muses so they won't catch a glimpse of us on the beach. A huge distraction is the only way both Cary and Balor will be drawn to this side of the house."

"I suggest doppelgangers," Alden mentioned. "If we send body doubles of you, Chance, and Kai out the front door, then that should allow you plenty of time to teleport to the beach and enter the tunnel to your Guardian boulder."

"I agree," Benedict said. "But I advise we stagger the departure of the body doubles and have them run in different directions."

Bob remained silent.

"Bob, are you good with this plan?" Jake asked.

"I can see only one flaw," the Cererian answered. "What if only one twin falls for the ruse?"

"Then you deploy a doppelganger of Hilly," Darrius replied. "The twins would love to get their hands on her."

"Speaking of Hilly, is there any chance she or Stygian will return to The Nine Muses during our little scheme?" Alden asked.

"No," Darrius and Jake responded in unison.

The two men glanced at each other before Jake explained. "Hilly and Stygian are taking care of other matters. Don't worry about them spoiling our little party." He flashed a weak smile before asking, "Any other questions?"

The Cererians shook their heads.

"Alright, meet us back here in thirty minutes. Chance, Kai, join me in the study. Darrius, I'd like you to come as well."

When the men entered, Jake closed the door and strode over to the bar. Silently he poured four drinks of bourbon and handed each man a glass. Then he raised his. "Gentlemen, I propose a toast. We may be crazy, we may be mad, but at the end of the day, better men cannot be had." They all clinked glasses and gulped their drinks.

"Will I drown?" Chance blurted. "We're going to be underwater a long time."

Jake patted Chance's shoulder. "You'll be fine unless you're claustrophobic."

"What if I am...claustrophobic?" Chance wiggled his glass for another pour, and Jake obliged. "I guess I could always flick back to this study."

"Yeah, you could," Jake acknowledged. "But then you won't be able to flick back to us because we'll be constantly moving through the ocean."

"Look Chance," Kai added. "I'll be with you every step of the way. I won't let anything happen to you."

"Thanks, Kai, but if I freak out, I don't think you'll have the strength to keep me calm. Jake, describe this contraption again."

"Sure." Jake curled his fingers as if holding a long tube. "Think of it as a transparent wormhole but with ever-adjusting ends. Once we're all inside, the entrance will automatically seal up leaving us standing in a cylindrical room. I'll propel the conduit forward using my magic."

"How big is it?" Chance asked.

"About ten-feet high and wide. The length will be determined by where we stand. The tube will always allow for at least two feet clear space around any figures within it. For example, the conduit will be longer if we're all standing in one line. However, if we bunch up, two abreast, then our space will shorten, but the tube will still allow two feet all around."

Chance slumped in a chair. "I'm not so sure I can do this, guys."

"How do you propose we get you to the Guardian boulder?" Darrius asked.

"I don't know, Darrius. Jake's glass tube is the only way to get my fat ass there. But I won't lie, I'm pretty nervous."

"Tick-tock, my friend," Jake blurted. "Bus is leaving, and you need to be on it." Jake and Kai reached under Chance's armpits and raised the reluctant man to his feet. "Focus, Chance," Jake ordered. "You're a warrior who stared down Ryan, Aaron, and the twins. You didn't hesitate. You withdrew your weapon alongside Gabe and stood your ground."

Chance nodded.

"You and Fen combined your powers to propel Stygian to Ceres."

Chance beamed.

Jake crossed his arms. "Don't tell me the warrior standing in front of me can't stay underwater in a waterproof tube."

"You're right, Jake!" Chance shouted. "Let's get this show on the road!" Chance dashed out of the study.

Jake looked around the room. "You heard the man, let's get to the Guardian boulder." Kai and Darrius followed Jake into the foyer where Alden, Benedict, and Bob awaited them.

The Cererians had already created the doppelgangers who stood in a row staring blankly ahead.

"This is really weird," Jake said staring at his duplicate. When Jake squinted, his doppelganger also squinted. Chance and Kai also examined their body doubles.

Chance stroked his chin as he checked out his clone. "Gee, Jake. Can my doppelganger go in my place?"

"No!" Jake replied as he grabbed Chance by the arm and pushed him between Kai and Darrius. "Make sure he doesn't go anywhere."

"Is everyone clear on what they need to do?" Jake asked. Everyone nodded. Jake turned to Chance, Darrius, and Kai. "You guys know where we're meeting?" They nodded. "Good luck everyone. It's time we introduced Chance to his Guardian boulder."

One by one, Jake, Chance, Kai and Darrius disappeared.

Alden opened the front door, and Jake's doppelganger raced away toward the tree line. Cary was already in the front yard and yelled for his brother. Just as Balor rounded the corner to join Cary, Alden released Kai's body double who sprinted for the cover of a thick hedgerow. Moments later, Chance's doppelganger darted for a section of the front yard near the destroyed fountain. As the Cererians looked on, Cary and Balor chased the runaways.

Alden shut the door. "Let's hope that distraction gave them the time they needed."

Seconds after leaving The Nine Muses, Jake, Chance, Kai, and Darrius appeared on the beach near the wall of boulders. They could hear Cary and Balor shouting in the distance. Jake ran to the water's edge and threw his hands up, palms facing the water. Instantly, the mouth of a large tubular structure appeared in front of him. The opening nudged against the sandy beach while the long body stretched into the sea, disappearing under the waves. Completely transparent, the structure blended into its surroundings. If Jake hadn't stood by the opening, no one would have known where to enter.

"Let's go everyone!" Jake shouted as he waved them toward the entrance. Kai plunged into the conduit followed by Darrius.

Chance trotted to the opening and stopped. "Nope. Nope," he said shaking his head and backing away.

He collided with Jake's hands. The shaman shoved Chance forward, his feet digging into the sand. "Come on, big boy, you can do it. I'll be right behind you."

"Jake, this thing disappears into the water…" Chance fretted. "This is not what I was expecting. Hell, it won't hold my weight."

"We're running out of time, Chance!" Jake yelled. "Get in or we're dead!" With a mighty shove, Jake pushed Chance into the opening, leapt in behind him, and sealed the entrance as Balor and Cary raced down the beach.

Jake quickly made his way to the front and urged the cylinder forward with magic.

The transparent structure carried the men swiftly into the sea.

Kai stood behind Jake. "Holy shit!" he exclaimed. "Look at the sea life. There's a school of great whites!" He pointed at the mammoth beasts as their tube slid beneath the grayish creatures. One shark whipped his head toward Kai as they passed.

Chance gripped Darrius around the waist and buried his face into the Cererian's back.

"I hope you don't mind, Darrius," Chance said. "But you were the closest."

"You're doing fine," Darrius soothed as he patted his hand.

"Try to relax and enjoy the scenery around you," Darrius urged.

"Look at the size of that squid!" Kai yelled.

Chance squeezed Darrius harder.

"How far away is the Guardian?" Darrius asked.

"Roughly two hundred miles," Jake answered. "If we were in your typical cruiser, it would take us about five hours to reach it. But this magical conduit will deliver us there in just under one hour."

"Impressive," Darrius replied. "Chance, do you think you'll be hugging me for one hour?" Darrius adjusted Chance's fingers, so they weren't digging into his ribs.

Chance pressed his forehead against Darrius's spine. Beads of sweat popped all over his cheeks. Pursing his lips, he drew in a long breath, filled up his lungs, and then slowly exhaled through his mouth.

Kai turned and walked toward the back. Because he changed his position, the supernatural tube readjusted its size to accommodate the movement. That action caused the structure to wobble slightly.

"Oh no!" Chance groaned as he gripped the Cererian tighter.

Kai maneuvered behind his brother. "There, there, Chance," he cooed while rubbing his brother's back. "Turn your head to the side and peek at what you're missing."

Chance shook his head.

Undeterred, Kai continued, "There are brilliant blues and greens and small fish with stripes of golden yellow. Damn, is that a humpback whale?"

Chance turned his head and opened one eye. A trio of jellyfish danced by. Bioluminescence made them appear blue. He opened the other eye. The cylinder had just entered a massive school of mackerel, their silver bodies shimmering as they turned one way and then darted another. Still hugging Darrius, Chance lifted his head and looked to either side and then upward as a hammerhead shark zigzagged across the top of the tube.

"Wow," he whispered.

"Look over there, Chance," Kai pointed. "We're passing through a deep section of the ocean. I betcha there's odd creatures down those crevasses."

Chance lifted away from Darrius. "Thanks, Darrius," he said sheepishly. "I hope I didn't hurt you."

"I'm glad I could help." The Cererian replied as he bent forward and stretched his back. The movement caused the cylinder to shudder again as it modified its outer skin to allow for two feet around all the occupants.

"Yikes," Chance muttered reaching out to steady himself and inadvertently grabbing Darrius's ear. "Sorry, Darrius."

"All is well," the Cererian replied as he seized Chance's arm and steadied him. "Are you okay now?"

"Yeah, I'm getting used to this see-through submarine."

Jake spoke over his shoulder. "Since we'll be stuck in this tube for an hour, feel free to sit down, or even lie down. But keep in mind the space will modify to your position."

Chance crouched. The cylinder immediately altered its shape so it was taller near Jake at the front and shorter where Chance hunched in the back. "Nope, this isn't going to work. Looks like I'll stand with the rest of you."

"Great idea," Kai agreed. "Check out these trenches and mountains we're zipping over." Kai pointed down. "You won't get another chance to see anything like this ever again."

Darrius maneuvered carefully toward Jake at the front. "You said Fen would be meeting us?"

"Yes," Jake nodded. "The earth spirt, Galena, will be with her. And I'm sure Fen's white bison, Bodhi, will be by her side."

"A bison underwater?" Darrius pondered.

"I know it sounds strange, but Bodhi goes everywhere with Fen. When you're dealing with magical people, anything is possible. *You* should know that!"

Jake slowed the transparent craft as it approached an underwater mountain range.

"Why are we slowing down?" Chance asked.

"We've arrived at our destination," Jake replied as he maneuvered the structure toward a large flat-top mountain. "Behold, Bear Seamount. It's an extinct volcano in a chain of about thirty."

"Wow," Chance muttered. "The Guardian boulder is somewhere on that thing?"

"Yep," Jake replied as he brought the craft to a stop at the midpoint of the seamount. The submersible hovered parallel to the side of the mountain, which soared four-thousand-feet above them and plunged two-thousand-feet beneath them to the ocean floor where the waters, devoid of light, swirled black and ominous.

Chance gazed around. At this depth, the light from above was faint and created different shades of midnight blue to navy. A tinge of vertigo swirled in his head, causing him to bump against Kai.

Kai caught his brother before he crashed against the side of the structure. "Whoa, Chance. Are you okay?" Kai noticed Chance's eyes twitching. "What the hell?"

"I'm a little dizzy," Chance said. "I feel like I'm whirling around on a carnival ride."

"It's a visual perception," Darrius commented. "Your brain is confused about what it sees. You're standing in water and to your brain, that doesn't make any sense because there's no firm structure under your feet, so it sends out signals to straighten you."

"Great," Chance commented. "I'll just keep my eyes closed."

"It'll get better," Jake offered. "You'll soon get accustomed to this space."

"I hope so," Kai muttered.

"When do you expect Galena and Fen to arrive?" Darrius asked.

Jake peered into the distance to the west of Bear Seamount. "They won't be long. You'll see them approach from that direction."

"Are they arriving in an invisible sausage casing as well?" Kai joked.

Jake smirked. "No."

"Then how will they get here?" Kai asked.

"Galena will deliver Fen in another dimension," Jake explained. "It'll be a parallel universe to the one we're in." Jake rubbed his chin. "I'm not sure how much it will look like this one. Hell, Galena might bring Fen in a realm that has no water."

"That would be interesting," Kai said. "How do you combine a watery existence with an arid region?"

"Very carefully," Chance joked.

"Looks like you've found your sea legs," Kai observed. "You good, now?"

"Yep," Chance replied. "Until the next thing comes along."

"Shh," Jake said, holding up his hand. He closed his eyes and mumbled under his breath. After several moments, he faced the others. "That was Galena. They're approaching." Jake pointed into the distance. "That's them."

Like phantoms shimmering underwater, the faint images of three figures appeared beside the submersible.

"What. The. Hell?" Chance uttered. "Are they real?"

"Yes," Jake replied. "That's Galena on the left with Fen beside her."

"What's that large four-legged thing to the side of Fen?" Kai asked.

"That's Bodhi, Fen's spirt animal," Jake replied.

"Impressive," Darrius added. "I've witnessed the effect of universes side by side, each world filling their unique spaces. But I've never seen a dimension that was fully integrated with the physical world."

The four men gazed at the two women. Inches separated them from the craft.

Chance reached forward, but Jake grabbed his hand. "Remember, our structure will modify its size based on the forms inside. If you reach forward, it will expand more toward Fen and Galena's universe. Stay exactly where you are."

A foreign voice spoke inside the submersible.

"I am Galena, one of three sacred sisters and guide to the Healers. I have delivered Fen, Guardian of Peace, so she can fulfill her role in uniting the Guardian boulder with its sacred gemstone."

Neither Fen's nor Galena's mouth moved.

"Welcome Galena," Jake replied. "This is Chance, Kai, and Darrius." Jake turned to Chance and Kai. "You may speak with your sister now."

"Hi Fenny!" Kai said, waving. "How are you?"

"Hi Fen!" Chance echoed. "I've missed you so much!"

A generous smile spread across Fen's face. She first faced Galena who nodded and then returned to her brothers.

"I am well," she responded. Her words echoed in the see-through chamber, but Fen's lips did not move. "My heart soars to see both of you are doing so well. I ache to touch your hand or give you a hug, but I am no longer able to be with you in your physical world. I'm at peace in this realm and sit alongside the ancients who guide me along my path."

"Sounds like gobbledygook," Chance said under his breath. He leaned toward Kai. "Does that sound like our Fen?"

Before Kai could respond, Fen answered. "It is me, Chance. I'm the same sister you've always known...but different."

Chance squinted at the woman smiling at him. "There are tricksters and doppelgangers everywhere. If you're really Fen, tell me something only you and I would know. Something from when we were little."

Fen gazed upward thinking of what to say and then grinned wide. "I'll share something Darrius told me when I was older. You were seven years old. When I first arrived at The Nine Muses, I was a frightened baby. My parents had been murdered, and I was ripped from my crib and brought to a strange house with strange people. I cried for days, and our adoptive mother couldn't console me. Darrius said you began creeping into my room late at night, after everyone had gone to sleep, and would stand by my crib and sing to me while holding my hand.

"Darrius said I immediately stopped crying as if you had cast a spell on me. Once I quieted, you'd climb the rails of the crib and snuggle beside me so I would fall asleep. Before morning broke, you'd awake, kiss my forehead, and hurry back to your bedroom."

Tears welled in Chance's eyes as Fen relayed her story. "Nobody should know that. How do you know about that, Darrius?"

"In the early days, both Prasad and I kept watch over each of you. We remained vigilant lest the Yfel Brethren find and kill you. I was keeping an eye on you while Prasad monitored Fen that night.

"But you weren't there," Chance protested.

"Both Prasad and I were there. To avoid disturbing the children as they slept, we'd shape-shift into small animals, so we'd be able to maintain watch without disturbing you. That night we had transformed into mice and watched your display of love from our perch atop the dresser."

"But why did you tell Fen?"

"Human hormones," Darrius replied.

"What do you mean?" Chance asked.

"As you became a teenager, you spent less time with your younger sisters, preferring to roughhouse with Kai, or run away into the woods. One day, I found Fen crying in her bedroom. She must have been around ten at the time. When I asked her what was wrong, she pointed out the window where you were swinging from a tree branch. Fen looked at me with tearful eyes and said, 'I miss Chance's snuggles'. You see, even though she was a baby, your selfless actions left a lasting effect."

Chance choked back a cry as tears rolled down his cheek. He dropped his head and swiped the wetness from his face. When he looked at Fen, his eyes were red and watery. "I'm so sorry, Fen. I never forgot about you...never."

"No apologies are needed," Fen said. "The sweetness of that memory sustains me."

"That's our sister," Chance acknowledged. "I don't care that she talks without moving her lips or that she appears like a ghost in the water. She is my baby sister, Fen."

The mood in the submersible quieted as everyone processed the sweetness of the relationship between the siblings.

It was Galena who broke the moment. "Shaman, we should proceed."

"You're right, Galena," Jake replied. "Fen and Kai will need to open the Guardian boulder before Chance can offer his gemstone."

"I understand. Fen will work with the Guardian boulder in our realm while Kai addresses the Guardian in your dimension."

"How is this going to work?" Kai asked. "I need to place my hand on Fen's shoulder so we're connected to the Guardian. That contact must be maintained. If we're in two different dimensions, how will I be able to touch Fen?"

Jake placed a hand on Kai's shoulder. "Galena and Fen have that worked out."

"Yes, Magician," Galena spoke. "While you don't have the ability to be in two dimensions at the same time, your sister possesses the powers to do so. She will be able to touch you to maintain the connection as required by the Guardian."

Fen nodded. "Yes, Kai. We'll be able to perform our tasks as usual, except we'll be side by side in different worlds."

"We have a challenge," Jake noted. "We need to remain within our transparent chamber, which means I'll need to push the pod against the Guardian so Kai and Chance can do their jobs. This means we need to coordinate our positions, so we don't interfere with Galena's world, and we don't inadvertently break the connection in our physical world."

"Shit, this sounds tough," Chance said. "Couldn't we just get into scuba gear and make it happen?"

"You'll explode at these depths," Jake commented. "Just do as I say, and we'll all be fine."

"Tell us what to do," Darrius said.

"Chance and Kai. Stand right in front of me as I push the submersible closer to the Guardian. Don't move until I tell you to. Do you understand?"

The men nodded.

"Shaman," Galena interjected. "Fen will await your command before she approaches the Guardian in our world."

"Understood, Galena," Jake replied.

Chance and Kai stood directly in front of Jake as he urged the chamber forward toward the side of Bear Seamount. The craft moved forward slowly as Jake jockeyed for the best position to approach the Guardian boulder.

"I don't see the Guardian." Kai whispered.

"It's there, but it's camouflaged," Jake replied. "A millennium of silt and debris has covered it. Just a few more feet."

The chamber crept forward until a slight shudder proved it had touched the side of the underwater volcano.

"The mountain is coming through the craft!" Chance exclaimed as he pointed toward a plant-covered rock that nudged into the front of the submersible.

"Steady, Chance," Jake assured as he guided the submersible even closer. As the craft engulfed more of the mountainside, wet earth fell to the floor followed by tiny crustaceans that scurried within the cabin. Soon, a rocky pillar covered with plants and organisms pushed into the craft.

"Behold the Guardian boulder," Jake announced. "Nobody move!"

The single spike of rock—about three feet high—appeared between Chance and Kai. Muddy and sodden, the pillar was unremarkable and unimpressive when compared to its brothers.

"I smell fish," Chance complained. "And not in a good way."

Jake glanced at Galena and nodded. "Kai, watch Fen and move together. You should touch your respective Guardians at the same time."

Fen kept a watchful eye on her brother as she leaned forward toward the Guardian that shimmered in her dimension. Likewise, Kai mimicked her movement as he poised his hand above the slimy rock that invertebrates still clung to.

Fen's voice echoed in the chamber, "One, two, three!" Together the siblings laid their hands on their Guardian boulders. A shiver raced up Kai's arm, and he threw his head back and gasped. His mouth fell open as if he was going to say something but although his jaw moved, no words came out.

Fen, too, had been caught in the throes of the connection to the Guardian. Galena looked on as Fen gasped and her eyes rolled back.

"Why is this experience so different?" Darrius asked Jake.

"Extreme depths and the fact Fen and Kai are touching two different aspects of the same Guardian. It's taking a while for the connection to be made."

Simultaneously, Fen and Kai fell forward toward their boulders, their foreheads resting gently on the surface. With eyes closed, the two magicians began communicating telepathically with the boulder.

I am Fen Kemp, Guardian of Peace.

And I am Kai Kemp, Keeper of the Keys. We have come to restore the Crystal of Earth to its seat of power.

Welcome my children. The Guardian's voice drifted through their heads like a gentle whisper. *I was informed of your mission by the Sentinel boulder, and I'm glad to assist you.*

The siblings opened their eyes. Holding their hands at heart center, they bowed toward the pillar. Fen gazed at Kai and nodded. "I've located the ancient symbols, and I'm preparing to touch the Guardian. When I do, I will also reach toward you. Do not flinch or break away or the connection will be gone."

"Okay, Fen," Kai replied. "I'm ready.

Fen started at the top of the rocky pillar, gently running her fingers along the algae and plant life searching for the ancient symbols that would allow her to open the Guardian. Finally, she located the ancient hieroglyphics and pressed her hand against the rock. She grabbed Kai's arm.

A chill raced up their arms, swirled within the pits of their stomachs, and exploded in their brains. The siblings gasped as the connection was established.

I demand the ethereal key from the Keeper, the Guardian announced.

"This is different," Kai whispered to Fen. "I'm usually the one to choose the proper key to open the boulder."

The ethereal key, Keeper...now! A violent bolt of energy coursed through their bodies causing them to convulse.

"This is different," Darrius said to Jake. "The Guardians have never been violent with them."

"It must be the ocean depths," Jake said. Helpless to assist Kai, he could only observe as Kai trembled from the earth spirit's power.

Forgive me, Guardian, Kai began. *The process has been different with your brothers. My delay is due to ignorance and not rudeness.*

Visibly shaking from the strain of the electrical bolts, Kai trembled as he slowly withdrew an antique ebony box from his shirt and set it on the floor of the submersible. The lid instantly popped open and displayed four skeleton keys. Kai's hand fluttered over each key as he engaged his intuition to help him select the proper instrument for unlocking the boulder. "The key's not here," Kai squeaked.

"It must be," Fen answered.

"None of these are right."

"Where do you keep the ethereal key?" Fen asked.

"Omigosh, you're right. I haven't used it in almost a year." Maintaining his touch with the boulder with his left hand, Kai began scribing symbols in the air with his right hand. He drew elements in the air faster and faster until a shimmering yellow light trailed his movements. Soon the energized outline of a small skeleton key floated right in front of his face. Using his magical powers, Kai urged the ethereal key toward the boulder. The instant the key touched the side of the rock, the instrument vanished and a loud, grinding noise rumbled inside the submersible.

"What the fuck is that?" Chance shouted as he jerked.

"Steady, Chance," Jake reminded as he stopped Chance from taking a step backward.

Pieces of rock fell to the floor as the pillar pulled apart, exposing a small obsidian recess. The crunching abruptly ceased, and a soft melody drifted throughout the craft. Barely audible, the humming, which sounded like a million honeybees, rose and fell like a comforting breeze. The hairs stood up on the men's necks and arms as electrical energy filled the submersible.

The thrumming suddenly stopped.

"Do you hear that?" Chance asked as he looked around searching for the source.

"The Guardian is communicating only with you," Kai confirmed. "As the holder of the jewel, the Guardian must now connect with you."

The Boulder messaged Chance:

Within this rock, an entity lies waiting,
Awaiting the one who will free the imprisoned,
Embracing the one who will lay the foundation,
And create life with the element of earth.

Chance's mouth fell open as the words drifted through his mind like a gentle caress. Not accustomed to telepathy, the words were both shocking and interesting.

The Guardian continued, *My son, the following sacred words are meant only for you. As I speak the words, your crystal will yearn to be reunited with me. You may step forward with your offering.*

Chance glanced over his shoulder. "The Guardian wants me to approach, Jake."

Jake adjusted his hands to prevent extreme modulation in the submersible. "Okay, take a small step forward."

Chance stepped nearer and withdrew a small vial from his shirt pocket. He held it up showing it contained a small bluestone chip, which was found in the Welsh Preseli Hills. "I'm ready to receive your message," he announced.

Very well, the Guardian replied.

I stand alone, one of four,
United, the four will be one.
The heart within you beats strong and resilient,
The world awaits your earthly gift from Gaia!

The bluestone chip rattled violently in the vial. Chance tilted the container, and the tiny stone tumbled into his hand and then jumped around his palm as if alive. He pinched it between his thumb and forefinger and guided it into the obsidian recess and gently placed it inside.

Instantly, crunching and grinding ensued as the two openings to the small recess slid together and sealed.

Silence.

Then the Guardian boulder sighed sending a shockwave around the globe. Carried in that magical vibration was a joyous message audible only to the magical populations of the world. *Earth has been restored. The third marker is secure!*

As with the other boulders, Fen lingered with her hand on the Guardian and imparted healing energy for any damage caused during the tortuous opening of the recess.

Her hand still gripped Kai's shoulder. He slowly raised his hand toward hers, but when his fingers touched the back of her hand, his fingers went through her flesh as though she was a spirit. He looked at her and found her peering back, her eyes sad. Her hand immediately disappeared, and she stood up beside Galena.

"Is all in order, Shaman?" Galena asked.

"Yes, Galena," Jake replied. "Without your help and without Fen's involvement, we would never have been able to seat Chance's family jewel. I appreciate your help."

"Ah, but our job is not yet complete," Galena added. "We still have the final phase of the Prophecy. Are you ready?"

Jake sighed. "Yes, I am. I need to prepare and will contact you for arrangement."

"Very well," Galena replied. "Fen, say your goodbyes to your brothers and friends. It's time to go home."

Kai and Chance faced Fen as her shadowy shape hovered inches away in her parallel dimension.

"I wish I could hug you, Fen," Kai said. "You were able to touch my hand. Is it possible for you to touch both of us?"

Fen glanced at Galena who nodded. Fen pushed her arms toward the submersible. Her phantom hands appeared on the shoulders of her brothers. She tenderly squeezed. Instinctively, they reached up to touch her arm. The second they did, the vision disappeared.

"Time to go," Galena remarked as she turned away.

The men watched the women and white bison slowly fade and disappear.

"Are you guys okay?" Jake asked as he searched the sibling's faces. They continued to gaze out into the dark waters well after Fen had disappeared from view.

"That was rough," Kai said, turning toward Jake.

"I won't be able to sing her songs anymore," Chance whispered as he stared into the ocean depths.

"Yeah," Jake replied. "It's only going to get harder." He patted the brothers on their backs. "Time to head home."

"Shit," Chance exclaimed. "I'm not looking forward to a one-hour trip back to the beach where Cary and Balor are probably prowling, waiting for us to return."

"Ah, but you forget one thing," Jake said, holding his finger in the air. "You can now flick back to The Nine Muses, and the rest of us can teleport. The moment we leave, this device will simply disappear."

"Perfect!" Chance shouted. "I'm a little hungry."

"Good grief," Kai exclaimed. "It's always about food, isn't it?"

Chance arched his eyebrows. "Isn't it always about the food?"

Chapter 28

A Cererian Response

THE SENATOR'S DYING SCREAMS echoed in the brains of all Cererians. Guards rushed to the Justice Hall but found only destruction and the remnants of the Senator's energy molecules.

Moments after the dignitary's death, an emergency meeting of the High Order of Truth was assembled.

We must find them! Orion demanded. With the Senator dead, Orion, leader of the High Order of Truth, was now the supreme leader of Ceres. He controlled all operations and could make all decisions independently.

Orion was omnipotent.

My lord, Mason began. *The assassins, Hilly and Stygian, escaped to Earth. Their whereabouts are unknown. They've cloaked themselves.*

We must send our best soldiers to kill them, Orion insisted.

Natural Cererians cannot survive for long in the harsh atmosphere of Earth and must use sustainable life pods, Luther explained. *Unfortunately, we are restricted on the number of pods available. Since the Senator disassembled all operations associated with the Earth mission—*

Silence! Orion yelled. Flashes of deep red pulsed throughout his body. *Send all we can. If Stygian and the Firewalker witch are not located and killed, we'll all be dead anyway.*

Mason and Luther drifted together. A myriad of bright colors pulsed within their bodies as they telepathically conversed.

My lord, Mason messaged. *Luther and I have created a list of ten Cererian warriors who would be ideal for hunting the murderess and the hybrid.*

Excellent! Orion replied. *When will they leave for Earth?*

Within the hour, Mason reported.

Keep me informed. I want results before the next moon in seven days.

Yes, my lord! Mason and Luther pulsed blue as Orion floated by them and exited the main hall.

Hilly and Stygian sheltered under the icy overhang on Denali's slope. A whiteout pummeled them from all sides. Occasionally, a ball of icy snow would glance off the rocky overhang barely missing the occupants.

"Denali is not pleased," Hilly shouted into the wind.

Stygian held her close. The proximity of their blood created a fire that smoldered low in their abdomens and slowly rose until it flared in their chests.

"She will forgive you," Stygian replied. "Eventually."

"Why did you bring me back here?"

"You said you would miss Denali's slopes. I hoped seeing them one more time would make you smile."

Hilly shielded her eyes from the relentless sleet. "If only I could see those beautiful slopes." She buried her head in Stygian's shoulder.

"Denali's tantrum is lasting too long. We need to move on."

"I know." Hilly sighed deeply.

Stygian tilted her chin so he could gaze into her eyes. "Are you troubled by something?"

"I wish we had more time together...to explore the universe and get to know one another. I had hoped I'd learn more about my family."

"You and me—we're the last of our family. You're the last of your kind." Stygian gripped her tighter. A surge of heat-fueled adrenalin coursed throughout their veins. "I finally found you, only to let you go."

Hilly leaned back and stared into Stygian's eyes. Many moments passed as they searched each other's faces, penetrated each other's souls, and delighted in the fire that swirled within their blood. With their chests pressed together, their hearts found each other's rhythm and pulsed slow, yet strong. Beads of sweat dotted Hilly's forehead, only to instantly turn into ice pellets.

Stygian nuzzled her neck and raised his lips to her ear. "It's time to go," he whispered.

"Yes," she responded. "It's clear Denali wants nothing to do with us." She wrapped her arms around his neck and the duo vanished from Mount Denali.

From the moment he saw Jake and the others escape into the sea, Balor assaulted The Nine Muses with renewed fury. He pounded the shingles on the roof while Cary hammered at the rear walls of the house.

"Doppelgangers!" Balor yelled. "I can't believe we were tricked by clones. But the magicians will be coming back. Keep an eye on the beach."

"We need reinforcements," Cary complained. "The moment I breach the exterior, Alden and the other benevolent Cererians deploy stronger magic and create more barriers."

"That's the same with the top of the house," Balor lamented. "My feet broke into the attic at one point. The next moment, I was blown out of the hole by Cererian magic. Then the opening sealed, and the shingles repaired themselves."

Balor jumped to the ground beside his brother. "You heard the message about the third gem finding its seat of power?"

"Yes," Cary replied. "One more and the Prophecy will reach completion. Where's Stygian? I've tried to reach him without any response."

"He's probably keeping out of sight," Balor replied. "After killing the Senator, I imagine he'll have quite a lot of bounty hunters on his trail."

"I heard the Firewalker killed the Senator."

"Stygian didn't stop her," Balor noted. "He's just as guilty."

"But if the rumors are true, the Senator was not innocent."

The twins stared at each other. Finally, Balor broke the silence. "I think Stygian has abandoned us, brother. We have been faithful to him. and he has run away with the Firewalker witch, leaving us to fend for ourselves. He no longer answers my messages either."

"What do we do, Balor? We are Yfel Brethren, and he is our leader."

"There are others."

"What do you mean there are others? Yfel?"

"Yes. Stygian once explained that rogue Cererians roamed all over the globe. These are ex-soldiers from the earlier expeditions who yielded to their human urges and murdered magicians and consumed their supernatural energy. If Stygian has abandoned us, then we are within our right to find our own way."

"What do you propose?" Cary asked.

"I suggest we reach out to find others of our kind. I suggest we forged other alliances so we can halt The Cererian Prophecy."

Cary jerked his thumb at the house. "What about our sworn oath to annihilate everyone in this house?"

"We've done our job. Now, it's time for us to look out for our best interests like our leader has done. Besides, I no longer care about the people here. To me, they are petty annoyances. The Firewalker witch should be our focus. Do you agree?"

Cary rubbed his chin. "You have a point, Balor. What's our next move?"

"Stygian has cloaked his whereabouts, but there are subtle markers whenever he makes an appearance. I suggest we hunt for him. Once we find Stygian, we'll locate the Firewalker witch and, together, we'll kill her and feast upon her magic."

Cary nodded. "Yes, brother. That's an excellent plan." The twins gazed at The Nine Muses one last time and vanished.

"The twins just disappeared," Alden noted. "When the pounding on the roof ceased, I investigated and found them talking at the back of the house. Then, they disappeared."

"What do you think it means?" Benedict asked.

"Either Stygian has called them away, or they have gone in search of him. In either case, I believe we'll have some peace and quiet."

"That's good news," Bob chimed in. "The spells required to maintain the roof were weakening. I wasn't sure I could reinforce them as fast as the twins were demolishing it."

"Darrius and the others are on their way back," Alden announced.

"I was pleased to hear they were successful," Benedict added. "Now we have one more Guardian boulder yearning to be united with its gem. It appears the Prophecy will be completed."

"I hope so," Darrius commented as he entered the room.

"Congratulations on a successful mission," Alden said.

"Thank you," he replied. "By now, you've heard Stygian and Hilly killed the Senator?"

"Yes," the Cererians chorused.

"Ceres will not take the Senator's death lightly. I'm sure there will be repercussions. Since we've been cut off from our Cererian contacts, we no longer receive information from home. This places us at a disadvantage."

"I wonder if the Yfel Brethren are also aware of this development," Alden mused. "I wonder if that's the reason the twins departed."

Chapter 29

An Impossible Mission

A LIGHT BREEZE TEASED the wildflower blooms. Hues of red and orange swayed back and forth brushing Fen's face as she stretched out in the middle of the meadow.

She gazed upward and watched puffy clouds cruise by unhurried.

"What do you see?" a female whispered.

Fen looked around and saw no one. A smile popped onto her face. "You always surprise me, Galena. You're not standing beside me, yet I feel your presence."

"I'm always by your side," Galena answered. "My reach has no limits."

"It's comforting," Fen noted. "You, the ancients, and Bodhi." The white bison stood nearby chewing placidly on a mouthful of flowers and prairie grass.

"You've been staring into the sky for hours," Galena continued. "What do you see?"

Fen shifted to a sitting position. "I was observing the developments on Ceres and watching my sister and Stygian on Mount Denali. I feel like I'm watching a head-on collision in slow motion. I have the power to divert their course but cannot change the outcome of the Prophecy."

"A conundrum," Galena said as she appeared on the ground beside Fen.

"Yes. I've had a lot of those lately." Fen's brow wrinkled in thought as she absently played with the grass. "I loved seeing my brothers again. I had almost forgotten how funny and kind they are. I wish I could talk with Hilly one more time."

"You'll see her at the final Guardian boulder."

Fen looked up at Galena. "Hilly's conflicted. Her shared blood with Stygian influences her judgment, especially now that they're together."

"The Firewalker has a responsibility to many and not just herself." Galena stood and turned her face into the cool breeze and breathed deeply. "Like the rocky spokes of the medicine wheel, each of you have a path to walk, but you'll all head for the same destination."

Galena abruptly turned toward the east. "The shaman is restless. Now that the third Guardian has rejoiced in being united with its jewel, he grows anxious for you to unite your gem with the final boulder."

Galena extended a hand toward Fen. "Rise, Fen. It's time to visit the medicine wheel."

Glass of bourbon in hand, Jake sat alone in the study. He swirled the fluid and gazed out the window. Hilly hadn't responded to his telepathic messages since she told him she'd killed the Senator.

He sipped the bourbon, grimaced from the burn, and gazed outside.

This moment of peace was welcome. Quiet moments alone with his thoughts without the intrusion of Cary and Balor pounding on the house.

Hilly, where are you? he thought.

Now that the Prophecy was nearing completion, he pondered the last steps of his journey and reviewed how far he'd come.

He recalled the first time he saw Hilly. She had just arrived in Alaska and seemed arrogant and demanding. But she was also refreshing, a capable and confident warrior who didn't mind getting her hands dirty. And during her vision quest, he'd also seen the demons that consumed her. Being the last of her kind meant she had no family to guide her and teach her the ways of the Firewalkers.

But she was a quick learner. And once Darrius restored her memories, her extraordinary abilities raced to the surface with unusual intensity.

The moment Hilly approached him at the hangar as he waited beside his plane, Lola, a powerful energy preceded her. He knew instantly that she was the Firewalker witch he'd heard stories about from the native shamans. Even then, he was keenly aware of her role in the Prophecy.

Jake gulped the bourbon. *Why don't you answer me?*

"Because I don't know what to say," she replied.

Jake bolted up from his chair and whirled toward her voice. Hilly leaned against the closed door.

"Why so secret?" Jake whispered.

"I don't want the others to know I'm here. I don't want to explain myself."

"Your brothers miss you."

"I'm aware. They've been reaching out to me, like you have."

"Please sit and let's chat." Jake gestured toward the sofa.

"I don't have time, Jake." Hilly walked to him. There was an unusual glow—an aura—surrounding Hilly and the moment she drew near, Jake's heart raced, his breathing quickened, and his cheeks flushed.

She offered a faint smile. "I have that effect on people lately. I wanted you to know that you can count on me at the end. I'll stand with you and my family." She turned to go, and Jake gripped her wrist.

"Please stay longer." Hope filled Jake's eyes as he searched her face.

She gently cupped his chin, caressed his cheek with her thumb, and vanished.

Not long after, there was a knock at the door and Kai entered. Jake still stood in the middle of the room with his face tilted upward, his eyes closed.

Kai passed him on the way to the bar, poured a drink, and then looked at his friend again.

Jake hadn't moved, but he'd opened his eyes and stared at the door.

"You okay?" Kai asked.

Jake didn't respond. Kai poured bourbon into another glass and brought it to Jake. "Need this?"

Jake silently took the drink, turned, and folded into a nearby chair. Without a word, he gulped the bourbon.

"You're freaking me out," Kai said as he sat opposite his friend. "What's going on?"

"I saw Hilly," Jake whispered.

"What! She came here and didn't see me?"

"Hey, what's all the noise about?" Chance asked as he burst into the study.

"Jake saw Hilly," Kai said.

"What?" Chance exclaimed. "Where is she?"

Jake cleared his throat and drew in a deep breath. "Look, guys. She wanted to stay but couldn't. She wanted to let everyone know she'd see you later when we're at the last Guardian boulder."

The brothers stared at Jake with sad eyes.

"Hilly said she'd stand with family and we could count on her." He joined them and patted their shoulders. "You should feel proud. Chance, you conquered your fear of small spaces, and Kai, you successfully teamed with Fen while you were in different dimensions. Those are extraordinary accomplishments. Now, it's time we plan for the next Guardian boulder where Fen will unite her gem on its seat of power."

"You're right," Kai agreed. "I wasn't sure how that dual dimension thing was going to work out, but we made it happen, didn't we?"

"I hope the next Guardian isn't underwater," Chance noted. "I don't want to plunge under the sea in a see-through condom again."

Everyone chuckled.

"I promise you won't need to be underwater," Jake replied. "I'll be leaving in a few minutes to talk with Galena and Fen about the particulars. Are there any messages you'd like me to take to your sister?"

"Let her know I love her so much it hurts," Kai said.

"Yeah," Chance added. "I love her a lot too."

"Okay, guys. I'll let Fen know. If I can, I'll give her hug from you guys as well. Hold down the fort while I'm gone."

"With Balor and Cary gone, there's not much going on," Kai pointed out.

"Consider this time a well-deserved break because things are going to get hectic soon." Jake's eyes twinkled with mischief, and he disappeared.

After Jake left, Kai and Chance meandered into the foyer where they found the Cererians gathered. With impassive, blank faces, the four men faced each other in a circle.

"Cererian coffee klatsch," Chance joked.

"I hope it's good gossip," Kai added.

They strode by the Cererians and went into the dining room. "I don't know why, but I kind of expected food to be sitting here," Chance noted as he slumped into a chair.

"Damn, Chance, do you always think of food? It's boring now that the twins have run off. I wonder if it's okay to go outside?" Kai peered at the Cererians. "They're still caucusing."

Chance stood. "Up for some exploring?"

"What do you mean?" Kai asked. "Like go outside?"

"Yep. Since the C-boys are still having their chit chat, let's go outside. It's been a long time since I've been able to run through the woods."

Kai peeked into the living room. “Yep, they’re still deep in conversation. I’m up for it.”

Chance led the way through the kitchen, so they wouldn’t disturb the Cererians. Behind a secret door disguised as a tall cupboard, old stone stairs led down into the basement. The siblings made their way past a maze of crates and boxes in the cellar until they reached a double door that opened to the outside.

“Do you think the Cererian spells will prevent us from exiting?” Chance asked as he switched on the single bulb that illuminated the cellar.

“Nah, their magic was specific to the Yfel Brethren.”

Chance lifted the massive iron chains that threaded through the handles of the double doors, snapped them easily as though they were made of kindling, and flung the doors open. “Ah, fresh air!” he exclaimed.

Kai followed him outside and opened his arms wide, basking in the warmth of the sunshine. “The sun has never felt so good.”

“I’ll be back soon,” Chance said. He sprinted into the pine tree forest that surrounded the property. Kai watched his brother dart away. The last time Chance was able to use his powerful legs was in Wales, and it made him smile to see Chance transform into a little kid running and jumping among the trees.

Kai strolled along the flower beds until he reached the destroyed Apollo’s fountain in the front yard. He absently plucked debris from the stale water in the basin. He swiped leaf litter and dirt off the marble ledge and sat down. In the distance he heard Chance whooping.

“A magician shouldn’t be caught outside unguarded,” a male warned.

Kai leapt to his feet and whirled toward the voice, his arms in defense position, ready to deliver a supernatural bolt of energy. The hairs on the back of his neck bristled as he glared at the person who spoke.

“Stygian,” Kai hissed. His eyes darted left and right, looking for Chance and calculating his options for escape.

The Cererian stood ten feet away on the other side of the demolished fountain and made no move to come closer.

"Why has Darrius allowed you to venture outside unattended?" the Yfel leader asked.

"He's watching from afar," Kai lied. Meanwhile, he telepathically messaged Darrius for help.

"I've already reached out to Darrius," Stygian replied calmly. "He knows I'm here."

Within seconds, Darrius materialized beside Kai.

"Why are you outside?" Darrius demanded. "Where's your brother?"

"I'm here," Chance answered as he emerged from the bushes.

"Get back inside now!" Darrius ordered.

"Sorry," the brothers chorused before returning to The Nine Muses.

Darrius turned his attention to Stygian. "You look well, brother."

Stygian smirked. "You're not a good liar, Darrius. I feel and look exhausted."

"Is Hilly with you?"

"No. I've come alone. This is a private matter between you and I." Stygian walked around the circular edge of the fountain basin and joined Darrius.

The two friends sat side by side in silence.

"It's odd sitting next to you civilly," Stygian blurted. "I've missed our all-night discussions about philosophy, the magical populations, and—"

"Your killing impulse?" Darrius interrupted.

"You can't wound me with your words, Darrius. I own what I've become."

"Balor and Cary departed earlier today."

"I'm aware. They desire to find Hilly and are rendezvousing with a few Yfel Brethren in New York. Honestly, I'm relieved to be rid of them." Stygian gazed at Darrius. "I'm tired." The Yfel leader dropped his head and sighed.

"Something has changed in you, brother," Darrius noted. "The fire has fled from your eyes and your thirst for adventure has disappeared."

The Yfel leader stared at the ground. His fingers gripped the basin edge tightly until his knuckles blanched. "I'm troubled, Darrius. I've come to seek your advice."

"How can I help?"

"You and I have been friends for thousands of years. You've been my brother...my family. Despite our differences, we loved each other."

"This is all true," Darrius commented.

"I was not prepared for Hilly and her influence over me. For years I dreamed of killing her and consuming her extraordinary powers. Then when she arrived at The Nine Muses a year ago, my cravings intensified. I needed to have her. I erred in attempting to enter her body. Even before you restored the memories of her magical legacy and abilities, Hilly's power simmered just below the surface and manifested as I tried to control her thoughts."

Stygian glanced at Darrius with sunken eyes and continued, "Hilly expelled me from her body. Then she captured and banished me to an interdimensional prison." Stygian dropped his head with a heavy sigh. "She bested me, the leader of the Yfel Brethren."

"But she died, if you recall."

"Yes," Stygian replied. "But I believe she was already aware of Prasad's role in the Prophecy and that he would trade his life for hers. For a few minutes, our thoughts were melded, and I could see how advanced she truly was.

"It was at that moment, when our souls were intwined, that I realized Hilly would advance to a level far beyond my abilities. And when Hilly dispatched the Senator, I witnessed power unknown in the universe."

"What are you saying, Stygian?"

"I serve Hilly now. She's being hunted by natural Cererian soldiers that arrived from Ceres earlier this morning. Additionally, once the Guardian boulder announced the third gem had been united with its seat of power, Yfel Brethren around the globe have been gathering in the hopes of trapping and killing Hilly."

"You're protecting Hilly," Darrius observed.

"Yes. Blood must protect blood."

"What about your desires for ultimate power?"

"Imagine being in the vicinity of a magician so strong she can crush you into dust just using her thoughts. What Yfel Brethren wouldn't try to obtain that magic?"

"But you resist the urge?"

Stygian peered at Darrius through red, tired eyes. "Yes. I must. I love her."

"You're not the only one," Darrius whispered. His thoughts raced to Jake, Kai, and Chance. And he couldn't deny the fondness that flourished between him and Hilly.

"Do you need help?" Darrius asked

"You're kind, brother, but no, we don't need your help."

"Where will you hide?"

"In plain sight." Stygian smirked, which made his sad eyes twinkle with mischief, although briefly. "Don't despair, Darrius. I'll deliver Hilly as is preordained by the Prophecy. She'll arrive alive and ready to do her job."

"Is this goodbye, Stygian?"

"I suppose it is." He stared at his friend for several moments before leaning forward and gently kissing Darrius's lips. Darrius wrapped his arms around Stygian and pulled his friend close."

When they parted, tears welled in their eyes.

"Goodbye, brother," Stygian said as he faded from sight.

Chapter 30

A Storm is Brewing

Jake scrutinized the central cairn in the Big Horn Medicine Wheel from his perch on the butte. Although he could see no one, his instincts assured him Fen and Galena stood in the vicinity. A dimensional traveler himself, he was impressed by Galena's manipulation of universes, bending them to her needs. He wanted to learn those skills, to exist simultaneously in all universes.

He sat down on the cliff's edge, his legs dangling over the side. Jake was weary. The physical and mental energy required to keep the Kemps alive and guide them to their Guardian boulders was taking its toll. He was exhausted. But an undercurrent of excitement to see this extraordinary adventure to the end ran just beneath the surface.

A light breeze drifted across the top of the mesa scattering gravel and dirt. Without looking up he greeted, "Hello Galena."

Silently she sat beside him, allowing her tanned legs to hang beside Jake's. The light scent of chrysanthemums tickled his nose, and he breathed in her perfume. "Is Fen ready?"

"Yes," Galena replied. "She has been preparing all her life. Are her siblings ready to perform their parts?"

"Yes, although they may not be fully aware what will happen."

Galena studied Jake's face and then looked over the valley. "That is of no importance. What will happen, will happen. The Prophecy will not be denied."

"Did you see the streaks in the sky early this morning?" Jake asked as he pointed to the western horizon. "The trails were visible for several minutes."

"I'm aware," Galena replied. "The natural Cererians have sent ten soldiers, their best hunters, to find the Firewalker witch and make her pay for her crime."

"Are you saying she's guilty?"

"I am neither judge nor jury. But Hilly dealt the death blow to the Senator. She does not deny this act."

"Will you interfere with the Cererians?"

"No, events must unfold as they are preordained."

"But what if she is killed? Then the Cererian Prophecy will not be completed."

"The Firewalker witch cannot be killed." Galena stood.

Jake jumped to his feet. "Hilly can't be killed?"

Galena laid a hand on Jake's chest, above his heart. Her touch sent a jolt of energy throughout his body, and he shuddered. "She has become what she was destined to be and so will you." She turned away and looked upward while raising her arms skyward. "All is as it should be."

Jake studied the sacred sister. Barefoot and dressed in a simple tan shift, she didn't appear like a powerful entity capable of destroying the world. Serenity and peace dripped from her pores and tranquility graced her face.

"You are perplexed, shaman," Galena said facing Jake. "But you are also resolute. The Sentinel boulder chose you to carry the sacred Word. The account of your world's future decorates your body, and you have not strayed from your mission to deliver it safely home." Galena smiled softly. "The chronicle will ascend."

A shiver raced up Jake's spine. Although the sacred words were tattooed on his body, they had never been spoken aloud, not until now when Galena uttered the phrase, "The chronicle will ascend."

"The sacred words must never be spoken aloud," Jake whispered while glancing around as if he was being watched. "I—we are not allowed."

Suddenly his hand jerked sideways as if an unseen force had grabbed it. His legs buckled and Jake crashed to the ground. Seizures rolled through his body, and he spasmed uncontrollably as foam sprayed from his mouth.

Galena stood above him impassively observing the tremors that wracked his body. After several moments, Jake's body quieted, and he curled into a fetal position with his legs pulled up against his chest.

The air was calm except for Jake's ragged breathing

Eyes closed, he lay still and wheezed.

"Wh—what...happened?" he stuttered.

"You have transformed," Galena responded. The entity hunched down and caressed Jake's shoulder. He flinched at her touch.

"Jake?" a female called out.

Jake opened one eye and saw Fen kneeling beside him. She lightly stroked his forehead and cooed, "You are well, Shaman, you are well." She folded her hand inside his. "Rise and stand with me, Jake." As she stood, she pulled Jake upright effortlessly.

Dazed, he stood on shaky legs with his hands out to the side for balance. He glared at the two women. "What did you do to me?"

"The Chronicle has been born," The two women responded in unison.

"What are you talking about?"

"The notch in the Prophecy wheel has moved forward," Galena spoke. "You are ready to lead the others to the fourth and final Guardian boulder."

"You are one with everything," Fen added.

Jake shook his head, scattering remnants of confusion. Then he drew in a deep breath. "Galena zaps me into a seizure and you speak as if everything is just fine! That's not cool, Fen. I expected more from you. I thought you were my friend."

Fen exchanged a glance with Galena before replying. "I'm your friend, Jake. What happened to you...it was necessary for the change required for the final Guardian."

"You two are crazy!" Jake angrily marched away to the edge of the butte, the tips of boots jutting into space. He'd been there only a second when Galena and Fen appeared on either side of him.

Galena held her hand up in front of Jake. Her palm had transformed into a mirror and Jake's face reflected in it. "Look in the mirror," she requested.

Frustrated and angry, Jake turned away refusing to do what the sacred sister asked.

"Jake, please look," Fen urged. "Your questions will be answered."

Jake looked at Fen. She smiled gently, her eyes pleading.

He sighed and turned toward Galena's palm. When his face came into view he leaned forward and squinted. Although his tanned face and laugh lines were the same, something had changed drastically. His vivid blue eyes were now a bright yellow, the black pupils had narrowed like the eyes of a feline.

"What did you do?" He yelled and then slapped Galena's hand away. "You've turned me into a monster!" In his anger, Jake stepped forward and slipped off the top of the mesa. He plunged downward and in those first few seconds of free fall he didn't care. He had been transformed into a creature, and he welcomed death.

But the rate of his plummet soon slowed until he came to a halt just above the desert floor. He hovered parallel to the ground. Slowly, he rotated and looked upward. Galena and Fen stood above him, evaluating.

He willed his body vertical then rose upward until he could walk easily onto the butte.

"What changed your mind about death?" Galena asked.

"My promise to the Sentinel," he replied tersely.

"You are *not* a monster," Fen assured. "You've emerged as your true self, a dual entity who walks in both the physical world and the realm of the shadows."

"I feel different," Jake observed. "Like I have no substance. I'm lighter than a feather."

Galena nodded. "You are one with all, Shaman." A broad smile brightened her eyes. "You are ready to gather your troops."

Abruptly the entity whirled toward the west and closed her eyes. She tilted her chin and sniffed the air. Fen did likewise. Jake searched the western horizon engaging his new powers to see, hear, and feel.

"The Cererians march eastward," Galena remarked.

"The Yfel Brethren march westward," Fen added.

"A storm is brewing," Jake whispered.

Chapter 31

The Final Plan

After returning to The Nine Muses, Jake brooded in the study. He gazed at the placid Atlantic Ocean, his hands on his chest, the fingertips tapping lightly together. Deep in thought, he didn't hear Darrius calling.

When Darrius touched his shoulder, Jake jerked.

"You're engrossed in something," Darrius observed.

"Yeah," Jake replied.

Darrius walked in front of the shaman and hunched down. "I'm aware you've transformed," he said, cupping Jake's chin and guiding his face forward.

Bright yellow cat eyes stared back at Darrius.

"Your eyes are captivating," Darrius observed. "Almost mesmerizing."

"Thanks?"

Darrius sat beside Jake. "Our time together is growing short. This year has gone by too fast."

"Yes," Jake agreed. "I feel like I've been shot out of a cannon."

"Is everything in order for the Guardian boulder?"

"Yes. We leave tonight."

"You've told Chance and Kai?"

Jake shifted uncomfortably. "Not yet. I'm not ready to introduce them to the new me."

"They won't care. They, too, know the final moments are arriving." Darrius sighed. "The Prophecy is a curious thing. It provides minute amount of information to some individuals and pours too much information into the brains of others."

"Try living with it tattooed on your body," Jake joked.

"It hasn't been easy, has it?"

The smile fell from Jake's face and his focus drifted to the floor. "I'm not complaining." He met Darrius's gaze. "I always hoped though..." Jake swallowed the rest of his words.

"Hoped for what?" Darrius pressed.

Jake fidgeted as he pondered Darrius's question.

"I had hoped Hilly and I would be together." Jake's voice was barely audible.

"Considering how you two met, there are many who are surprised you haven't killed one another." Darrius grinned until Jake frowned at him. Then seriousness filled the Cererian's face again.

"Your attempt at humor? Nice, Darrius. I appreciate that."

Knock, knock, knock.

"Jake, are you in there?" Chance asked.

"Ugh." Jake grimaced. "I'm not ready for this."

"It will be fine," Darrius assured as he stood and opened the door.

Chance and Kai rushed in and joined Jake near the window.

"Holy shit!" Chance exclaimed.

"Damn, Jake," Kai added. "Your new look is...interesting."

Jake rushed to the bar. He grabbed the Woodford Reserve and poured a double. He tossed the drink back and stared at the mirror above the bar. Brilliant yellow eyes with black slits stared back. Images of Kai and Chance appeared behind him as everyone studied his reflection.

"Sorry, Jake," Chance apologized. "It's a bit of a shock."

"It's just eye color, Jake," Kai added. "Hell, if we were at a fantasy convention, people would be impressed."

"A fantasy convention?" Jake hissed. "I'm in hell. That's what this is—hell!"

Jake whirled and pushed past Kai shoving him aside. Kai flew toward the window.

"What the hell?" Kai yelled. "Why did you do that?"

Jake stopped. He gazed at his hands and then at his friend on the floor. "I didn't mean to do that."

Kai leapt to his feet and rushed toward Jake. Darrius jumped between them. "Relax, Kai. Jake didn't mean to shove you." Darrius glanced at Jake who backed up against the door staring at his hands. "Apparently, his transformation has encompassed more than his eyes."

"Transformation?" Kai asked.

"Jake is still the shaman and friend we know," Darrius explained. "But he's acquired additional powers as you can see."

"Now, I need a drink," Chance said as he poured bourbon into his glass.

"Me too," Kai added.

"Pour one for me, Chance," Jake said as he joined his friend at the bar. He turned to Kai. "I'm sorry Kai. I only meant to get by you, not throw you across the room."

"Now that everyone is together," Darrius began, "It might be ideal to discuss your plans for the fourth Guardian boulder."

Jake grew serious as he carried his drink to the window. He gazed first at the ocean to gather his thoughts before turning around. "Darrius is right. We'll leave tonight to assist Fen in uniting her crystal with the fourth Guardian boulder."

"Wow, that's fast," Chance exclaimed. "We just got back from the third one."

"We're running out of time," Jake continued. "Cererians are advancing from the west coast, and Yfel Brethren are approaching from the east coast. Both groups are intent on killing Hilly and preventing the completion of the Prophecy."

"Damn," Chance uttered.

"Be prepared for a fight," Jake cautioned.

"We're ready, Jake," Kai said. "You can count on us. So, how do we get to the boulder."

"That's the tricky part," Jake explained. "I'll provide coordinates to a nearby location and then I'll lead you the rest of the way. Chance, you'll need to travel with Darrius."

"Oh, no," Chance groaned. "Why? You know I get sick with Cererian teleporting."

"Sorry, brother," Jake replied. "We need everybody for this gathering. I could use your sword and magic. We'll be exposed as we trek to the last Guardian boulder, but Darrius and I will deploy cloaking magic. Hopefully that will be enough to keep both the Cererians and Yfel Brethren from detecting us."

"You mentioned they're after Hilly," Kai noted. "She wasn't at the third boulder. What makes you think she'll be at the fourth boulder? She hasn't answered any of my messages."

Jake and Darrius exchanged glances.

Kai and Chance aren't aware of what will happen as the Prophecy reaches its completion, are they? Jake messaged Darrius.

The Prophecy reveals only what is necessary to each person, Darrius replied.

"She'll be there," Darrius answered. "As Jake noted, we need everyone present to ensure the successful completion of the Prophecy. Hilly has assured us she will be there."

"That's wonderful news," Kai said. "It'll be nice to catch up with her."

"It'll be nice to have the entire family together again," Chance added.

Jake glanced briefly at Darrius before responding. "You're right, Chance. It will be nice to have everyone together."

Jake raised his glass and offered a toast. "To the Kemps, remarkable magicians who dared to save the world."

"Cheers!" everyone chorused.

Chapter 32

A Guardian Boulder Awaits

Later that day, Bob surprised everyone with a feast. Every imaginable meat filled the buffet: roast turkey, honey ham, grilled steak, juicy hamburgers. Vegetables of every color had been placed on the sideboard and a five-tiered tray of desserts decorated the center of the dining table; each level filled with sugary confections.

"I've died and gone to heaven," Chance exclaimed.

Pop!

Bob pulled the cork from the champagne and filled a line of glasses. "Enjoy, everyone. Today is a special day."

Jake, Chance, and Kai filled their plates sky high.

I've never been so proud to be a benevolent Cererian, Alden messaged Darrius, cloaking his mindful conversation from the others.

Darrius nodded. *I've waited a millennium for this moment.*

Do you regret your choice?

Not one minute. I've enjoyed watching the Kemps evolve into who they were destined to be, and I've been proud of my role in their journey.

Still, to finally reach the end, to know what will happen, do you question your decision?

Darrius searched Alden's eyes and saw doubt darkening them. *I suppose I will miss the conversations and the moments when the Kemps made me laugh, a human trait that I didn't use often.*

I recall when I met Chance for the first time, Alden remarked. *Here was a half-naked magician, standing in the pouring English rain because he'd locked himself out, using simple magic to retrieve a key that lay just inside the house. I wasn't accustomed to frivolity of any sort, but at that moment, I couldn't contain my laughter.*

Still, you have doubts..., Darrius commented.

You've always been intuitive, Darrius. Yes, I will miss this world. There are still countries I've not visited, and the beauty of the natural spaces is unparalleled.

I agree. Our journeys have taken us to extraordinary places with different species of flora and fauna. While Ceres will always hold a special mystique for me, Earth and all it offers has enriched my senses.

I've been considering bringing Chance's cousin, Gabriel, back from his interdimensional prison.

Interesting. What prompted your change of heart?

Gabriel will be useful as an observer to the Prophecy's completion. Since he's a magical soul and related to one of our chosen, he's ideal as the official storyteller, sharing the tributes and accolades of the Prophecy participants. He can guide the next Keeper of the Records.

That's an excellent idea!

Chance will be pleased. He's avoided me since the incident in Wales.

Kai walked up to the Cererians. "Aren't you going to eat? I'm concerned Chance is going to devour the entire spread."

"You're right, Kai," Darrius replied. "Come on, Alden, let's take part in the celebration."

Meeting in the foyer just before midnight, Jake briefed Kai, Chance, and Darrius. "Since the Prophecy restricts me from speaking of the location of the Guardian boulder, here are the coordinates for where we'll assemble. He handed slips of paper to each of the men. "These are the longitude and latitude directions."

"What the hell?" Chance complained.

"Don't worry, you'll be with me," Darrius consoled. "I know how to get there."

Kai looked at Jake, his brows furrowed. "Wyoming? Isn't that where Fen is from?"

"Lovell, I believe," Chance added.

Alden, Benedict, and Bob entered the foyer. "We've come to wish you good luck," Alden said. "And I have a surprise before you leave." He curled his fingers, gesturing for someone to join them.

"Gabe!" Chance yelled as he scooped his cousin up in his arms and swung him around.

"Ya can put me down, Chance," Gabe sputtered. "I'm feeling a wee bit dizzy."

"Thank you, Alden. I appreciate you releasing my cousin. This is the greatest gift."

"You're quite welcome," Alden replied.

"Is Gabe coming with us?" Chance asked, his eyes wide with hope.

"Cousin," Gabe replied. "I'll be staying here in The Nine Muses."

"Oh. Then I'll see you when we get back. We'll catch up then." He hugged Gabe one more time and then joined Darrius. "I'm ready. What about the rest of you?"

"Remember," Jake announced. "When you arrive, be on the lookout for Yfel Brethren and natural Cererians. Both groups might be prowling around."

"The natural Cererians will appear quite odd," Darrius added. "They won't have human bodies. They will be encased in metal alloy vehicles that are propelled with their minds."

Darrius wrapped his arm around Chance and nodded at Jake. One by one the men disappeared.

Interesting, Benedict messaged Alden and Bob. *Chance is not yet aware he will not be returning to The Nine Muses.*

The Prophecy informs each person at the rate they can process the information, Alden explained. *If Chance had known what fate awaits him, I'm sure he wouldn't have left.*

The Cererians glanced at Gabe who peered at them suspiciously. "What? Have ye been talking about me or something?" he asked.

Alden wrapped his arm around Gabe's shoulder and guided him toward the dining room. "We were just discussing what we should do with all the leftovers."

"Ah," Gabe replied. "If food's involved, I'm yer man!"

It was risky gathering on the butte within sight of the Big Horn Medicine Wheel, but Jake needed to be close to the Guardian boulder and avoid trekking over a long distance, when they might be easily found by the Yfel or natural Cererians.

He and Kai arrived almost simultaneously. They hunched low and scanned the area for anything suspicious.

Because of a new moon, the landscape was bathed in shadows and darkness. "Good timing," Kai whispered. "The new moon will keep us hidden...hopefully."

"Damn," Jake cursed under his breath. "Where's Darrius and Chance?"

"Yeah. They left at the same time."

Jake crept along the ground, his belly inches from the dirt, as he made his way to the edge of the mesa and peered down. His pupils enlarged like a cat in the night as he squinted into the blackness. Employing his psychic abilities, he surveyed the area, sensing for any entities—magical or Cererian. He detected nothing, not even Galena or Fen. He scurried back to Kai who sat on the ground looking off into the distance toward the west.

"Did you see something?" Jake whispered.

"I thought I saw something in that direction. A pinprick of light flickering into view now and then."

Jake peered into the western sky. "Cererians," he hissed.

"Natural Cererians?" Kai asked, as he flattened on the ground beside Jake.

"Yes. That glint of light you've been seeing is the reflection off their transports. There are only ten of them."

Darrius and Chance sidled up.

"About time you arrived," Jake mumbled. "We've got company." He pointed into the distance.

"Sorry for the delay," Darrius replied. "There were complications during teleporting."

"What's that smell?" Kai asked.

"It's me," Chance replied. "I threw up on the way here. God, I hate teleporting."

Kai grimaced and fanned the air. "Stay over there for now."

"Darris, how long do you think it will take for the Cererians to reach us?" Jake asked.

"About an hour. Right now, they're moving at a slow pace as they scan for Hilly. If they catch her scent, they'll arrive in minutes."

Jake rolled onto his back and groaned. "This is going to be tricky guys. Really tricky."

"Why?" Kai asked. "How far are we from the Guardian boulder?"

"We're not far away, but the hard part will be completing our task before the Cererians arrive." Jake crept toward the edge of the cliff. "Galena and Fen are nowhere to be seen," he confirmed.

"Perhaps they're also aware of the Cererians," Darrius noted.

"I'm sure they are. After all, Galena is aware of everything."

Jake sat up and stroked the stubble on his chin. Then he closed his eyes. Moments later, he gestured to the others.

"Okay, listen up. I've chatted with Galena. We're heading to the Guardian boulder now. I'm sorry, Chance, you'll have to travel with Darrius one more time. We can't risk being detected hiking to the boulder."

"Not again," Chance groaned. He belched loudly. "My stomach isn't going to take more of that tilt-a-whirl."

"You're not permitted to tell us the whereabouts of the Guardian," Darrius cautioned.

"I know and I won't," Jake assured. "While I'm forbidden to speak the location of the Guardian, I'm not aware of any restrictions to gesturing."

"Fascinating," Darrius replied.

"Gather 'round." Jake signaled for the others to come closer. "We don't have much time, so we'll teleport to the Guardian. Once we arrive, Galena and Fen will appear." Jake's voice lowered. "Listen to me. This will not be easy. You thought uniting Chance's gem underwater was difficult, this undertaking will be more dangerous. Darrius and I will cloak our whereabouts the best we can, and Chance, be prepared to battle anything that comes near. Kai, you and Fen need to work quickly, and don't stop no matter what you see or hear. Is that clear?"

Everyone nodded.

"Will Galena be able to assist us if we're besieged by Cererians?" Darrius asked.

Jake shook his head. "Nope. We're on our own." He gazed into everybody's eyes and saw determination and confidence staring back at him. "Any questions?"

Everyone shook their heads.

"Okay, we leave immediately. There." He pointed toward the Big Horn Medicine Wheel in the distance.

Jake disappeared. Then Kai. The last to depart was Darrius as he yanked Chance to his side and vanished.

One by one, the men appeared near the central cairn of the medicine wheel.

"Stay low," Jake whispered.

"What's that?" Kai asked as he pointed into the darkness.

Three figures slowly approached. In the blackness, they appeared as shimmering shadows hinting of something substantial but otherwise indistinguishable. As they neared, familiar shapes came into view.

"It's Fen," Chance said as he rose to meet her.

Jake pulled him back. "Stay here." Chance nodded and kneeled on the ground beside Jake.

Galena arrived first followed by Fen who gripped the shaggy neck of the white bison, Bodhi.

"Shaman, our time is short," Galena said. "Not only do the natural Cererians advance closer, but the Yfel Brethren are arriving from the other direction." She pointed east.

"How do you know?" Darrius asked. "I don't sense the Yfel."

"You're not a sacred sister," she replied bluntly.

"We saw the natural Cererians," Jake confirmed. "How far away are the Yfel?"

"They will descend upon us first."

"Get ready," Jake instructed. "Kai, you and Fen prepare for the ritual. Chance, stay with me and Darrius."

Holding onto Bodhi, Fen approached the central cairn. Because she, Galena, and the bison resided in a parallel universe, her form appeared like an outline with faded features.

"Hi Fenny," Kai greeted as he joined her at the Guardian boulder. "Fancy meeting you in a place like this."

"Always ready with a joke? I love that about you. Live life and don't take it too seriously."

"Because it can always bite you in the ass when you're not looking." Kai chuckled into his fist, careful not to make much noise.

Fen giggled and then grew somber. "We're actually going to see our mission to the end."

"Almost a year ago, I wouldn't have put money on this happening. But now..." Kai stared off.

"Please quicken your pace," Galena urged as she joined them. "The Yfel are not far away." The sacred sister touched their shoulders. The siblings gasped and fell to their knees. Consecutive waves of electrical energy passed through their rigid bodies, their hands spasmed into fists, their teeth clenched in hideous sneers.

Moments later, the convulsions ceased, and a blue dome of light glowed around their bodies and the Guardian boulder.

"Shit," Kai wheezed.

"You may now work together within the same realm. I've created a space where your universes are united." Galena vanished.

"Bitch," Kai seethed.

"Kai!" Fen admonished. "She's only doing what's necessary."

"I think she enjoys her job too much."

"Come on, Kai, let's get to work." Fen reached through the thin veil demarcating their dimensions and pulled her brother closer.

"Chance isn't aware of what will happen today," Kai mentioned.

"What? He doesn't know?" Fen looked toward Chance who stood with Jake and Darrius. "How can he not know?"

"The Prophecy reveals only what the individual can absorb at the time," Kai replied. He followed Fen's gaze. "It's better this way, Fenny. Let's get to work, or Galena will zap us again!"

After leaving the siblings, Galena appeared beside Darrius. "The Brethren are approaching. Don't let them penetrate this sacred circle. Fen and Kai are preparing to open the Guardian boulder, and their work cannot be disturbed."

"They've already arrived!" Jake yelled as he ran to the perimeter, whipping out his battle daggers, Cathal and Cadmar. Darrius and Chance joined him as they sprinted to the northeast section of the wheel.

One by one, fifty Yfel soldiers appeared in a long line in the dark desert.

The twins, Balor and Cary, stood in the middle of the imposing group of Yfel warriors. Each soldier carried a different weapon, which they waved threateningly.

Balor stepped forward. "Hello, Darrius," he sneered. "As you can see, I've brought friends."

"When do we attack, Balor?" an impatient soldier asked.

"Steady, comrade. The Firewalker witch is not here. Why waste our time on these meager appetizers? The main course is worth the wait."

"Quick, Fen," Kai uttered. "We need to complete this ritual as fast as possible." He pressed his hands together at heart center.

Fen followed her brother's lead and drew her hands together in front of her chest. Simultaneously, the siblings bowed to the Guardian boulder. Then Fen leaned forward, her fingers feeling for the ancient symbols hidden along the stone's surface. As her fingers inched along the rough surface, she engaged her intuition to sense where the sacred message was hidden.

"I think I found it," she whispered. "Kai, place your hand on my shoulder so we can establish the connection to the Guardian."

Kai gently touched Fen and a jolt of electricity rushed through them.

Welcome my children! a gruff male voice spoke into their brains. *I was informed of your imminent arrival by my underwater brother when you restored the Crystal of Earth to its seat of power. You may now proceed with the ritual.*

Fen bowed her head and recited the sacred incantation to open the Guardian. Her lips moved swiftly, mouthing an inaudible conjuring.

Vibrations rolled back and forth between the pillar and the magicians. Fen continued her soundless spell and the quakes magnified and quickened, which jostled Fen and Kai sideways. Fen fought to keep her hands on the Guardian as her fingers slipped on the moss-covered surface. Kai dug his fingers into Fen's shoulder to maintain the connection.

Fen completed the incantation.

Clunk.

A muffled thud rippled throughout the circle. Darrius and Jake glanced toward the sound and then turned back to the Yfel. The Brethren had gathered into a circle around Balor and gave no indication they had detected anything.

It doesn't appear they heard that sound, Darrius messaged Jake.

Galena joined the men. *The Yfel cannot hear anything that occurs within the sacred circle. I've cast a noise suppression spell preventing the Cererians from hearing anything.*

We need to remain vigilant, Jake cautioned glancing over his shoulder toward the Cererians.

Grinding and growling, two rocky slabs slowly pulled apart, one lifting upward and the other retreating downward below the ground. When the shaking stopped, Fen stuck her fingers into the cavity, probing carefully for a notched recess. In the intense darkness, everything was shadowy and imperceptible.

"Kai, I think I found the keyhole," she whispered.

"I can't see anything, let me feel." He reached forward and followed Fen's hand into the cavity. "You're right. A skeleton key is needed."

Kai withdrew a small ebony box from his shirt and placed it on the ground. Reciting a sacred spell, he slid his fingers around the edge of the box, clockwise, until the lid popped open and revealed four skeleton keys. Eyes closed, Kai hovered his hand over the keys and waited for a gentle vibration to poke his palm.

"Ah, that's the one," he said. Then he reached into the box. Careful not to disturb the others, he pinched the appropriate key with his thumb and forefinger.

Following Fen's hand once again, Kai relocated the notch and maneuvered the skeleton key into the keyhole. He turned it to the right.

Click.

The key vanished and reappeared alongside the others in the ebony box, which then slammed shut. Kai picked it up and tucked it back into his shirt.

A low grumbling emanated from deep within the ground. Tremors rolled through the medicine wheel, shaking the Guardian boulder violently. The siblings closed their eyes as stone shards pelted them from above.

An explosion blasted from the base of the pillar, knocking Fen and Kai backward breaking their connection with the Guardian. The violent burst of energy opened a gap beneath the sacred stone. A luminescent blue light flickered from underneath the boulder, mesmerizing the siblings with its pulsing glow.

"That's different," Kai whispered, his eyes wide.

"Quick, Kai," Fen urged. "We need to finish our ritual. The Yfel will notice the illumination."

The siblings quickly scrambled back into position alongside the boulder with Fen placing her hands on the pillar and Kai laying his hand on her shoulder.

The Guardian vibrated in recognition. *Time grows short,* it warned.

Kai reached into the recess and located a smooth-sided chamber with a small groove in the middle. The skeleton key had done its job in revealing the seat of power on which Fen's family crystal would lie.

A subtle humming filled the air around the pillar. Barely audible at first, the soft melody intensified in volume and soon resembled the thrumming of a million honeybees.

Fen closed her eyes and wept.

"You're hearing the Guardian's song, aren't you?" Kai asked. "I can't hear it, but your face says something special is happening."

"Yes." Fen nodded.

The Guardian boulder connected with Fen:

Within this boulder, an entity lies waiting,
Awaiting the one who will remove the barrier,
Embracing the one who will quench our thirst,
And change the world with the element of water.

Tears trailed down Fen's cheeks as she listened to the beautiful words the Guardian boulder shared only with her.

My daughter, this sacred text is meant for you only. As I speak the words, your crystal will respond and yearn to be reunited with me. You may present your offering.

Fen removed the necklace from around her neck. Then she carefully plucked the pendant from the strand and separated the bluestone chip from the miniature feather. The diminutive stone was smaller than a dime. Pinching it between her thumb and forefinger, she raised it toward the Guardian.

I'm ready to receive your message, she reached out.

Very well, my daughter, the Guardian responded.

I stand alone, one of four,
United the four will be one,
The droplet inside you carries life,
Quench the world with your gift of water!

An explosion detonated high above the medicine wheel. The concussion catapulted Fen and Kai away from the Guardian with Fen tumbling further into her dimension while Kai flew back several yards into Jake's legs, knocking the shaman to the ground. During the commotion, the bluestone chip fell from Fen's hand and disappeared in Kai's physical realm.

We are in peril, the Guardian boulder warned as it recalled its granite slabs, first hiding the inner recess and then sealing the outside access to the boulder.

"The Yfel are firing above the Guardian boulder!" Darrius yelled.

Chance gripped his battle sword. "If it's a fight they want, I'm gonna make sure they get it."

Before he could move, another fireball exploded in the sky. Its concussion waves pinned everyone to the ground in a barrage of tornadic winds and searing heat.

Twisting against the force, Jake glanced up to see Hilly descending from the sky with Stygian by her side. She lingered above the central cairn, her body slowly rotating as she surveyed the area. She stopped and glared at Balor.

"Leave this sacred space or die!" she thundered.

"I knew you'd be drawn to our fireballs, Firewalker," Balor replied. "And I see you brought your lap dog."

Kill them, Hilly, Stygian sneered.

Patience. They will die soon enough.

"Attack the Firewalker!" Balor cried as he launched into the air followed by his brother, Cary. The remainder of the Brethren soared from all angles above the sacred circle until they had surrounded Hilly and Stygian.

"We need to help Hilly!" Jake yelled.

"Wait!" Darrius replied, gripping his friend's shoulder. "Look." Darrius pointed upward at Hilly and Stygian who stood back-to-back, hovering ten feet above the Guardian boulder. Hilly raised her hands outward to the side, fingers splayed and ready to deliver lethal doses of powerful energy.

She spun clockwise like a toy top. With his back pressed against hers, Stygian kept pace while protecting her flank. As they spun faster, they soon resembled a blurred column.

"The witch plays games!" Balor yelled. "Kill her!"

A large roar erupted as the Brethren rushed at the spinning duo.

The first bolts of fire from Hilly's hands vaporized Cary and three other Yfel. With each revolution, she discharged streams of flames forming a firestorm that incinerated Brethren with each turn.

"Die, Firewalker!" Balor screamed as he rushed her. But Stygian stopped the Cererian with a forceful blow momentarily stunning the Yfel soldier until Hilly incinerated him.

In less than a minute, the battle was over.

Hilly's flame-fueled cyclone of destruction transformed the night sky into an eerie red glow. Extreme heat and stinging smoke floated throughout the medicine wheel while the acrid smell of burning flesh drifted.

Charred bodies lay strewn along the outer boundary of the sacred circle.

Hilly descended to the ground with Stygian by her side.

Her eyes loomed black and menacing. Her hands glowed dark red, and heat waves radiated from the fingertips ready to deliver another bolt if a Yfel moved. A red aura shimmered around her as flames licked up her arms leaving momentary streaks of char before crimson skin returned.

Hilly panted.

"Hilly?" Kai carefully approached his sister.

"Halt, magician!" Stygian barked as he stepped in front of Hilly. "Stay clear. This is your only warning."

"What the fuck!" Chance cursed joining Kai. "She's our sister."

"Do as Stygian commands," Hilly boomed in a voice so loud everyone covered their ears and turned away. Abruptly, she marched toward Jake. Stygian paralleled her steps while watching for threatening moves from anybody.

"Jake," Hilly said in a softer tone as she approached. "We don't have much time. The Cererian army is almost here." Her eyes transitioned to emerald green and the glow around her body vanished. She stepped closer to the shaman. Residual heat from her body caused him to break out in a full body sweat.

"What do you need?" he asked.

Hilly reached forward and took his hand in hers and squeezed lightly. Then, cloaking her thoughts from the others, she messaged him. *This will be the last time we touch. The battle is nigh, and once I transform, I will see the fight to its completion.* She cupped his face and lightly ran her thumb across his cheek.

Jake gasped.

I've always loved you, Shaman, Hilly said. *From the moment I saw you at the airplane hangar, I knew our lives would forever be intertwined.*

I knew you were a Firewalker before you knew yourself, Jake's cockeyed smile crinkled laugh lines around his eyes. *You were naïve but determined.*

I found you arrogant, conceited, and often, an ass. She smiled.

Is this foreplay? Jake asked as a dimples popped in his cheeks.

She caressed his cheek one more time. *Time is short,* Hilly cautioned. *The natural Cererians are almost here. Don't let them kill you.* She leaned forward until her mouth lingered an inch from his face. She hesitated before lightly pressing her mouth on his.

Jake closed his eyes and swooned, surrendering to the feeling of freefalling into a volcano. His blood boiled and a flame, that started in his abdomen, raced up into his chest.

Hilly pulled away and rejoined Stygian. She dropped her head and clenched her fists. When she raised her head, her eyes had transformed to solid black. "The natural Cererians are minutes away," she announced, her voice gravelly and hoarse. "Since Stygian and Darrius are not permitted to kill their brothers, I suggest that you both stay out of our way so we can battle our adversaries unimpeded."

"Welcome, Firewalker," a female voice greeted.

Hilly whirled toward the sound. "Who—what are you?" she demanded.

"I am Galena."

Hilly bowed her head. "I'm honored by your presence sacred sister."

"Your arrival was expected," Galena replied. "I appreciate that you didn't violate the sanctity of the medicine wheel with your carnage. Through your intervention, you have released the imprisoned spirits within each Yfel soldier."

Galena gazed upward. "Behold a wondrous sight. Fireflies of freedom. Thousands of souls seeking the ether and eternal peace."

Everyone looked into the night sky which was illuminated by thousands of tiny lights swirling first above the sacred circle and then spiraling upward into the heavens.

An intense calm descended over the area.

Galena broke the trance. "The ritual must continue, or your efforts are in vain."

Hilly turned west. "The Cererians will be here soon. Jake, join me. We need to take this battle to them." She faced her brothers. "Chance, protect this sacred space. Kai, protect Fen as you two connect with the Guardian boulder."

"Darrius and I will join you," Stygian announced. "We may not be able to kill, but we can stun and perhaps buy you more time."

"I welcome both of you," Hilly agreed. Then she vanished.

One by one, the others followed her.

"Kai, get to work," Chance directed. "I'll stand guard. Whatever happens, don't stop. Promise me."

"I promise," Kai said. The brothers hugged.

Then Chance pulled Kai closer and whispered in his ear. "I now know what will happen. I'm disappointed I won't see Gabe again, but I'm proud to stand with my family one more time." He pushed Kai away, and the brothers gazed at each other with tears welling in their eyes. Chance swiped his face, turned, and marched away.

Kai sniffed back his tears as he watched his brother leave. He looked up to see Galena observing him. "Brothers," he said. "Just when you think you've got them all figured out, they go mushy on you."

"Yes," Galena nodded. "Humans are unpredictable. Do you remember you have a job to complete, magician?"

"Shit," Kai cursed. "Sorry, Galena, I meant no disrespect."

"Nothing offends me, magician. Fen awaits you at the Guardian." She gestured toward the central cairn.

"Are you ready?" Kai asked as he approached Fen.

"I am," she replied. "Except, there's a problem. I've lost my family crystal."

"What?"

"That last explosion threw me to the ground. I must have dropped it. I've searched my dimension for it. I must have dropped it in your physical world."

"Galena, can you help?" Kai pleaded.

"Alas, I cannot," she replied. "You must hurry. The others are already engaged in combat with the natural Cererians."

Kai dropped to the ground, moving his hands back and forth through the dirt searching for the dime-size bluestone chip. In the pitch black his eyes were useless, so he engaged his intuition and mindfully hunted for the elusive gem.

Fen knelt in front of the Guardian boulder and placed her hands on its rough, granite surface. Starting over from the beginning, she searched for the hidden symbols once again. "Hurry Kai," she urged.

"I'm hurrying, Fen. Chance, come and help me search for Fen's gem. She lost it when the Yfel exploded those fireballs."

Chance rushed to his side. "What am I looking for?"

"A dime-sized bluestone chip."

"Bluestone? That's the stone of my family. I'm sure I'll find it." Both men crawled around, their hands pushing in front of them as they moved back and forth sifting through the dirt.

"Kai, you need to place your hands on me so we can reestablish the connection with the Guardian boulder," Fen insisted.

"Go on, Kai," Chance said. "Get set up.I'll find your gem."

Kai knelt beside his sister and placed his hand on her shoulder. A soft vibration rolled through the ground and into their bodies.

My children, the Guardian boulder spoke. *We have reestablished the connection. We were interrupted, so I'll begin again. But first, I will expose the receptacle.* Grinding and growling ensued as the two rocky slabs pulled apart, screeching until a small recess was visible.

"Kai, we need your key again," Fen said urgently. "Please hurry."

Withdrawing the ebony box from his shirt, he opened the lid and placed the container on the ground. Then he held his hand over the skeleton keys until one psychically poked his palm. He deftly plucked it from the box and carefully maneuvered it into the small recess then turned the key to the right.

Click.

Again, the key disappeared and reappeared with the other keys in the ebony box, which slammed shut. More stones moved apart on the

Guardian until a smooth-sided chamber with a small notch in the middle was revealed.

My daughter, this holy text is meant for you only. As I speak the words, your crystal will respond and yearn to be reunited with me. You may present your offering.

Fen glanced at Chance who crept along the ground on his forearms. "Anything Chance?"

"I'm still looking...don't worry."

Fen faced the boulder. *I'm ready to receive your message,* she replied.

Very well, my daughter, the Guardian responded.

I stand alone, one of four,
United the four will be one,
The droplet inside you carries life,
Quench the world with your gift of water!

"Found it!" Chance yelled. He pinched a tiny blue sliver between his thumb and forefinger.

"Give it me, Chance," Kai requested, extending his hand. Chance carefully placed the chip into his brother's palm.

Keeping his hand as steady as possible, Kai maneuvered the crystal to Fen's shadowy hand protruding through the veil separating their worlds.

"I have it, Kai!" she said.

She placed the bluestone chip onto its seat of power within the Guardian boulder. The instant the gem fell into the notch, the inner and outer slabs slammed together while stone shards showered the siblings from above.

The Guardian boulder was whole once again.

Silence filled the sacred circle.

The siblings gazed at each other, relief brightening their weary eyes. Fen raised her hand against the magical veil between their worlds. Kai pressed his hand against her palm. Then Chance placed his hand on top of Kai's.

Then the ground shuddered.

Kai and Chance jumped to their feet. Chance withdrew his battle sword and held it in front of him while Kai held his hands up ready to deliver bolts of magic. The brothers searched the darkness for intruders, but nobody had penetrated the medicine wheel.

The ground convulsed again as seismic waves, originating at the Guardian, fanned outward in all directions. The shockwaves, deep within the ground, delivered an important message throughout the world: *Water has been restored. The final marker is secure!*

"Did you hear that?" Kai asked Chance.

"Yeah. We did it!"

Light exploded from the top of the Guardian boulder stabbing deep into space illuminating the dark night with a surreal glow. The Kemps covered their faces, shielding their eyes from the brightness.

"What's going on?" Chance asked. "This didn't happen at Bear Seamount."

The laser beam split and strobed, pulsing shafts of white light into all directions, replacing the darkness of night with the brightness of an artificial day.

"Brothers," Galena softly spoke as she laid a hand on their shoulders. "Come with me."

"Why?" Chance challenged.

"It's time," she replied.

"Oh." Chance dropped his sword and slipped his hand into Galena's. She led him to the cairn facing north. "Stand here, Keeper of the Records. Do not leave your post, no matter what you see."

Taking Kai's hand, she brought him east to the next stack of stones. "Stay here, Keeper of the Keys. Do not move no matter what occurs."

Kai nodded.

Galena crossed the wheel to the cairn facing west and gestured for Fen to join her. With Bodhi leading the way, Fen took her place by the tower of stones. "Guardian of Peace, remain here."

The entity returned to the Guardian boulder, which shuddered and shook as more laser beams exploded from its core illuminating a column of small pebbles rising into the sky.

Galena gazed westward. *Hilly and Jake are needed so the Prophecy can reach completion.*

A shower of lasers struck the ground just outside the sacred circle pelting the Kemps with clouds of gritty debris.

"Look!" Chance yelled pointing into the distance.

Ten Cererian travel pods loomed on the horizon. Pinpoints of light bobbed up and down as they advanced forward. They fired again. Thin streaks of light peppered the desert floor pushing clouds of dust into the air.

"Where's Hilly and Stygian?" Kai yelled.

"Where's Jake and Darrius?" Chance shouted.

"Don't leave your posts!" Galena ordered "Stay where you are." Galena raised her arms toward the advancing armies, her palms facing outward. *Come to me, Firewalker. Come to me, Chronicle.*

Hilly flickered into view beside Galena. Flames licked from her skin while fire engulfed her head and hair.

She hurried to Chance. "You will always be my big brother, the dependable soul who always made me feel safe and secure, and the only one who could comfort me when I had nightmares. I love you. Be well, brother."

Not waiting for a reply, she trotted to Kai. "Kai, without you, there would be no joy in my world. Your creativity and humor opened my eyes to a fanciful world I would never have known existed. I love you. Be well, brother."

Kai began to speak, but Hilly had already run to Fen. "Fen, my studious big sister. You taught me how to view nature through a different lens, and how to appreciate the quiet moments when only the sound of our breaths was enough to sustain us. I love you. Be well, sister."

Without another word, she marched to the vacant cairn in the south, turned and faced the center of the medicine wheel.

Stygian, Darrius, and Jake arrived simultaneously.

Jake slumped to the ground. Blood oozed from a gash on his forehead and from his arm where it had been amputated below the elbow. Blood spurted from the gaping wound.

"Help me, Stygian," Darrius urged as he gripped Jake's arm to stop the bleeding. Jake groaned but did not cry out.

Stygian placed his hands over the raw stump and mouthed words. The conjuring quickened until the bleeding eased and the ragged edges of the stump crusted over. "This will have to do for now. I don't have time to complete the healing process."

A barrage of laser beams fired over their heads, forcing everyone to flatten to the ground.

Everyone, except Galena.

The sacred sister stood patiently by the Guardian boulder holding her hands upward toward the eruptions of luminescent light that shot from the top of the pillar.

"Stygian...Darrius...you must leave the sacred circle," she ordered.

The Cererians hesitated. "NOW!" she screamed as another barrage of lasers passed through the medicine wheel.

They gently placed Jake on the ground and hurried beyond the outer ring of the medicine wheel.

Galena raised her arms toward the Guardian boulder and conjured her magic. "As it was a millennium ago, let it be now."

The Guardian boulder pulsed violently, jetting more white light into the atmosphere. The intense beam exploded into the stratosphere and then arced in all directions like a dome. Another stream of light shot upward into space before looping back to the boulder and then radiating into the four cairns of the medicine wheel: north, south, east, and west.

The shafts of light penetrated Hilly, Fen, Chance, and Kai and the magicians shuddered violently against the ferocity of the blast. Their heads flung backward, their eyes squeezed shut, and their hands splayed out to either side. After several moments, intense white light discharged from their fingers, each beam penetrating the adjoining siblings on either side, completing the connection between the Guardian and each magician.

Jake hunkered down by Galena's feet, his breaths ragged and erratic.

"Rise, Chronicle," she ordered.

He rolled onto his back and stared up at her. Holding his injured arm, he grimaced as he forced himself to stand. "I...am...ready," he said haltingly.

"Ascend," the earth entity ordered. "Ascend my Chronicle and begin a new millennium of peace!" Galena raised her hands, sending Jake upward in the air until he hovered just above the Guardian boulder.

The shaman floated outside the intense beam of light shooting from the top. Deep shadows framed his face, which was bathed in a soft glow. Although battered and bloodied, his expression was steadfast.

He gazed westward. The Cererian transport pods lingered outside the sacred circle. Without further hesitation, he stepped into the brilliant beam of light.

Instantly, a dome of light exploded over the medicine wheel. Fed by luminescent streams coming from each magician, the Guardian boulder, and Jake, the entire area was engulfed in energy. The light-filled dome pulsed as it connected with each life force, finding their rhythm, and synchronizing their heartbeats.

Shockwaves rocketed in all directions. Like wind tsunamis, these invisible waves rushed outward in all directions covering the entire planet.

Magic and death rode the crest of these energetic swells, vaporizing any Cererian they encountered—benevolent, Yfel, and natural. The force of the blast pushed the seismic ripples further into space, engulfing the dwarf planet of Ceres and annihilating its inhabitants.

The pulses continued for five minutes and then stopped.

Quiet returned to the desert.

A smoky haze hung over the medicine wheel. A quiet breeze born from supernatural origins swirled, cleaning the sacred circle of smoke and debris, collecting its contents and drawing them up into the air and pulling them far away from the sacred site.

Stillness returned.

Galena walked through the medicine wheel, lightly touching the giant monoliths that had replaced the smaller cairns in the north, east, south, and west directions. Constructed of granite, each standing stone soared ten feet high. Symbols had been carved into each side. And as Galena lightly brushed the markings, they illuminated in recognition of the sacred sister. Once she had visited all four monoliths, she walked into the center. A twenty-foot stone pillar crafted from granite and bluestone had replaced the original Guardian boulder. It, too, had symbols etched into each side and as she drifted upward she lovingly stroked each marking, the symbol responding with a pulse of light.

Galena spoke softly. "The Chronicle has ascended. Peace has been restored to our world." She gazed upward. Thousands of tiny lights swirled into the heavens as freed souls spiraled into the ether.

Gabe was in the study at The Nine Muses. He slept soundly in a comfy chair with his arms wrapped around his body, hands tucked into his armpits, and his chin drooped upon his chest. When he snorted awake, he scratched his head, yawned, and stood.

What time is it?

He sauntered into the foyer.

"Alden," he called out.

A haunting echo replied to him.

A light burned in the dining room, and the door was ajar. He walked in. "Bob? Benedict?"

Some food remained on the table, but he noticed a platter of potatoes had crashed to the floor in the doorway leading from the kitchen. *That's odd,* he thought. Glancing around the room, he noticed other things out of place: a glass of wine had crashed to the floor in front of a chair, food bowls and plates on the table had been shoved close to the edge as though something, or somebody, had fallen and pushed them to the side.

What happened?

Frowning, he backed out of the dining room and returned to the foyer. As he passed the chair and telephone table in front of the fireplace, he noticed a bright white envelope. When he picked it up, black elegant cursive spelled his name: Gabriel.

He turned it over, lifted the flap and pulled out the folded sheet of paper that had been tucked inside. He recognized Alden's signature at the end of the note.

Dear Gabriel,
By the time you read this, I, and my colleagues, will be no more. Depending on your beliefs, we are in the ether or someplace where all souls go to rest. Jake, Hilly, Chance, Fen, and Kai have fulfilled their mission to ensure the Prophecy reached completion, allowing the Chronicle to ascend.

Peace has been restored to your world.

As part of the agreement forged a millennium ago, this day also meant that all Cererians were erased from existence, including those on Ceres. The Yfel Brethren are no more. Darrius and Stygian are gone. And it pains me to inform you that Jake and the Kemps are also gone. But they now watch over and protect the earth in their new forms. I hope, one day, you'll be able to travel to where they are and honor their sacrifice. I've provided directions.

Gabe withdrew a folded card where Alden had scribbled a name and a rough map. "Big Horn Medicine Wheel," Gabe whispered. He turned the paper over where Alden continued.

It's your turn to perform your part for the Prophecy. You are the Speaker of Truths. It is your responsibility to inform the world about the accomplishments of Jake, Hilly, Fen, Chance, and Kai. You will visit their families and reveal the truths of the five magicians who saved the planet. As a member of the Earth tribe, you'll continue your cousin's teachings and educate Chance's gifted children in using their magic appropriately and growing up in a world that embraces uniqueness. You will be instrumental in guiding Chance's son, Wyatt, as the next Keeper of the Records.

I've included the contact information you'll need.

I wish I could have said goodbye but then that would have spoiled the surprise.

Be well, Gabriel.

Yours in spirit,
Alden Stark

"Blimey," Gabe uttered. He folded the note into the envelope and tucked it inside his shirt pocket.

The house loomed large and deathly quiet as though he stood inside a three-story mausoleum. He shuddered and walked to the large picture window where he watched the placid surface of the ocean, allowing pleasant memories to return of him and Chance meeting for the first time, the two cousins exploring Stonehenge, and the two of them battling the Yfel.

"No!" he cried slumping to the floor. "Chance! Chance!" He sobbed uncontrollably.

Eventually, he rolled onto his side and hugged his knees to his chest. After decades of searching for his cousin, he found him only to lose him without even being able to say goodbye.

"Rise, Speaker of Truths," a female commanded.

Gabe choked on tears as he gazed upward and found a strange woman standing in the doorway. Barefoot and wearing a simple tan shift, the black-haired woman extended her hand.

"Take my hand, Gabriel," she said softly.

"Who...who are ye?" he asked, his voice quavering.

"I am Galena."

"A sacred sister?" he asked, gripping her hand and rising to his feet. "Is that truly ye?"

The entity smiled. "Yes."

He bowed his head. "Why have ye come here?"

"The Prophecy is completed, and the Chronicle has ascended. You must now spread the word of the heroics that were performed today."

"Aye, Alden left me a note about that."

"But how can you sing their praises if you don't know what happened?" Galena took a step forward and Gabe backed up.

"Whatcha mean?" he asked shakily.

"The Speaker of Truths must have firsthand experience before he can celebrate the accomplishments of the warriors." Galena stepped closer.

Gabe tried to move backward, but his feet seemed stuck to the floor.

Galena placed fingers on either side of his forehead. "You will now see what I witnessed."

Gabe went rigid, and his eyes rolled back. A soft white glow formed around the sacred sister's fingers and engulfed Gabe's head.

After several moments, Galena removed her hands, and Gabe slumped to his knees.

The sacred sister knelt beside him. She lifted his chin and gazed into his eyes. "You know everything, Speaker of Truths. The world must know what transpired."

"I...don't know...if I...can," Gabe gasped.

"If you are a true cousin of the warrior, Chance, you'll be honored to share the truth of his selflessness and the courage of the noble warriors who joined him in their final battle so the rest of the world could finally live in peace."

Galena gripped his arm and hefted him to his feet.

"Go in peace, Speaker of Truths," she said as she quietly faded away until she vanished.

Stunned, Gabe stared at the empty space the sacred sister had occupied. He squeezed his eyes against the fresh memories she had fed him: the fire, the death, the sacrifice.

"Aye," he uttered aloud. "I promise, cousin, I'll make sure the world understands what happened today. I won't rest me bones until I've told everyone how ye and the others sacrificed your lives so the rest of us could live in peace.

Chapter 33

The Speaker of Truths

Three Months Later

GABE NERVOUSLY SIPPED HIS Guinness while watching the entrance of Flanagan's Irish Pub from his barstool. He glanced at the door every time anybody entered. Then he'd rush toward them, introduce himself, and watch the patron stroll away shaking their head, and eyeing him suspiciously.

He was expecting some important guests but had no idea what most of them looked like.

"Paddy, another if ye please," he asked the bartender as he slid his glass down the bar.

"Righto, Gabe!"

Since Galena's revelation at The Nine Muses, Gabe had thrown all his energy into his new role as Speaker of Truths, determined to inform everybody about his friends' accomplishments. He had something to prove and atone for. Embracing this important position would give him the opportunity to make amends for betraying Hilly and disappointing his cousin, Chance.

He began first with their family members. It took some effort, but he managed to contact the relatives of Jake, Hilly, Chance, and Kai. Fen's husband, Lance, had passed away years earlier, so she had no other living relatives.

Jake's relatives were already aware of his sacrifice and had sung his achievements at a clan meeting. Jake's kin declined attending Gabe's gathering. Instead, they honored their shaman privately in the shadows of his beloved Sentinel boulder.

Gabe yearned to personally meet with Chance's wife, Janet. Since she was a Folk—a non-magical person—Gabe knew she'd be vulnerable during this period when her magical children would be aware of the Guardian's message that raced around the world.

During their brief chat on the phone, Gabe discovered that her two oldest sons were also Folk, and all of them had struggled processing Chance's death amid the barrage of information the supernatural community shared every day with her children with incredible powers.

Their initial meeting was awkward and painful.

As he walked up to Janet's house, he noticed the pleasant garden in the front yard with a variety of colorful flowers and fragrant herbs, a bubbling fountain, and several pentacles dangling in the breeze.

A proud magical family lives here, he'd thought as he mounted the steps to the front door. He knocked and waited. A shadow appeared through the translucent glass. First the figure hesitated and then opened the door.

"Gabe?" a young man greeted.

"Aye. Are ye, Wyatt?"

The young man nodded. "Come in," he said, waving Gabe into the hallway. "Mom and my sisters are in the living room."

When Gabe entered, Janet stood behind her twin daughters, her arms protectively draped across their chests.

"Hello, I'm Gabriel. I'm Chance's cousin."

Janet's bottom lip quivered, and she clenched the girls closer.

"This is my mom, Janet, and my sisters Maeve and Myla," Wyatt offered as he led Gabe to the sofa. "Please sit. Would you like anything to drink?"

"Thank you, kindly, but no." Gabe smiled and nodded at the women.

The girls took a step forward, but Janet pulled them back.

The sisters turned and looked at their mother.

"It's okay, Mom," Maeve reassured.

"Gabe's going to tell us about daddy," Myla added.

Reluctantly, Janet released the girls, and they sat on either side of Gabe.

"Yer eyes are just like your daddy's," Gabe began. "And you share his stunning smile. Lights up a room."

Janet sobbed and held her hand up to her mouth as she rushed from the room.

Wyatt watched her leave. "I'm sorry, Gabe. Mom's having a hard time dealing with all of this." He strode over to the large, overstuffed chair—the one his father had once claimed as his own—and sat down. He leaned back, crossed his legs, and stared at Gabe.

"Ye have your da's manner," Gabe said. "Kind but direct. I wager you also have a wee bit of your da's love of fun."

Maeve and Myla giggled.

"Girls!" Wyatt shouted.

"Wyatt is just like his father." All heads turned toward Janet who leaned against the door frame. "He's been my rock since...since it happened." Janet smiled sweetly at her son who beamed back at her.

"I find it difficult to understand why he did it," Janet continued. "How can a man choose to leave his family..." Her voice trailed off as she brought her hand to her mouth and sobbed.

Wyatt hurried to his mother's side and folded her into his arms. Although he was only sixteen, he was six feet tall and broad shouldered—a mirror image of his father.

Maeve tapped Gabe on his shoulder.

"Yes, little miss?"

"Daddy once told me that all the members of the Earth family have a triskele birthmark on their foot."

"Aye, ya da was correct."

In seconds, both Maeve and Myla pulled off their socks and sneakers and waved their feet in Gabe's face.

"Like this?" they screamed in unison.

Gabe laughed as he removed his boot and sock. "Aye, just like this!" The trio waved their feet around and laughed until tears ran down their cheeks.

Wyatt cleared his throat, prompting everyone to stop.

"What?" Maeve asked.

"Gabe, as you know, Mom doesn't possess powers like we do," Wyatt explained. "But she is head of this family and that will never change. I took Mom somewhere so we could make her an official member of the Earth family."

The twins jumped off the couch.

"What did you do?" Maeve asked.

Wyatt nodded at his mother and Janet slipped her right foot out of her sandal and held it aloft until the bottom of her foot was exposed.

"Mom had a triskele tattooed on her foot," Wyatt said. "Dad would be so proud."

The girls examined the tattoo against their birthmarks. Then they hugged their mother tightly. Janet wove her arm around Wyatt and drew him into the group hug.

A proud magical family, Gabe thought. "Please sit down everyone, I have a story to tell you."

Now on his fourth Guinness, Gabe anxiously awaited his visitors: Janet and her family, including her two older, non-magical sons, Kai's husband, Jeff, and Hilly's estranged husband, Curtis.

"Gabe, when are ye guests arriving?" Paddy asked.

"Soon, I hope. I've got butterflies all in me stomach." He sipped his beer and smacked his lips. "Ah, much better."

The door opened. The glare of the sunshine momentarily blinded Gabe as he strained to see who entered.

"Gabe!" Janet shouted. She entered followed by a throng of family members, including her son, Wyatt and Maeve and Myla.

She hugged Gabe and introduced her family. "You already know my youngest, now let me introduce you to my two oldest boys, Chad and Jason." She shepherded her sons toward Gabe.

Gabe shook the young men's hands.

Janet continued with introductions. "This is Chad's wife, Mary. They have beautiful twin baby girls who aren't here today. They're being watched by Mary's mother."

"A lovely family, Janet," Gabe replied. "We're waiting for a few more people but please help yourself to the buffet in the back room and order anything you like from the bar."

"Thanks, Gabe." Janet smiled at him through weary but determined eyes. Her family walked away, but she still gripped Gabe's hand.

"Mom, it will be okay," Wyatt soothed as he untangled her fingers from Gabe's. "Let's go get some food." He nodded at Gabe as he led his mother to the back room.

A few minutes later, a man entered the pub.

He took off his hat and ran his fingers through his thick, brown hair as he gazed around allowing his eyes to adjust to the dim light.

"Could you be Jeff?" Gabe asked approaching the man.

"I am," he replied flashing a brilliant white smile. "How did you know?"

"The mole on your left cheek," Gabe replied. "I had that in me notes."

"I see," Jeff softly said as he looked down at the floor.

Gabe noticed tears welling in Jeff's eyes and blurted, "Kai told me about Beatrice Brandy"

Jeff glanced up, dabbing the tears from his eyes. "He did?"

"Yep. And how he got you into trouble during his opening night."

Jeff nodded and smiled. "The scamp did. He left me holding the lush and went off dancing into the night. What else did Kai tell you?"

Gabe's eyes twinkled. "Come with me Jeff, I have a story to tell you." He guided Jeff toward a private room, first stopping at the bar to collect some drinks. "Here," he said, pushing a vodka and tonic into Jeff's hands. "You'll need this." Gabe turned to the bartender, "Paddy, please make sure we're not interrupted."

"Righto, Gabe!"

A half hour later, Gabe and Jeff emerged with their arms around one another. "Paddy, another drink for me mate, Jeff," Gabe requested.

"You're too kind," Jeff replied.

"Come on, Jeff, let me take you to Chance's family." Gabe led Jeff into the back room.

"You must be Kai's husband," Janet said as she approached them. "I'm Janet. Chance was my husband." The two briefly gazed at each other before falling into each other's arms sobbing.

Gabe returned to the front of the bar and found a curly-haired man sitting by himself. He hunched over a pilsner and didn't look up when Gabe approached.

"Might you be Curtis?" Gabe asked as he leaned on the counter.

"Who wants to know," the man replied without looking up.

"I'm Gabe, the one who invited you here."

Slowly, the man lifted his head. Weary eyes framed by dark circles stared back. "I don't know why I came," he said. "Hilly and I parted on bad terms.

"May I join you?" Gabe asked as he motioned for Paddy to pour more beers.

"Do what you want."

Gabe pushed a beer toward Curtis and sipped his own. "I'm glad you showed up."

"Sure...whatever." Curtis gulped the remnants of his beer and slammed the glass on the counter.

Paddy frowned.

"It's okay, Paddy. We're cool," Gabe soothed. Then he leaned toward Curtis. "You have a choice. You can listen to what I have to say about Hilly, or you can leave. I won't bother you again. But before you make that decision, understand that Chance and Kai's spouses are already here and would love to meet you."

Curtis glared at Gabe through bloodshot eyes. "Understand this, Gabe. I'm done with Hilly and her magic shit show. She left me for some god-damned vision quest and a shaman who's probably stealing her blind. She's dead to me!" Curtis rose to leave but Gabe grabbed his shoulder.

"Hilly *is* dead," Gabe said solemnly.

Curtis's mouth dropped open. His lips moved but no words came out.

Gabe quietly guided him back to his stool.

"Wha—what happened?" Curtis stammered, sniffing and rubbing his eyes.

Gabe's eyes twinkled. "Come with me, Curtis. I have a story to tell you."

Curtis followed Gabe to the private room. "Paddy, see to it we're not interrupted, okay?" Gabe asked.

"Righto!"

Thirty minutes later, Gabe and Curtis emerged from the back room. Curtis leaned into Gabe's embrace, his face red and wet from tears. They stopped outside the room where Chance's family and Jeff were chatting and laughing.

"Why don't you pop in for a quick hello?" Gabe urged.

Curtis's gaze flicked around the group. His eyes brightened, then darkened when sorrow returned.

"No, that's okay," he replied as he headed for the front door. "I appreciate you telling me about Hilly. There was more to her than I could imagine. She was always the strong one, and I'm glad that's the role she played even to the end."

Laughter erupted from the back room. Curtis glanced up but turned away. "It's best that I leave. I've never had a connection with those in Hilly's life. I've learned to be on my own."

"I'll honor your wishes," Gabe said as he patted Curtis' shoulder.

"Thanks." A weak smile fluttered on Curtis's face as he extended his hand. Gabe shook it and watched Curtis leave.

Gabe reflected for a moment. How did some Folk embrace their magical relatives while others turn their backs on the supernatural abilities of their loved ones?

More laughter erupted from the back room.

This time, Gabe joined the others, so he could share more stories of the five extraordinary individuals who saved the world, and the Cererians who sacrificed their lives to ensure the magicians were successful.

Chapter 34

The Cererian Prophecy

"GABE, PLEASE TELL US the rest of the story," Jeff urged. "We know bits and pieces of The Cererian Prophecy, but I still don't understand how Kai became part of it."

"Gather 'round, if you please," Gabe called out, gesturing toward a white board.

Everyone obediently pulled their chairs closer.

"How did Dad know what to do and when?" Wyatt asked.

"How can something invisible prompt people to...to willingly die?" The room quieted after Janet's question. Her sons, Chad and Wyatt, sat on either side of her, and she gripped their hands tightly.

Gabe took a long sip of his Guinness while pondering the questions. He ran his tongue over the frothy mustache coating his upper lip. "The Cererian Prophecy. 'Tis a complicated subject. So, I'll start at the beginning." Gabe pulled the movable white board closer and studied the various colors of markers lined up on the ledge. He chose blue and held it aloft. "This was me cousin's favorite color."

He drew a circle with the numbers 1013 on the left side of the board and tapped it with his marker. "This is when evil came to our world." He drew a larger circle in the middle of the board with the numbers 2012 and four smiley faces. "This is when the chosen four were awakened." He added another circle to the right with the number 2013 and a peace symbol. "And this is when The Prophecy was completed.

"What's complicated is everything that happened between these three events." He slurped his beer and studied the crowd.

As if on cue, everyone also took a sip of their drinks.

"What was the evil?" Maeve asked.

"Yes!" Myla exclaimed. "How did it get here?"

"In one word...Cererians," Gabe replied.

Disgruntled murmurs spread throughout the room. Gabe frowned as he heard "good riddance" and "glad they're dead."

"You sound mad at the Cererians," he observed.

"Why shouldn't we be?" Chad spat as he jumped from his chair. "They caused this mess that killed my dad." The word *dad* was barely out of his mouth when he crumpled to the floor in tears. Wyatt ran to his side.

"That's the first time he's cried since it happened," Janet noted as she knelt and stroked her son's hair.

"But there were benevolent Cererians like Darrius!" Jeff proclaimed. "My husband, Kai, spoke fondly of Darrius, Alden, and Benedict."

"Aye," Gabe said. "As ye can see, there's many sides to this story."

Wyatt guided Chad back to his chair. Janet placed her head on his chest and rubbed his arm. "Go on, Gabe," Wyatt prompted. "Tell us what happened."

Gabe withdrew a leather-bound notebook held together with a long brown strap, which was tied in a perfect bow. The book cover was smooth and shiny in some places and had obviously been used often. He held it up. "This is Darrius's notebook. He kept meticulous notes dating back to his arrival on earth."

He untied the bow and flipped through several yellowed pages. Then he tapped the circle on the left side with his marker. "One thousand years ago, our planet flourished in peace and prosperity sustained by earth spirits like Mount Denali, Mount Shasta, and Yr Wyddfa to name a few. These natural entities sustained the world through an endless supply of positive energy that allowed magical people to enhance their powers and provide for their families and villages. Folk—non magical people—contributed as much as their magical counterparts. There was no famine, no poverty, no hatred.

"But our future was altered when a Cererian exploration team arrived in the Alaskan region now known as the Mat-Su Valley." Gabe paused and sipped his beer while peering at Chad who sneered back at him. Janet stroked his arm.

"Their original mission was benign. They were to observe the inhabitants while collecting information on the flora and fauna. It's important to note their main directive was not to interfere. Period.

"To blend in, they arrived in a human form, which was created by merging human DNA with their Cererian lifeforce."

"How were they able to do that?" Jeff asked.

"We're getting closer to the root of the issue." Gabe winked. "Human DNA had been collected from cadavers by Cererian Harvesters, who arrived months earlier with the sole responsibility for locating DNA from a diverse population of deceased humans. This meant that the Harvesters travelled the globe collecting samples from all the continents."

"Wait," Chad interrupted. "If they were already here, why didn't they collect their flora and fauna data then?"

Gabe sighed. "See. It's rather complicated as I promised. Cererians in their natural state resembled spheres of energy and required the use of specially constructed transport pods that sustained their life while visiting Earth. But the vehicle's power would last no more than twenty-four hours. These limitations forced the Cererians to find a solution so they could explore our world for longer periods of time. The result was a hybrid form, one that merged Cererian energy with human DNA.

"Nobody could have predicted what would happen. Darrius notes that the Cererians should have devoted more time researching the possible side effects. But they were under pressure by the government to expedite the mission. So, they cut corners."

Gabe glanced around the room. Expressions ranged from fascination to smoldering anger. He swallowed the rest of his Guinness, walked to the door, and yelled, "Another round, Paddy!"

"Righto, Gabe!"

Gabe strolled back to the whiteboard.

"I have a question," Wyatt said raising his hand in the air. "Because the Cererians rushed creating these hybrids, did the evil you mentioned earlier develop on Ceres as a result of them skipping steps, or did the evil evolve here on Earth?"

"Excellent question, Wyatt. And it brings us to the core of the issue."

Paddy burst in with a tray full of drinks and distributed them to outstretched hands. He handed Gabe a Guinness and left.

Gabe swallowed long and hard before starting again.

"The evil was born on Ceres but matured here on earth. The Cererians who came to our planet carried the essence of two cultures within their bodies—their strict Cererian sensibilities and the traits of the human donors. Almost from inception, their bodies struggled adapting to the clash of these extreme characteristics. Human DNA was more influential over personality development and many of the soldiers found themselves either more aggressive or docile depending on the donor's temperament.

"Stygian was the leader of the exploration team, and it was he who developed into the evil that plunged our world into darkness."

"How?" Wyatt asked.

Gabe rustled through the notebook, found the page he was searching for, and answered. "From Darrius's notes, it appears Stygian struggled with his body's transformation, becoming more agitated each day. He beat his soldiers for any violation although physical punishment was not a Cererian discipline method. He became more erratic and unpredictable as time went on."

"I'm confused. Is that the evil you mentioned?" Jeff asked.

Gabe held up his hand. "I'm getting there, I promise."

He flipped several pages in the notebook and continued, "When the peaceful villagers invited the Cererians to one of their feasts, that's when Stygian's personality truly transformed. He became savage and brutish, abandoning his polite Cererian manners altogether. Then, later that day while attending the funeral of a warrior who possessed incredible powers, he inadvertently breathed in the man's spirit as the soul sought the ether."

"Ether?" Maeve asked.

"Yes. The place where souls go. The heavens."

"Where Daddy is," she stated.

Gabe smiled gently. "Yes. Where ya da stands watch over you and yours."

Maeve turned to her twin. The two girls chatted softly with each other.

"Darrius had a choice." Gabe's voice grew serious. "As the deceased warrior's spirit tried to escape Stygian's body Darrius could have killed his friend and allowed the entrapped soul to flee into the ether or wait to see what would happen. Since Cererians are forbidden from killing each other Darrius chose to wait.

"That's when the evil took flight. While Darrius slept, Stygian escaped the Cererian camp with two soldiers. Together they attacked the villagers who had been cordial and friendly toward them, killing them and consuming their magical essence.

"Stygian and his soldiers were the beginning of the Yfel Brethren."

The room became uncomfortably quiet. Even the twins ceased their soft chatter and stared at Gabe with puzzled eyes.

"And The Cererian Prophecy?" Jeff asked.

Gabe sipped his beer and looked at Jeff over the mug's rim.

"That's an easier question to answer," he responded. "But it's still quite complicated."

Gabe pulled a chair closer and sat down. "You can imagine how Darrius felt. His closest friend had become something akin to a monster and was killing humans—a direct violation of their mission. It was Darrius's responsibility to report him to his superiors. But instead of supporting Darrius, the Cererian government turned on him accusing him of impropriety and not supporting his commander. They instructed him to stand by as they determined how to neutralize the situation.

"But while he awaited his fate, a familiar voice drifted into his brain. He had received a message from the same earth spirit when he first arrived."

"An earth spirit?" Wyatt asked.

"Denali to be exact," Gabe replied. "When Darrius first arrived with the exploration team, his body adjusted in a different manner becoming more attuned to the energy that thrummed throughout the area. One day, a voice spoke to him, contacting him telepathically, and identifying itself as Mount Denali. This earth spirit recognized the shaman energy within Darrius.

"Once Stygian and his soldiers began their killing spree, the earth spirit reached out to Darrius and demanded retribution for introducing the evil to her land." Gabe paused and referenced the leather tome.

"Darrius wrote, 'I was besieged with new human emotions: guilt, shame, and an intense responsibility to correct the wrong. I had no choice but to help in any way I could for I was now possessed with an overwhelming sense of duty to the inhabitants of Earth.'"

Gabe studied the crowd. Even Chad who was surly minutes earlier seemed saddened.

"In a somber ceremony, the spirits of Mount Denali, Mount Shasta, Yr Wyddfa and Darrius developed a plan that would become known as The Cererian Prophecy. In one thousand years, peace would be restored through the selfless sacrifices of four magicians and a shaman.

"This prophecy created by powerful earth spirits was a living, magical entity capable of influencing both humans and Cererians. Throughout the years, the Prophecy would drop pieces of information into the consciousness of individuals providing them with only the information they needed at a particular moment.

"Chance, Kai, Fen, and Hilly were born with knowledge of their magical families but, under the direction of the earth spirits, Darrius and other beneficial Cererians masked the children's memories so any connections to their supernatural lineages would be broken making it impossible for the Yfel Brethren to find them.

"Well, *almost* impossible. Stygian's link to Hilly was discovered later. A surprise to many.

"Once Darrius and Prasad, another benevolent Cererian, unlocked the repressed memories of the four magicians in a ceremony known as the Revelation, the knowledge and understanding of their powers flooded into their consciousness. Each person continued to transform into the people they were destined to be, but at different rates. This was a peculiarity of The Cererian Prophecy."

Gabe eyed the crowd who appeared deep in thought processing the vast amounts of information he just shared. He had expected many questions at this point, but everyone was silent.

Gabe referenced the notebook and continued, "But there were strict conditions to The Cererian Prophecy. Darrius and other benevolent Cererians were solely responsible for protecting the chosen four and ensuring they survived to complete their final task. And the Cererians complied though they were aware their success also meant death for themselves and the Cererian race."

"That seems harsh," Jeff observed. "It wasn't Darrius's fault."

"Yeah," Chad agreed. "I mean, I'm pissed off at these Cererians, but Darrius didn't do anything wrong. He couldn't kill Stygian. It went against his beliefs." Janet beamed at her son.

Gabe finished the remnants of his beer. "Are there any questions?"

"I have one," Jeff said. "You mentioned standing stones when you and I chatted about Kai. Can we visit them?"

"Yes," Wyatt chimed in. "If Galena was able to communicate with the pillars, would we be able to talk with Dad and the others?"

"Yes and no," Gabe replied. His eyes twinkled. "Any of ye can visit the sacred site but only ye with magic in your veins will be able to converse with your loved ones."

Janet's lips trembled, and she blinked back the tears welling in her eyes. Gabe grabbed her hands. "Ah, but ye have magical children. All they have to do is place their hand on the stone while holding your hand and the connection with your loved one will be established."

Hope filled Janet's face as she glanced at her non magical sons. "You still have a chance to talk with your Dad!" she proclaimed.

Jeff listened intently as Gabe explained the process. "What about me?" he asked. "I don't have any magical family members. How do I talk with Kai?"

Gabe patted him on the shoulder. "Ya do have a magical family...me and them!" He gestured toward Janet's family. "We're one big family now."

An hour later, the pub was quiet as everyone left for home.

Except for Gabe and Paddy.

Midnight was minutes away as the two men cleaned up the back room. "Seems like a successful gathering," Paddy noted while plunking glasses onto his tray.

"Aye," Gabe replied. "That it was."

"Ya doin' this again next week?"

"Aye. I'll be speaking every week for the next month in this area, then I'll move on to the next town and talk with more folks."

"That's a lot of blathering."

Gabe laughed out loud. "Aye. I reckon I'll be having meetings until I'm dead and in the ground. People need to remember what happened. They need to know the truth."

"I reckon ya want to have ya meetings in the pub?" Paddy asked.

"If ya be willing to come with me. The folks feel at ease when they're in Flanagan's."

"That would be the magic! Now that the Yfel are gone, me and the pub can flit wherever we want. I'd be happy to join you on ya mission."

"I miss him badly," Gabe blurted. His eyes misting.

"Who?"

"Me cousin, Chance. He had wanted his whole family to visit the pub and now..." Gabe swiped his eyes.

"I have an idea," Paddy whispered as he peered both ways.

"Whatcha doing?" Gabe asked. "There's nobody else here."

Paddy leaned close. "How 'bout taking the pub to the standing stones? What a celebration that would be."

Gabe's eyes grew wide and then softened as the idea percolated. "Paddy, that's the best idea ya ever had! When should we do it?"

"How about the one-year anniversary."

"Brilliant! We'll invite the world."

Thank You

Thank you for taking the time to read Ascension of the Chronicle, book 5 of Chronicle of Ceres.

If you enjoyed it, please share your thoughts with others.

It's so important for a book to have social proof, and I'd love your help sharing this series with others who embrace their magic.

Leave a review or star rating at your favorite book retailer

For new releases, giveaways, and fun info, subscribe to my newsletter by visiting www.cllavigne.com

Acknowledgements

My readers and my fans who challenge me in my writing and keep the spirits of the Kemps and Cererians alive.

My husband, Chris, who weathers my emotional storms, calms me, and urges me to finish my fantastical tales.

John, Judy and Steve—how could the Kemps come alive without having you in my life?

Super Jimmy who lives on in my fictional Flanagan's Irish Pub.

Brittany and your amazing editing. Imagine my stories without your intervention.

About Author

Born in Alaska and raised in England, CL writes horror and fantasy that have supernatural overtones. Her stories feature real people and natural magic, all controlled by the spirits of nature and otherworldly beings.

Residing in the Sunshine State with her husband, four cats and six goldfish, CL incorporates elements of magic, mysticism and mythology into her writings. It's not unusual to encounter dragons, elemental spirits, glowing orbs, and even bigfoot as you follow her characters on their adventures.

Her current magical realism fantasy series is Chronicle of Ceres, which features 5 books.

Tales From the Crows, her first collection of horror stories was recently published.

Embrace your magic!

Stay informed about special deals, giveaways, and other great updates by subscribing to her newsletter via her website.

www.cllavigne.com

Also By

Chronicle of Ceres Magical Realism Series

Beginning of Tomorrows, book 1

Denali Rising, book 2

Shasta Beckons, book 3

Bluestone Shadows, book 4

Ascension of the Chronicle, book 5

Tales From the Crows

Horror short story collection

www.ingramcontent.com/pod-product-compliance
Lightning Source LLC
LaVergne TN
LVHW010641110826
845149LV00014B/2918

* 9 7 9 8 9 8 8 4 8 4 5 8 5 *